Minimal Damage

WESTERN LITERATURE SERIES

Minimal Damage
Stories of Veterans

H. Lee Barnes

UNIVERSITY OF NEVADA PRESS

Reno & Las Vegas

Western Literature Series

University of Nevada Press
Reno, Nevada
89557 USA

LIBRARY OF CONGRESS CATALOGING-
IN-PUBLICTION DATA

Barnes, H. Lee, 1944–
Minimal damage : stories of veterans /
H. Lee Barnes.
p. cm. —(Western literature series)
ISBN 978-0-87417-721-3 (cloth : alk. paper)
1. Veternas—Fiction. I. Title.
PS3552.A673854M56 2007
813'.54—dc22   2007004972

The paper used in this book is a recycled stock
made from 30 percent post-consumer waste
materials, certified by FSC, and meets the re-
quirements of American National Standard
for Information Sciences—Permanence of
Paper for Printed Library Materials,
ANSI/NISO Z39.48-1992 (R2002).
Binding materials were selected
for strength and durability.

University of Nevada Press Paperback Edition, 2013
22   21   20   19   18   17   16   15   14   13
5   4   3   2   1

ISBN-13: 978-0-87417-911-8 (pbk.: alk. paper)

*To John and Joyce Standish, with
thanks to the generous, good-humored
family they welcomed me into*

Contents

Acknowledgments

The author would like to express his appreciation to Amy Sage Webb, Alberto Rios, and John Zeibell for their wise advice; to Tim Schell, who never wrote his "crabbing" story; and to Rich Logsdon for the many conversations about writing and literature. In addition, the author would like to extend a sincere thanks to the editors of the literary journals that published the stories in this collection.

Five of these stories were first published in similar form in the following journals: "The First Hunger," *Connecticut Review*; "Ground Work," *Words of Wisdom*; "Minimal Damage" (published as "Silence"), *Red Rock Review*; "Private," *The MacGuffin*; and "A Pulling Thing," *Black Ridge Review*.

Minimal Damage

Into the Silence

'm doing my shift at Charleston and Decatur, holding up a sign that says, CRAZY. SAW GOD. HELP A VETERAN, when I spot a guy in a black Beamer in the far right lane giving me the squint like he's got a problem. At times my sign stirs wrath—honking, a few middle fingers. It's part of the job. Someone flips me off, I scratch my forehead and then my crotch to confound them. No one knows for sure if I'm crazy or messing with minds. Either way, it doesn't matter.

The driver of the BMW heads to the next turn lane and swings a wide U-turn, shifts to the right lane and glides to a stop. Depending on what's on his mind, I'm ready to back away. The kid—not a kid really, but a kid to me—stops at the curb, rolls down his window, and says he fought in the Gulf War. He's clean-cut, blends in with the gray designer suit he's wearing. I ask why he has to tell that to a crazy man. He says because it wasn't war enough for most people, and no one gives a shit; now America's back in the region and everyone's forgotten we were there before.

"Ain't it the truth," I say. I hold my bucket a little closer to his open window so he'll take the hint and come up with some change if not a buck or two.

His eyes have ten miles of sincerity in them. He asks what it was like not to make it when I came home, as if my botched life is some kind of badge of honor. I look at my pail, empty except for the seed dollars, and tell him it's been a real comfort to my mother and sister, who, I'm reminded, haven't talked to me since I barbecued Mom's iguana, ugly biting thing that it was. He says something else I don't catch because I'm thinking, Is he going to spring for a buck or not?

It looks like he wants to talk is all. Some guys are that way. There's a story one of the regulars at the VA laid on me about a cave in the desert somewhere where vets gather and talk. A cave. Maybe this guy should look for it and let me make a living. The woman driver behind him wants to turn right. She scowls in our direction from behind her steering wheel. I step back from the curb in hopes that Beamer Man will take the hint and move on. Instead, he holds out a folded five-dollar bill and says that after

Kuwait he slipped right back into civilian life, doing an eight-to-five every day for two grand plus a week. He can afford to be generous. I know numbers and calculate his generosity at one-twenty-five thousandths of his weekly income. But I'm not about to complain. A five for me is a turn for the better.

"It'll go straight into my four-oh-one K," I say.

He drops the bill in my bucket and tells me too many comedians are out of work.

He looks at my sign and nods. "Crazy," he says. "Sure, like a fox."

I thank him. The woman behind him buries her palms on her horn. He drives off, and I think that's all there is to it, a yuppie who wanted an audience. If I were crazy like a fox would I be standing here with a bucket? Ask me, the guy in the group who spun that story about a cave full of veterans trading stories is the one who's crazy. Probably a bunch of winos with tattoos pretending to be someone, I told him. He couldn't let go of it, claimed where he was from vets gather at night in the woods, spark up a fire, and then form a circle and tell their tales.

Doctors at the VA don't call me crazy. "Delusional," they say. I'm still working with whether it's true. In the meantime I handle my crazy as an asset, and I believe people deserve something for their money. It's capitalism. I invest in my business, spend time on my signs, write them with neat letters, use colors, and I put a happy face on them, a yellow circle with a smile. Crazy is my currency in the world, and the function of my job is to mediate guilt and self-righteousness and make others feel sane. I thank each person—dime or dollar—for what goes in my pail. I don't judge those who choose not to donate. And I don't use that woe-is-me look to shake down housewives who just want me to go away from their window.

In group sessions guys tell me, Hank, you're an educated man, which isn't true exactly, but I did complete almost two years at a community college where I was saner than most. You pay much attention to two-year college professors, you know exactly what I mean. I once told one that I saw God. He says to prove it. I stood up and told the class they were looking at the proof, that I was all they needed to see, eleven dead and me unscratched.

Some guys at the shelter say, Where's your pride? Get a job. Like they're wearing suits and ties and doing a nine-to-five in banks! Well, I've had jobs. Some I disliked, some I liked. A while back I mowed lawns and trimmed shrubs for Rich Nettles, a good guy. But the job was a washout, like the other jobs. It's inevitable. I'm washing dishes and suddenly I'm back in 'Nam. I'm posting handbills or turning dirt with a shovel, and wham, it's like the weather inside me changes. Something triggers the memory, a memory lacking one important detail.

Last spell I chased Rich around this woman's yard with my shovel, shouting he'd better tell me where he hid the canned peaches. I loved them. Full of syrup and preserved with good old chemicals. They slid down your throat like a piece of home in a can. Ever wonder why they color C-ration cans olive drab? I mean why camouflage cans? Rich didn't care about peaches or olive drab, just getting away, but in my mind I was west of Dak To and he'd stolen my peaches. Finally I tripped over a hose, and Paulo and Lime held me down till the crazy wore off.

Rich was a good guy and didn't file charges, but the lady whose yard we were working on called the cops. Officers took me to University Medical. The ward nurse, Ms. Braun, says, "Hi, Hank. Who you trying to kill today?" Like that's all I've got to do with my life. Great sense of humor, Ms. Braun.

I march my station, usually the northwest corner, good weather or bad. I have no respect for those who won't go out and work their corners because it's too hot or too windy or too cold. I stand erect in the wind and swallow car fumes and humiliation. Like right now that guy who hooted and told me to get a job. I hold up my sign and wave. No hard feelings, I think. If it weren't for guys like me around to give people the creeps, how could they be so smug about their own civic selves?

What's left that I can do? I flunked institutions. I'm an institution dropout. I went north one summer when the heat was too much. A deputy picked me up in Boise for panhandling. Day later the sheriff kicked me out of jail, said the likes of me would give a host like him a bad name, said criminals belong behind bars and bums belong elsewhere. He bought me a bus ticket to Reno and told me God might be waiting for me there. I told him I hoped not.

Within minutes I forget about Beamer Man and go about my business. A woman gives me a quarter. I tell her God bless, something she needs to hear. Two teenage boys, smacking away on some gum, roll up and call me Pops. I hold out my bucket. The driver spits his gum in his hand, looks at it, and tosses it in my pail. I thank him, but leave out the God bless. A woman in a Buick stops a few feet away and shouts, "You're insulting believers." The light changes, she turns left, shouts, "Liar, idiot," and something else that I can't quite catch.

Two hours later I'm looking at the near empty bucket when the guy in the BMW drives up again. I'd forgotten him, but when I recognize him I extend him my bucket and my finest smile. He looks out his widow and says he wants to take me to lunch. I shake the bucket, three dollars I put in, a five-dollar bill, and loose coin. Lunch would be okay, but I've got to take care of business.

"I'm really crazy," I say, hoping he'll drop in another five and scoot.

"I want to take you to lunch." He's very insistent.

I'm wondering what this guy's orientation is, and can't he do better than me? "I saw God in Vietnam," I say.

"I want you to be my father," he says. "My Vietnam father. You paved the way."

"Paved the way to where?" I squint to take a close look at him. I need glasses, but they're not a priority to the Veterans Administration, who tells me come back when I need a white cane. I nod a few times when I see he's serious. "You crazy, too?" I ask.

He explains how he wants to do something humanitarian for someone whose dignity is a bit shattered. He says the lunch includes cocktails. I glance up the street. I should mention I do drink as a hobby, only because I can't find a way to make it a profession. That's why I stopped the meds. Booze and mood kickers make a crazy man a zombie. The day's not likely to treat me any better—car fumes and staring eyes and honking drivers. Why not? Lunch, sure.

Where? I ask. He says Le Petit Affair, which happens to be a swanky yuppie joint on Paradise that I never in my life entered or expected to. I look at my jeans, soiled for appearance's sake, and my boots, scuffed up for the same reason. The black T-shirt isn't so bad. I don't mind putting the gross on people, figure it'll be a bit like picking my nose in church, so I say sure, thinking, No way they'll let me in.

He unlocks the passenger door. We drive the speed limit, no one talking at first, Annie Lennox playing on his CD. Ms. Braun used to play her to us in the wacko ward even though most of us wanted to hear Iron Butterfly or Pink floyd, which the nurse insisted would contribute further to our problems.

Thinking I should know if I'm going to be his father, I break the silence, "What's your name?"

"John, John Sebastian," he says. "Yours?"

"Hank, Crazy Hank," I say.

He smiles. "Great," he says and turns down the radio.

"So, what do you need a father for?"

"You'll see," he says. "What is it that makes you crazy?"

"If I knew, I wouldn't be crazy, would I?" I say.

"Guess not," he says.

But I can tell by his expression he doesn't believe me, so I volunteer "Doctors say it's a post-stress disorder complicated by paranoia and delusions. I say it's because I saw God."

"A God sighting?" he says, his tone real doubtful. "God? Wow, that's pretty far-fetched. Kind of heretical, wouldn't you say?"

Sometimes my burner turns on when people doubt me too much. I lean toward him and say real sharp in his face, "Hey, I'm crazy but not about that part."

"God?" he says.

"Yep."

He goes silent again. I crank up the volume on the radio. It's me, Silent John Sebastian, and Annie Lennox. Like always, my head reels off images fast as the white stripes on the road zip by. A mountain trail. One Cong all by himself strolling our way, me, Plumber, and nine South Vietnamese. And there's no sound in the world. The music in the car stops. It's there, but I can't hear it. I wonder, if Beethoven was deaf, did he know how the music he wrote sounded? flowers, hibiscus, I think. Trees clumped thick as fur. Was it math in his head? Tangles everywhere. Jackson Plumber bending down to pull off a leech. Fill in the blanks? Tuan, the Vietnamese sergeant, with an M-79 tucked into his shoulder ready to do what? Plumber's hand going up. Everything freezes. No motion, breath, sound. Heartbeat. Maybe Beethoven was crazy, too.

John Sebastian says, "What did you really see?"

I realize he's been talking and I hope he's not patronizing me. Never think crazy and stupid are one. "In the Highlands," I say. "Probably the best place to see Him."

"God, you saw God? You believe it?"

Call me a profligate, a fool, a heretic. I've heard it. Heard it more than once. But I have seen Him. Not the God a woman in Texas claims is in her toaster. You know, the woman holding up a piece of burnt toast she claimed was the image of Christ and another slice that read "666." Headlines read "Good and Evil Battle in Toaster." Like a toaster's a handy gadget to salvation or hell. Hard to know what to believe in this world when the news is peddling the claim of miracles in a toaster. The lady got herself on network TV, headlines in Star and National Inquirer. No one called her crazy. She had proof. Toast didn't even look like Christ. More like Geraldo Rivera with a beard. That guy's everywhere. Probably paid to have his image put on bread. A miracle?

The truth is I can't believe in small miracles from Him, especially toast. Start with the parting of the Red Sea. Impressive, especially when you consider it wasn't a special effect some baldheaded movie director ordered up. You can bet I'm real rational on the subject of miracles, having been part of one. On the other hand, doctors say it's a delusion. Fact is, what I have is spells. Spells I don't even see coming.

Of course, people in their starched and well-ironed sanity must distrust every word I say. Actually what I witnessed was the swift hand of God, which I view the same as seeing God. But I'm not going to quibble about it. No one sees God. The sight would blind us. Why else burning bushes, voices in the clouds, messages from angels? When you think God, you got to think big, think out of the box, get confused a bit. But don't think toast that looks like Geraldo.

"You want me to cross my heart or something?" I say.

"Wow." He whistles through his teeth. "You think you should find some help for it?"

"Help for what?"

"A doctor." He taps his head with a index finger.

"I told you I've talked to doctors."

VA. doctors listen, jot comments on a pad. Mostly they doodle and pretend to take notes, then write prescriptions for me and reports for the VA. What the VA expects from them is notes, reports, conclusions. Hank, stay on your meds, they say. I don't. I got good reason. I mean, what do they know? Doctors weren't with us seven klicks west of Dak To on a Sunday in March of 1970. And I was quite sane at the time.

John pulls into the entrance at Le Petit Affair.

"I'm not one for formal affairs," I say. "No high hat, no tails."

John says not to worry.

The valet greets him as Mr. Sebastian and says his party is waiting. Then the valet opens my door and sees my clothes. "Some ties hanging inside my booth." He points to something that looks like a guard shack with a chalet roof. I grab one of the pre-knotted ties and loop it over my neck. It's extra wide and has a lavender and blue diamond design. I show it to John, who says it looks great. On a black T-shirt? Great? Wouldn't look great on an Armani shirt.

Inside, the maître d' bows his head and says we're expected. The room we enter is set for a banquet of twenty-two—white tablecloth, china, and real silverware gleaming under a crystal chandelier. It's not a lunch but a banquet. I've been to one other banquet in my life and that was a Little League awards dinner when I was eleven. The good thing about this banquet is everyone has a drink in front of him. Twenty are seated and John Sebastian and I are twenty-one and twenty-two.

Thing about the table that strikes me right off is that every other man is John's age, dressed in suit and tie, while the others, those my age, wear borrowed ties around their necks. They might, under other circumstances, look like any group of middle-aged men headed toward retirement. Some wear T-shirts. Others wear casual shirts buttoned at the collar. Only one wears a suit. Among them are the gaunt and the obese. Some are bearded, some bald, and others gray. I don't recognize any of them from the VA, but I figure they're all vets.

The guy at the head of the table, one about John's age and dressed in a black suit with black shirt and tie, stands up and says he's glad we made it. John introduces me and says I'm the guy he spoke about, his Vietnam father. I'm not real happy to hear this spoken aloud because I have no idea what's going on, and to my knowledge I never fathered anything but bad luck and bad choices.

Next thing, the guy standing up points us to the two empty seats as if we weren't smart enough to figure out where to sit on our own. He says we've got to get started. Right away, waiters seem to fall out of the ceiling, pouring water, setting salads and soup down on the plates in front of us. They swarm around us, and the room fills with a lot of delicate little clatters as the plates and glasses touch down. The younger guys don't seem to appreciate what's in front of them. They ignore their guests and lean across them and talk to one another about golf. A few open up cell phones and carry on loud conversations. Guess they never had to eat ham and lima beans out of an olive drab can. None of the older guys talk. We eat our soup and salad and drink.

When it's time for the main course, the emcee announces that everyone's to turn off his cell phone. The young men make a ritual of this as the room fills with the bleeps of tinny notes. Soon enough a rare slice of prime rib about the size and shape of a baby grand is set in front of me. I tell John I'm a vegetarian. His expression goes limp. Panic sets in his eyes.

"We can get . . ."

I wink and slice off a bite of meat. "Just joking," I say and stuff that rare side of cow into my salivating mouth, then motion to the nearest waiter to make my wineglass a little damper.

For dessert we have coffee and seven-layer chocolate cake with frosting so rich and thick it sticks to the top of your mouth. After that comes brandy or Grand Marnier. It doesn't register on me till I've downed one shot and am holding the second one in my hand that no one has spoken a word, and except for coffee and water, the young guys aren't drinking.

The guy who greeted us stands up and tinks his spoon lightly against his still empty wineglass. He calls for silence. I wonder why he bothers since the room's been silent for twenty minutes. He offers each of us a broad smile, like this is kickoff night for his political campaign.

"Gentlemen, fellow soldiers, veterans of America's conflicts," he says.

The young guys applaud while the old guys look at each other, getting familiar with faces, before clapping. I notice one about my age. He's got a beard that hangs to mid chest much like mine and the soulful look of a prophet or a addlebrained ascetic who lives off vermin and water. I figure he probably works a corner somewhere, likely has a file with the VA and county shrinks.

"For you Vietnam vets, it was Agent Orange and baby killing, while for some of us in here it was Gulf War syndrome and liberating oil. Are we tired of being the warts on America's ass?" the host speaker asks.

We Vietnam vets look at our empty snifters and screw up our faces. This guy says it's time for our stories to be told. One of the young men two seats over stands up and says to his right is Bobby, and Bobby was a Marine at Khe Sanh. Bobby is a black man with a grandfather face, round cheeks, and eyes as sad as a burned dinner. The guy goes on to explain how Bobby got the Bronze Star but now works as a janitor in an office building where the speaker works as a stockbroker. He says he's proud to have Bobby as a father.

Waiters keep the coffee and brandy coming, which makes us older guys smile. Next speaker says he was a lieutenant and platoon leader in the late eighties, never saw combat, but would have been proud to have served with his Vietnam father, Arnie Spouts. He goes on to say that Arnie was in the Delta. This is followed by others, who one at a time stand up and say who they were in the service. Each Gulf War vet states what his guest did in 'Nam and how sad his Vietnam father's life has been since then, and I wonder why the old guys aren't talking. I study a few of the faces on the men my age. Some roll their eyes. Some stare at their hands. Bobby's eyes meet mine. He nods. I nod.

Walls begin to slide away. The room's a blur. I try to bring it into focus again but can't. I don't know what's happening, but it's not a spell coming on because I never foresee *them*. In the background I see the thick brush in the Highlands, a dumb kid, a VC, marching up a trail, oblivious, his rifle resting on his shoulders, his arms extended across it as if it were a yoke or the thwartwise beam of a cross. Plumber's just behind the Vietnamese on point. One behind Plumber calmly goes down on a knee and gut-shoots the dumb kid.

The emcee introduces the next host, then the next, but what I see floats right above the room and no one else sees it. It's a glow inside that chandelier, something electricity can't do, stories caught in the crystal prisms, stories half trapped. The introductions go all the way around the table until the emcee comes to John Sebastian, who stands and clears his throat.

"This is Crazy Harry, my Vietnam father," he says. "He thinks he saw God in the Highlands."

"It's Crazy Hank, and I did," I say, fully aware that I was the first Vietnam vet in the room to talk.

The master of ceremonies says, "Let John talk. He has to explain."

"He wasn't there," I say.

"Well, you're his guest," the guy says.

"Thank you, John," I say.

John narrows his eyes on me, takes a sip of water, and clears his throat. "Now he stands at Charleston and Decatur and begs money." He takes his seat and folds his arms.

"That's only part right," I say. "I stand there, but I don't beg."

John Sebastian gives me a look that has shut up written all over it, but I don't have shut up in me. I see it clear, my life and their lives, and I feel words welling up. I stand.

"John said I think I saw. But that's not the whole measure of it. I saw what *God* did, which is the same as seeing."

"Sit down," the emcee says.

"Can't," I say. "See, God was in the Highlands that day. And . . ." John grabs my tie and yanks it, and I feel the air go out of me as I collapse in my seat.

"So," the emcee says. He makes a speech about service and a bunch of blather that I barely hear because I'm up there on the peak again, the Vietnamese packing the boy Cong dead and dangling and swaying on a pole. And we enter a village, and an old man comes running up, crying and one of the South Vietnamese shouts and pushes him aside. Then we're outside that village. With a girl.

The emcee goes on to read, "And that concludes our tribute to our Vietnam fathers."

"No, it doesn't exactly," I say.

"Thank you for coming. Stay around for a few social drinks," he says, and all the young men applaud and a few of the old guys look at me like I'm ruining something. Bobby and a couple of others give me a thumbs-up.

I think one of the vets in the room must have seen Him too and has the memory, maybe the one that looks like a prophet. And maybe he'll speak up. "It was God, I tell you, God!"

They come, four of them and a waiter, and grab my arms. I struggle to stay on my feet. I feel my toes dragging on the marble floor. One unlaced boot slips off, and for moment I don't see the room, but I see the Vietnamese drag the girl screaming to the side of the trail. One tears her silk *au dai* from shoulder to waist. I scream at Plumber to stop them, and God comes, and I start hollering about getting them off her, and no one listens. There is one big flash.

By then I'm at the back door and the maître d' is holding the door open. I have no breath. I'm moving across the floor turning over and over, like a fat ham on a rotisserie. I hear rattling. A helicopter. And I feel the hands pulling me onto a stretcher. They lift me up. Suddenly I'm launched out the back door. I clear the first step entirely and tumble over the second, then fall facedown on the asphalt. One throws my untied boot to me. I see that John Sebastian is one of my tormentors. I start to sit up, but the door slams shut, so I lie down instead.

My thoughts drift between the closed door and the closed canopy beside the trail in the Highlands. They said I called a dustoff over the radio, said there were casualties, wounded. I don't remember that. All I know is that none were alive, except me. All of them there spread out on the red clay, slain by the Righteous Hand. A miracle. If anyone wants to know where He can be found, it's seven klicks west of Dak To, negotiating for souls with the devil. If you're wanting real hard to find him, forget miracle toast. Go there. Or you can look at me and believe.

I look at the surface of the pavement in the alley. It's hot and sun-softened, and my hands and my cheek burn on it. I notice that if I look very closely, because of the angle of the sun, I can see sparkles in the blacktop. They look like little diamonds in a field of tar. Or stars maybe in a blackened sky. It's all in the seeing, all in the angle. I crawl a few steps and get to my feet.

One doctor said, maybe, Hank, you're seeing it but not seeing it. Were there bombs? he asked. Bombs? I remember getting to my feet, and looking around. There were pieces of people. And the girl was half buried, and her face was looking up. Like the Virgin, if Mary had been Vietnamese. Her mouth was open, and her lips formed an oval as if she were holding a high note in an endless song. I touched her.

Sometimes I think it was the devil, but the devil would have claimed me too. They say I was babbling when they lifted me onto the Huey. I don't know. Section Eight, they said, recycle him into the World. And here I am. I realize that my sign and my bucket are in John Sebastian's BMW. I rub my head, stand and start looking for a piece of cardboard. I need a sign. Everyone, I think, needs a sign. So I rummage in the Dumpster for a good piece of cardboard, but they're all crushed or bent.

I notice the tie hanging from my neck. I lift it off my neck and look at the knot and the oval loop. I picture that dead girl, her mouth open. I think of Beethoven. The doctors insist the pills help, but meds don't stop you from knowing or seeing. They help you to forget and stop you from living. I hold the tie upside down and swing it back and forth. Plumber once said that a hangman is waiting for all of us. I drop the tie and as I look down, I see my feet buried in trash and wonder how someone would picture me, a man digging in garbage.

I hold my shoulders back, slip away from the trash bin, and leave the alley without a sign or a bucket. There's plenty of day left, and plenty to remember. This time I'm going to try, really try to remember. That cave? I wonder if they light a fire, if they stare at the flames as they speak. I know now that the guy was telling the truth. I know where the veterans go. Into the silence. That's where my tribe waits. I won't need a map or a sign. I'll march out there where the cave is, and maybe, if I remember and tell my story clearly, one of my kind will hear the words the way Beethoven heard the notes, and he will tell me why God did that, or if not God, who.

Punishment

Silence defines the cellblock designated Unit 12. It can be hard on a man, can break the weak, a quiet interrupted only by the occasional rattling of keys and grinding of steel doors, sounds that herald the same few things—a tray of food, an attorney with a document, a guard hefting a wrist box and twenty pounds of shackles. This is where the hard core are punished or those facing the last walk spend their last days. For seven days it has been Billy's home.

He rips the page from the pad, balls it up, and flips it on the ground. Then he stands and walks to the door, where he wheels about and returns to his cot, four steps in all. He picks up his pad and pen and again scratches a greeting and a first sentence: "Brenda, Sorry I wasn't around the last eight years to help celebrate your anniversary." He pauses, then composes the next terse sentence. "See, I've been occupied several years now trying to save my neck." For the next two minutes he taps the pen on the paper and stares at the wall, thinking of a night, not the one in the desert that he too often remembers, but a humid night in 1989 when in a muddle he stepped from the skids of a helicopter and stumbled into an open ditch, a fall that saved his life, and for the first time since playing car tag with his brothers he'd felt wondrously alive.

He had planned to spend that Christmas with his family, their first reunion since he was fourteen. He had hoped for a reconciliation. Billy was dressed in his class-A uniform, boots and brass shined, waiting to catch a ride to the airport when his platoon sergeant entered the barracks to announce that all leaves were canceled. The sergeant smiled and said, "Get your gear ready. I want every swingin' dick standin' at attention by his bunk in thirty. We're goin' into action."

He wonders how life's course might have altered had the president not decided to capture Noriega. His plans to patch up matters with Maury and reunite with his brothers ended on the night of December 21, 1989. The following March Maury died while pressing a bet on a losing poker hand at the Sahara. All that was left Billy was to hold Arden's hand at the funeral and share a last dinner with Drew and Alex. Ridiculous, he thinks, believing that large events determine the path of a small life. He would like to write that in a letter, but not one to Brenda. He snorts. It is small events that mold a life—meeting the wrong person at a particular time, getting lost on a highway, beating up a stepfather.

One of those small events turned bad and brought Billy to this day—if the last-minute appeals fail as all the previous ones have. The courts do not look fondly on men who kill. He tears the sheet off the pad and crushes it, sets pad and pen aside, and faces the corner. How, he wonders, would Tennyson say it? With subdued passion? He clears his throat. "'We are not now that strength which in old day . . . '" His words bounce back at him sounding like the bark of a drill sergeant, not at all the way he would expect a poet to perform. He whispers the remaining verse, then sits on his cot, gathers up his writing pad, and starts afresh.

Often, he recites the poems of Eliot, Stevens, and Tennyson. In days when he thought his mind might disintegrate if he didn't occupy it with something other than the grimness of prison life, he committed lines to memory. Anything, he figured, even memorizing recipes, might ease the banality. The poems came from an anthology sent by a graduate student named Erica who'd read newspaper articles about him. She enclosed a note that read, "You are not a monster. I hope the book will soften your days."

This letter he's composing is the second he's written to Brenda in thirteen years. It's been hard writing all the way. Five sheets of paper lie wadded at his feet. Initially, when he'd read her letter, he'd been tempted to correct spelling and grammar and mail it back. But he didn't. It would be cruel. No point in that. He wonders what she looks like now. At first she'd seemed the woman he'd hoped would stumble into his life and build a future with him. Later, she'd been a sharp stone pressing on his ribs. Now she's a letter that's difficult to write.

No one dances in Unit 12, Billy thinks, no one laughs. Lockdown—no inmate contact, no television, no radio. It's all no here. In the early days of his incarceration, when he sought truth in everything he read, especially the Bible, he came upon Ecclesiastes, and after a month of reading, determined that what was missing in the text was that there is a time for musing, and more time for musing, until . . . Until is the word.

On a bulletin board at the entry to his cellblock is a Polaroid of an inmate slain by a fellow prisoner. Guards say, "Right here. Stabbed right here." The hint is stay in line even if this is your last day on earth. The murdered inmate, black and homosexual, was killed by a white prisoner for no other reason than those two facts. The strong rule the yard. The wise let the strong rule. The weak get fucked. Nonetheless, a man needs human contact, even if with the worst elements of society. Presently, he is the celebrity in Unit 12. Others are here as punishment for infractions. Billy misses the hard core at Ely, the stupid grandiose proclamations and posturing.

He stands and paces. He pauses at the iron door, puts an ear to it. Nothing. An overhead bulb recessed in the ceiling is all the light he has. When it goes out, darkness ensues. Elsewhere there is utility. Prisoners work, interact, and are allowed to raise puppies that will become seeing-eye dogs. Here there is silence, isolation, and light or dark. The distinction between the prisons in Carson City and Ely is the difference between a sweatshop and a slaughterhouse.

The outer door rattles. He turns toward the sound but remains seated. Procedure calls for him to wait on his cot. If he approaches the door without being instructed to, the guard will order him back to his cot to be cuffed, perhaps beat him to the floor. He follows rules. What is to be otherwise gained? The staff views him as a model inmate who goes along with "the program." He's been here before for appeals and hearings, the last time for a clemency board. He smiled at the governor, who then looked away. Grim, Billy thinks. Serious stuff to serious people.

In prior days he had read Genesis repeatedly and marveled at the power rejection has over the psyche and the struggle for self among siblings. If the Bible is correct in human flesh being one, we, like Cain, are killers of brothers. How, he once asked a chaplain, would the world be if God had shown generosity and the smoke from Cain's sacrifice had ascended? "Man cannot question the ways of God," the priest said. But what if those ways don't make sense? And if not man to question the ways, then who? The cockroach? The rat? "You don't believe," the priest said, as if that crystallized the complexity of doubt. Billy answered, "I want to, desperately, but I can't find Him."

Billy is not Cain. Nor—and he knows he's not deceiving himself—can he kill. But he did once, a cop. The fact grants him status among inmates. He has come to accept his confinement, has adjusted to routines, eight-by-five cells, and each uneventful day sliding into the next. The mind has to adjust or get calloused or cluttered with worry. But he can't adjust to the idea of being a killer. He accepts that he did what he did, feels remorse, takes responsibility, but refuses to see himself as a cop killer. Why, he wonders, can't he see himself as one? Shame? Is that why he didn't look at Drew in the courtroom, and why for eight years he declined his brother's requests for a visit, because cops too are brothers? Shame leaves us in shambles. Sure, that's it. Or maybe he still resents Drew for that night.

His door grinds open. He looks up momentarily and goes on writing. The clash of metal on metal is immutable. In the beginning the sound of bars opening struck terror in him, as if the sound itself were announcing his fate. He measures the idea up against his current state. Was this his fate? Was he irresistibly drawn to a confrontation on a darkened desert highway?

He sets the letter aside. When done, it will be the third he's finished that afternoon, the twenty-second in a week, notes to strangers, people who wrote saying how unfair his punishment was, how cruel, how insensible, inhuman and inhumane. Strange, but as he neared this day, he became some curious figure in the lives of people he'd never met. Some correspondence left him feeling awkward. He turned down a proposal from a woman named Elizabeth who claimed her life would be unfulfilled if they didn't marry. He figured her life would be unfulfilled if she married a handsome millionaire who loved her desperately and showered her with attention. He wrote back that he was flattered, but marriage without at least the illusion of a future would do no good for either of them.

His door grinds to an abrupt halt. "Billy," the voice says over the intercom, "stay in your cell. I'm coming for a visit."

Billy stands. "Yes, sir."

Without investing much chance in his hopes, he wonders if the warden will bring good news. He reminds himself that rule number one is do not hope. Time is a slow fire that consumes it. A moment later the warden and Officer Cramer enter and stand to either side of the door. The warden looks at the wadded letters and books piled beside Billy's cot.

"Get enough reading and writing done?" the warden asks.

It seems a silly question. Billy is unsure how to answer. "Enough for what?"

"Never mind. Your brothers are sitting inside my office. You want to see them?"

"Alex too?" Billy takes a moment to consider what Alex's coming may mean. He knew Drew had come, but his younger brother's appearance is a surprise. Since Billy beat Maury with the plumber's pipe, they have not spoken more than a dozen words. "Alex? We haven't spoken in . . . thirteen years. Drew's a cop, you know."

"In an hour or so we'll be moving you. They can see you then if you choose."

"I don't know."

The warden glances at Officer Cramer. "Leave us for a moment."

Cramer holds up the wrist box. "Should I restrain him, sir?"

"We'll be fine."

After the officer leaves, the warden leans against the wall. He seems quite relaxed. "Last chance, will you want a spiritual advisor?"

"No," Billy says without hesitation.

"A Bible, then?"

Billy gazes at the wall. "I read it twice, looking for something to explain this. Couldn't find it."

"Okay, then. Your one brother flew all the way in from the East."

"Alex married a girl from Vermont. About a year before . . ." He's bottled up words for so long he feels a hunger to speak but fears what he may say, so he stops.

"Before?"

It strikes Billy as strange that he has nothing to lose but can't talk about what happened before because by *before* he means before he killed. "It's not important. The appeal?"

"We haven't heard anything. Sorry."

"No. Guess the undertaker's the only one in a hurry."

"Billy, your brother, the cop?"

"Drew?"

"He's worked at helping, you know. Pretty hard, him being an officer. He got some heat."

Had to be tough, Billy thinks, a cop's brother killing a cop. It wasn't the first time Drew picked up Billy's fight for him. In his sophomore year, Billy grew four inches from May to December. His ankles showed at the cuff of his jeans. "Hayseed," a boy in school called him. They met after classes. A crowd gathered across from the campus, cheering for the other boy because the Debeckis were scum. To their disappointment Drew stepped through the circle and eased Billy aside. He punished the boy with quick jabs, taunting him as he did, until the boy's face was bloodied and swollen, and then he made Billy's antagonist apologize. Like flint, Billy thinks, that's how Drew was.

"I wanted to be like him," Billy says, hoping he does not sound jealous.

"What should I tell them?"

What, Billy wonders, can he say to his brothers? Will they talk about Maury? He pictures himself seated on the couch wrapping electrician's tape around a pipe as Drew helped Arden from the bedroom to the front door, her face covered by a bloodied towel. Billy offered the pipe to Drew, said he could take care of Maury if he wanted. Someone had to. Drew shook his head, picked up Arden, and carried her down the stairs.

"I can't make you, but you should see your brothers."

"I'll think about it."

"Don't take too long deciding. I've got matters to attend to."

"It'd be nice to talk, I guess." He looks at the expression on the warden's face and sees his situation clearly. Every choice he makes now is perhaps a last, no room for error, no time for correction. "Okay. I'll see them."

"Do you wish to make a last statement to the press if the appeal is denied?"

"Can I go on *Larry King Live* or *Oprah* to do it?"

The warden smiles. "Is there something you want that I can do?"

"Can I go to the exercise area? I'd like to see the mountains before it's dark. You've got a great view here. And I'd like a fresh deck of cards when we go up."

Go up is the term for it, as if ascending into a better place, a better social position. Ironically, Billy thinks, it is also the term gangbangers use for tagging their territory with graffiti. Go up. Does it mean he will leave his mark, make a claim to the room?

"I'll give you twenty minutes. Officer Cramer, come in!" the warden says.

■

The occasional car sluices over the road that traverses the prison. He watches the day transform into night and smiles as he conjures up the past.

It is the narrative of three boys, a narrative of sadness and anger and laughter. He and Drew and Alex inseparable, latchkey kids crammed into one bedroom of a two-bedroom apartment. They folded newspaper to cover holes in their shoes, washed shirts and socks and underwear in the sink and dried them overnight on the rails of their bunks. Kids mocked them. Teachers belittled them.

They snuck into movie theaters. Alex, youngest and much shorter, constantly fell behind. Billy or Drew would hoist him to their shoulders, and seeing who could carry him farthest turned it, as they did most everything, into competition. There were sorties into supermarkets. Alex's role was to distract clerks while Drew and Billy stuffed cold cuts and slices of bread under their shirts. Alex once walked the aisles of the store hunched over, dragging one foot as if he had muscular dystrophy and saying, "Step aside for Jerry's kids." People stared or turned their carts around when they saw him coming. Drew and Billy laughed so hard they didn't boost any food. The three of them went to bed hungry, but warmed by laughter. Now Drew's a cop and Alex a counselor who works with Down syndrome adults.

He gazes at the Sierras. In the bowl formed by the peaks is Tahoe, where he and Brenda once shared a romantic weekend. For a time he blamed her, reasoning that if she had not called and insisted he find her, had she waited a day or two and met him somewhere, he would have slept off his drunk. She dialed from a phone near a women's shelter, said her husband had beaten her, insisted this time it was really over. She was in a shelter for abused women, where exactly she was unsure, but waiting wasn't part of her opera. She begged him. In his foggy reasoning, Billy figured Drew would help him find her.

He closes his eyes, pictures the night they met. Her at a lounge bar at the Rio, two drinks in hand. She bumped into him, called him a gorilla. He apologized and offered to replace those she had spilled. "What about my dress?" She twirled a lock of hair in her finger, studying him, and asked if he wanted to join her and her friends. He lit a cigarette. She took it from him, puffed on it once and stubbed it out in the ashtray, then asked for his pack, which he handed over. "You should quit," she said, tossed the pack on the floor and crushed it underfoot. But he didn't quit cigarettes until the last date with her. He figured out too late that he expected Brenda to reward him for loving her, but she was incapable of it. He can't blame her for that. She was like Arden, like his mother that way. No wonder the two of them clashed.

"Officer Cramer, do you have a cigarette?" Billy asks.

"Don't smoke, Debecki. Never did."

"Quit them myself. Wondered if it was the way I remembered it being. Figured . . ." Billy hears himself, and what he's saying sounds silly.

"I can get you a cigarette," the guard says.

"Thanks all the same. I don't want to take up the habit again." He looks to see if Cramer is amused. No sense of humor, none. Lost it or never had it.

He smoked his last cigarette while sitting in a booth beside Brenda at the Athens Grill, stubbed it out in an ashtray, and picked up a slice of bread. They'd been arguing. Her ex-husband had showed up at the movie and seated himself behind them. A confrontation followed, and Brenda had insisted on leaving before it escalated. Both were still distraught from the encounter. Brenda said, "Jesus, I can't control what he does." Billy said that he could control him if Brenda gave the word. He took a bite of bread and said it would be nice not to have to look over his shoulder. He asked why she married a loser. That set her off.

In the midst of her defending Kevin, the ex-husband, Billy looked up and saw him barge through the door to the restaurant. He bulled his way across the floor, intentionally bumping into the backs of occupied chairs. They locked eyes. Billy said, "Speak of the devil." The second confrontation of the night ensued, this time a waiter and the manager caught in the middle. After a heated exchange, Kevin turned toward the door as if to leave but then wheeled around and clipped Billy above the eyes with a straight right. An anger akin to the one that drove him to beat Maury welled up in Billy. He butted Kevin with his head. In the aftermath, Kevin went to the hospital, Billy went to jail.

"You've got about five minutes," Cramer says.

"Do you play chess?" Billy asks.

"Tried, didn't like it. You know, I'm not out here to socialize."

Billy considers the possibility that Officer Cramer too has suffered. That may account for his not having a sense of humor. Or perhaps he's just miserable. Or hates his job. "It doesn't hurt to be civil."

"Debecki, you killed a cop. That just doesn't sit well with me."

Billy nods twice. "You should try chess again. It's a great way to pass time."

The guard grunts.

"Officer Cramer, you may not care, but I was awarded a medal in Panama, a Bronze Star."

"Okay, so you're a fucking hero."

"No, no hero. But I did do something right in my life. Thought I'd say that."

Again Billy stares at the mountains. The sky is cast in a neon red. He recalls sunsets in Las Vegas, vibrant oranges and pinks in the backdrop as the Charleston Mountains turned brown to gray to black. He doesn't lament what is ahead of him so much as what is not. He wanted to be a father, once thought Brenda would give him children. He wanted to bring a child the comfort of being loved. His had been a childhood of punishment without reward.

He speculates for a moment on things he would change, what he would accomplish in that never-future. Kids. College. Build a house. Kids, he thinks, kids, and then he pictures the highway as he invariably does, the desert opaqued by clouds. He doesn't know even now how he ended up on that lonely stretch east of Death Valley. Drunk, he was drunk, but more than that, he was tired, tired of everything, the dance that Brenda constantly re-choreographed. He had avoided alcohol for months, but that night, of all nights, he went on his first binge since leaving the army.

"Three minutes, Debecki," the guard says.

■

Why, Billy asked on his first trip back to Carson City, didn't they just move the death chamber to Ely, where the condemned are housed? It seemed a logical question, especially because it affected him. The officers transporting him asked what it was to him. "I don't like traveling. Never know what can happen on a highway." The guards didn't think he was funny. Now, as Officers Cramer and Harding clamp the manacles on, wrists and ankles, connecting chain secured to a strap on his waist, he wants to say something humorous. Anything.

"You ready?" Officer Harding says.

Billy's heard guards talk about Starbucks coffee, speak of it almost with reverence. He's never tasted it and wonders what the fuss is about.

"Can we stop at a Starbucks?" he asks.

"Funny, Debecki," Officer Harding says.

"Well, it'd probably keep me up all night anyhow."

"Let's go," Officer Cramer says.

The chains force him to slouch forward in a semi-fetal position. Each officer takes an arm, and they lead him out of the cell to the outer door. Neither guard looks at him nor talks. They guide him to the walkway between the bays of the secure units. They progress slowly because his shoes remain unlaced. He shuffles. There's no hurry. It's seven o'clock, dark now, and cool. The dance isn't until past midnight. He enjoys the cool air and wishes the walk could last a long while. Spring, he thinks, a good time.

Two-hundred seventy-one feet of asphalt pathway separate the door of Unit 12 from the stairs. It takes them seven minutes, the officers holding his arms loosely to catch him if he stumbles. Escape is impossible. In the otherwise silent night, he hears the buzz of the spotlights, the rattle of the chains that bind his ankles, and the heavy scrape of his shoes on the asphalt. As they approach the flights of stairs that ascend to the death chamber, it occurs to him that every book he has read will vanish, just as if it had never been written or read. The blanking of the mind troubles him. Why learn just to forget? He looks up the stairs that end at a single steel door. It seems absurd to make a man climb these bound up as he is.

He says, "Sure be embarrassing if I broke my neck."

"We won't let you fall," Officer Harding says.

Billy nods. "I broke a finger once. You ever break a bone, Officer Cramer?"

The guard smiles. "A few, but none of my own."

"Officer Cramer, you've got a sense of humor after all."

They nudge his elbows, and he begins the climb. It takes three minutes to climb to the final landing—two flights, forty-eight steps. Officer Cramer holds Billy as the other guard unlocks the door. Billy looks up at the sky. It's difficult to see stars. Too many lights. He would like a better look, wishes he knew more about the constellations. What he remembers most clearly about that night is that it was starless and pitch-black when a flashlight in his face blinded him. He takes a last glimpse at the sky as the guards ease him inside.

He has prepared himself for the sight. Still, his knees buckle when he sees the steel shell painted an innocuous cream color. The convex door enters into what was formerly a gas chamber. Instead of a chair it is furnished with a stretcher large enough to accommodate one body. The door is open, exposing the viewing windows in the room from which twelve witnesses in total, reporters and strangers, will watch his final breaths. Harding grips Billy's arm a little tighter and says his reaction is normal.

"One guy shit himself," Cramer says. "You're not going to make us clean up that kind of mess, are you?"

"Will that disappoint you?"

"Not too much."

Billy scans the stark quarters, bare concrete walls, steel reinforced, two barriers of steel bars facing north, one forming a corridor between the room and the split cells. One cot each is in the two separate cells. Why two cells, two cots? Maybe they had a two-for-one day.

"I'd hate to see what it looked like before they remodeled."

Cramer grunts. They march Billy to the left, where two layers of bars stand between him and escape. He wonders, why two? No one had gotten this far and escaped, unless in movies. As the cage door opens, he notices the black telephone on the wall. It has no dial. Its sole purpose is to transmit word of a last-minute stay to the warden. Billy is fully informed on the procedure. All makes sense except one small matter—the executioner. The man who sets the plungers into action is not an employee of the prison system or associated with law enforcement or medicine. No nurse, no paramedic, just a volunteer who has been scrupulously screened for the job and who will remain anonymous. He will be the last to enter the room and the first to exit. Neither Billy nor anyone in the room will ever see him except for the warden, whose job is to stand over the executioner's shoulder and give the final order.

The cell door is opened. It will remain so until his visitors arrive, and they will be locked in. He's glad his mother is unable to see him. He would not want her to see what he will spend the next few hours viewing. He stares at the death chamber and wonders what happened to the poisonous gas. Did it vent into the air? Did the man's soul follow it, drift through an aperture in the roof into a finer realm? He doesn't believe so, wishes he could but cannot.

"Medieval," he mutters.

"What's that?" Cramer asks.

"Nothing. How often do they change the sheets?"

"What sheets?" Then Harding glances over his shoulder at the rack. "Oh," he says as if having seen it for the first time. "You need anything, speak up. We'll be here the duration."

Billy's glad Harding has the duty with Cramer. "Warden promised cards," Billy says and holds up his wrists. "Can't play with cuffs on."

"We'll take them off."

"And maybe a folding table to play on."

"We'll see."

They remove the cuffs and chain but keep his ankles shackled. So, he thinks, as he sits on the cot, this is it. He's struck with the thought that he may soon be an oddity, one of a fraternity of healthy men dying in the prime of life by order of a court. He did what he was accused of, never denied it. Though part of that night is a blur, he remembers winning and winning in a casino and drinking and stumbling out into the parking lot and walking around the garage unable to find his truck. And then he found it. But it wasn't his truck at all. If only, he thinks, they had made it easier to locate a car in the parking lot. Later they claimed he'd stolen it out of the valet lot. It looked like his, keys on the visor where he kept his.

He pictures the stretch of desert, gateway to Death Valley. Even now he can't remember the drive there, one hundred miles from his apartment. Was he lost and still looking for Brenda, or running away? He has no idea what clouded his mind as he drove out of the Imperial Palace. Three hours later when the flashlight beam hit him, he didn't know where he was or how he got there. A hand was pulling at him. At first he thought it was a dream, then came the struggle. And the shot. He looks at the room some five short paces away and wonders if he and Trooper Riggs had been on a collision course all their lives, two men on a lonely highway.

"The cards are coming," Harding says. "We'll have a phone here to call out. Do you want to see your brothers first or order your last meal?"

"What about the appeals?"

"How would I know?"

"Right."

"Your attorney will be here, I assume."

"Can I have ice cream, French vanilla with fudge, and cole slaw and an artichoke?"

Harding squints. "You sure you're not pregnant?"

"I'll take a steak, rare and corn, ice cream for dessert. Then I'll see my brothers."

■

As he shuffles cards, Billy relives his mother's testimony. She thought she was helping when she told the jury that Billy was "a good boy." Then on cross-examination the prosecutor asked, "Isn't it true Billy once tried to kill your husband with a metal pipe?" She looked at Billy. Incapable of an intentional lie or an exact truth, Arden said, "I didn't think so. You see, Maury only had three broken ribs and a concussion." And when the attorney asked, "Would you call that a good boy?" she became like Silly Putty for the state and Billy became, in the eyes of the jury, a man incapable of stemming his rage.

Officer Harding unlocks the cell door and steps in. "I guess you're finished."

"Yes."

"What game you going to play?"

"Blackjack or poker. We only had two games when we were kids—cards and car tag."

"Never heard of that one."

"Probably not." Billy pictures the corner of Eastern and Desert Inn, the green light signaling cars through in north-south lanes. It's a sunny autumn afternoon, traffic thin. Drew, who always won, was ahead. Then a black-and-white came barreling their way, slowed as the cop anticipated reaching the crown in the middle. Billy sees himself step out, Drew hollering, "No."

"So, I'm curious."

"We used to run out in the street and tag moving cars. The side was one point, front fender or bumper, two, a side view mirror was three."

Officer Harding stares at Billy. "Why not baseball?"

"There were no balls to play with, no mitts, no bats. We had cards, decks and decks. Our stepfather was a poker player and a card cheat, though not much of either. Watch this."

Billy deals out three hands of blackjack and quickly plays them through to the finish. He gathers up the cards, shuffles three times, strips the deck, and shuffles again. Again he deals out three hands, each the same as the previous deal.

"I saw it. How'd you do that?"

"False shuffles. Magic one-oh-one, kindergarten stuff for a magician. Maury, that was my stepfather, he taught us. Drew and Alex never learned, thought it was boring. I liked learning tricks. Never did anything with them except pass time."

"Yeah, well. If you need something."

"My brothers?"

"Sure."

"Officer Harding?"

"Yeah."

"I know you're not supposed to . . . get personal . . . involved with inmates, but you've been good. I appreciate it, appreciate your interest."

"I'll get your brothers."

"Check them for files," Billy says.

"You think this is funny?" Cramer says and stares angrily at him.

"Officer Cramer, you know a laugh now and then might add some time to your life."

"Maybe. It's not adding any to yours. People like you been on this path a long time."

On death row in Ely the population played "If you could pick a way to die." Castañeda chose a firing squad. Garve opted for a crystal meth overdose. Smith said he'd line up a hundred naked whores and fuck himself to death. Billy said subduing a hijacker at the controls and crashing an airplane like the men who'd gone down in Pennsylvania on 9/11. "You're a romantic, Billy," Peppers said, the only insightful remark he'd offered in eleven years. Once Billy explained car tag to the others. Smith said, "You been headin' here a long time." That, Billy thought, from a lunatic!

The door buzzes. Cramer looks through the window, nods, and presses the button to open the door. The warden enters with Sylvester Chartres, Billy's attorney. Billy doesn't have to guess what it means, the two of them arriving at the same time. But the news has to be announced, has to be discussed.

The attorney stands at the bars, his eyes red. He's been working around the clock for days, living on hot dogs and brandy and coffee, all of which Billy smells. Billy starts to stand but sees no point in it. "That's it?"

Chartres shakes his head. "The governor can still . . ."

"He won't. You've done what you can."

"The widow and the brother got an audience with him this evening."

Billy remembers her from the trial, staring at him, hate in her eyes. Who could blame her? Two kids. "She'll get to witness it. Maybe that'll make it better?"

"It's not like the movies. Do you want me to give a message to anyone?"

Billy swallows. Brenda? What would he say? The widow? Tell her it was all an accident? He stands and offers his hand to the attorney. They shake.

"In my personal property is a book a graduate student sent me. Her name and address were written inside the front cover. She may have moved. I don't know. If you can find her, say that it meant a lot, that it was good company."

"That's it?"

"Guess I should start making calls."

Chartres lingers at the bars. "Drew met with the governor after the widow and told him he was the one who put the bruise on your cheek that night, and that Riggs couldn't have known the truck was stolen because the dispatcher was trying to tell him after the stop. There's still a chance for a stay. If we get it, I can try another appeal. After the shot was . . ."

"My stepdad was a cross-roader, cheated at cards or dice or . . . If he taught me nothing else, he taught me odds. Thanks for everything." Billy takes a long breath and looks at the telephone on the wall. Everyone else's eyes stray in that direction. He can guess their thoughts.

The door sounds, and third guard enters with a folding card table. He hands it to Harding, who asks if it will do.

"Perfect," Billy says.

■

Billy has forgotten Drew's home number. Fortunately someone on the staff, anticipating the need, kept it in a file. Officer Harding reads the number off a sheet of paper and dials it. When the number rings in, he hands the receiver to Billy. Drew's wife, Megan, answers, which throws Billy off for an instant because he expected to hear his mother's voice.

"Hello," she repeats. "Drew, is that you?"

"It's Billy."

"Is Drew with you?"

"No. He's coming, I think. And Alex too."

"Good. How, ah . . . how are you doing?" Megan asks.

He looks at the open door and the stretcher. "Okay, I guess. Thanks. How about you?"

"I'm okay. Reporters keep calling."

He likes Megan, thinks she is the ideal mate for Drew. They shared good times for a while, Drew, Megan, Brenda, and he. Barbecues on Drew's patio. Billy once stood behind Brenda's chair eating a hot dog and dripped mustard on her hair. The only one who didn't laugh was Brenda, who stormed off, muttering that it wasn't funny.

"Is Arden there?"

"Yeah. She's been waiting all day. Hold on."

He looks at Harding as he waits. When Arden speaks, he's surprised at how weak her voice sounds. "Arden, what happened to your voice?"

"Comes and goes. I'm not thirty-nine anymore."

"Neither am I," Billy says.

"Guess I know why you're calling."

"Yeah."

"So what do you have to say for yourself?"

"Say? Well, I guess I should apologize."

"What for?"

"Missing your last thirteen birthdays and Mother's Days. I've been busy."

"Stop it, Billy. I'm your mother. Not a good one. You never heard that before."

"No. Can't say I have."

"Are you . . . are you okay?"

"I don't have time for that, Mom."

He hears Arden say to Megan, "He called me Mom."

"Mom?"

"Yes, Billy. I'm sorry. When they started asking all those questions, I got confused. I couldn't help . . . Can you forgive me?"

He understands that she truly loved Maury and that loving someone who's bad for you is not uncommon, that he himself shares his mother's weakness for loving the wrong one.

"Sure. It's no big thing."

"I did the best I could."

"You did. It's not your fault." He feels an old bitterness well up. Maury, he thinks, you're the one I can't forgive. From hustling drinks in a casino, Arden earned plenty to keep the family in better circumstances, but Maury had a habit of winning until he lost. There was never enough money, never time for meals, never time for caring about three boys.

"But I . . ."

"Arden . . ." He can't continue in this direction. "Mom, don't. Look, I gotta go. You take care of yourself."

"Billy . . ."

He hands the receiver through the bars. He thinks of people he's loved, including Arden, thinks it queer that he couldn't tell his own mother he loves her. But we loved one another, Drew, Alex, me, he thinks. What is a childhood where no one said words of love?

But Drew and Alex came through it. Maybe, Billy thinks, if he'd not had such an ingrained sense of justice he might have fared better.

■

Harding sits in a chair and leans back on the legs. Billy's tempted to say something, but why? Because insignificant matters gain importance? He recalls Maury thumping him with the knuckle of a middle finger for leaning back. "You'll ruin the furniture," Maury said. Billy stood, wiggled the rickety chair, turned his back to Maury, and said, "Why don't you pick on grown men?" Maury muttered something about "Someday," which echoed exactly Billy's feelings that someday matters would come to a head.

Billy looks at the phone. "Officer Harding, what's taking them so long?"

"Can't say, Debecki."

"I thought they were downstairs."

"Don't know. Maybe there's no parking spaces. There's a bunch of protestors outside the gates singing Christmas carols."

"It's May."

Officer Harding shrugs. "You know, peace songs like at Christmas."

"Christmas? One Christmas I boosted some jeans. Store cop caught up to me. We shared a cigarette. I had three pairs on. I stripped to my undershorts and handed over the jeans. He tossed one pair back, said, 'Merry Christmas.' That was about the best Christmas I ever had."

"The best?"

"Pretty much, but," Billy says to no one in particular, "I loved Fourth of July. Summer, no school."

He imagines the park in Blue Diamond, sky alight with fireworks bursting overhead—red to blue to brilliant white—a breeze ruffling through the tall elms, the grass cool and moist. Crystal, a girl he'd met just that day, whispered she had a joint. Would he like to try some? He and Drew ditched Alex and rode in her car with her and her friend to Calico Basin, where they climbed to the peak of Red Rock. The brothers smoked grass for the first time and watched fireworks go off in the distance. Crystal stood, slipped off her tank top, and pulled Billy into an embrace. The dome of light over Las Vegas seemed ethereal as they swayed back and forth to a song she hummed. There was a sweetness to her and her breathy voice that went into and through Billy and warmed him, a feeling he'd never before experienced. As Drew took his companion's hand and led her away, Billy spread his arms and spun around, shouting, "I love it. I love it."

A week later Drew and he jumped off the forbidden cliffs at Lake Mead, plunging into water fifty feet below as Alex screamed that he was going to tell. It seemed they were emerging into something wondrous. Billy, imagining the possibilities of life, convinced himself the fearless Debecki brothers combined could conquer anything. Then early the following autumn he beat Drew in a game of car tag and broke his little finger on his right hand. He wore a cast for three weeks, wore it with quiet pride, refusing to tell anyone how he'd broken the finger. He was going to be okay. They all were. Another year of high school for Drew, and two for himself, then out of the apartment and on to college. Where didn't matter.

Then the first Friday afternoon in October the world shifted when Billy found his mother lying in bed, sobbing, blood on the sheets and pillowcases, on the carpet, on the bedspread. She insisted that she would be fine. Billy left her and walked to a hardware store, stole a three-foot pipe and a roll of electrician's tape. When he returned, he cut the cast off his hand and covered the pipe with tape, doing so slowly and ritualistically. Over a three-day period Maury called from various poker parlors in Gardena, checking on Arden and asking if cops were looking for him. Billy assured him Arden was fine, said it was safe to return, but all the while he looked at the plumber's pipe he'd neatly wrapped in electrical tape for Maury's homecoming.

Billy blinks and gazes at the steel door that resembles those used to seal passages on ships. Doors, he thinks, the symbols of poets. He remembers lying on his back, Brenda unclothed next to him, both of them exhausted from lovemaking. As he stroked her pubic mound, the Doors sang in the background. She had reopened in him that which he lost in the autumn the year he beat Maury. He thought, Here is the woman I can talk to, tell her what it was like in Elko, locked away for two years, or the night he ran across a field to save two wounded Panamanians, one a teenage girl. He rolled on his side to see her face in the dim light. She'd gone to sleep. He lay on his back and listened to her soft snoring.

Now nothing seems more important than seeing his brothers. He wonders what was causing the delay. He scoops up the cards and deals out three five-card poker hands, which he gathers up one card at a time. He places those on the top of the deck, sets the deck on the table, and lies back. He stares at the door, thinking of a stray he brought home, a mixed terrier with orange spots in its fur and an always-wet black nose. He named him Oliver Twist. The boys had never had a pet, and for once Arden sided with them against Maury and said they could keep it. Maury refused them money for dog food, so Billy and Drew panhandled or earned money helping elderly women load the groceries in their cars. They claimed to be Boy Scouts working for donations to aid stray dogs. The blue-haired ladies, charmed and disarmed, never doled out less than a dollar.

Billy loved the dog, let it sleep in his bunk, but after two weeks passed by Maury took it out to the desert and turned it loose. Billy wonders how bad Oliver suffered. What kind of man makes war on animals and women and children? He pictures his stepfather slouched on the couch, a smile on his lips as he calmly said that Oliver would die of thirst before dying from hunger. Billy sauntered to the kitchen and lifted a carving knife from the drawer. He casually walked to the couch, and just to let him know, drove the blade in the cushion between Maury's outstretched legs, an inch from his crotch.

■

The guard looks through the slot and slides the lock. Billy sits behind the second row of bars, in front of him on the table a deck of cards. He looks up casually as his brothers enter. He does not want to appear anxious or worried, so he masks his feelings behind a dry smile. Drew enters first and walks straight for the cell as if he knows his way around. He appears as he always has, tall and assured. Alex, obviously struck by what he sees, hesitates at the sight of the room, seems nervous.

Still grinning, Billy stands. "What brings you two here?"

Drew looks at the cards. "We heard there was a card game."

"This is Nevada. Card games everywhere."

"Okay, we came to see you. How goes it?"

"Can't recall having a worse day." Billy glances at Officer Harding. "Look here, a couple of suckers. Well, come on. We have time for a little game of chance."

Drew looks around. He licks his lips. "Arden wants you to call."

"We talked." Billy picks up the deck and appears to shuffle. "Let's see. They call one of you Drew and one Alex, right?"

Alex says, "We talked to the governor. Didn't we, Drew?"

"Yeah, and he listened. Or seemed to."

Billy drops his smile. "He listened to the Riggs widow and his brother, too." He motions for them to sit. "I don't want to talk about that. . . . Know what I want?"

"What?"

"I want to pretend we've got cigars to smoke and some Jack Daniel's to drink, and there's a tomorrow for all of us. Crazy as it sounds, that's what I want."

"Fine," Drew says and nods to Alex.

They seat themselves on the two open chairs. Billy deals out the round of cards. Without peeking, the brothers leave them facedown on the table.

"A nine for Drew, the old man, and a three to Alex, a ten for the house. That's me." he lets the deck rest in his hand. "Can't say who's my favorite. Hemingway? Steinbeck? Kesey? Thing about all of them is they didn't know how to write about gambling."

"Why do you say they didn't know how to write about gambling?" Alex asks.

"Gambling isn't about hope. It's about odds. You win with the odds. Right, Drew?" Billy smiles at Drew. "And because their characters always had the upper hand. But mostly because we grew up in a house where every deck was stacked."

"Brenda came to the house. A week ago," Drew says.

Billy deals the second cards around. "Two to the old man, a five to Alex, a card for the house." He settles his gaze on Drew. "Double down?"

"Always on eleven."

"I cheat, you know. What did she want?"

Drew shakes his head. "Drama."

"You sent her away, right?" He deals Drew a card. "You got another deuce. Turn it over."

"I'll take a hit," Alex says. "Gotta hit a twelve."

Billy deals Alex a four and glances at the guards, who silently watch every move as the skit plays out. Their grim expressions are part of the ritual. He smiles at them and holds the deck out but doesn't hit Alex's hand.

"So, Drew, you sent Brenda packing?"

Drew nods. "Actually Arden did. You remember how they were. Peas in a pod."

"You could say that. Good for Arden. She didn't mention it." Billy lays a seven on Alex's hand. "I wrote Brenda a letter today. Know what I wrote?"

"How would we know?" Drew asks.

"It was a rhetorical question." Billy shuffles the deck, this time giving it an honest shuffle as he riffles the edges. "I told her I hope she finds a path, but if she doesn't, keep up the shopping. It's good for the economy."

Alex shakes his head. "That's your girl who got together with her ex-husband?"

Billy pictures the glass window at the county jail, Brenda seated on the opposite side, a telephone receiver to her ear. Drew arranged her visit. The first words from her were that she wouldn't be able to pick him up upon his release. He said that was fine, that Drew would take him home. She shook her head, said that wasn't what she meant, and raised her left hand, on it a wedding band. Kevin was deeply sorry, she claimed, promised he would control himself. They were reunited. It was best for all.

"That's the one," Billy says.

Alex holds his card below the table's edge.

"Okay, Alex, rule number one is don't hold cards away from the table. I don't want you making any gypsy moves on me."

Alex lays the cards on the table. "Billy, we've got to talk."

"That's what we're doing. We're talking."

"No, *talk*. Drew told me."

"Drew told you? Told you what?"

"Why you beat Dad. It wasn't a car accident that hurt Arden."

Billy finds this amazing. After all the years, he assumed Alex had to realize Arden wasn't hurt in an accident. He shakes his head. "Hell, Alex, everything's an accident. Or nothing is."

"I'm talking about Arden."

"So am I. If it's not all accidents then everything's planned, including human events." To Billy that means a drunken fool and a cop with a wife and kids were predestined to meet on a dark highway, and that is unacceptable. "Think about it. What that would suggest about a God."

"All I'm saying is I'm sorry. I should have trusted you. It's just that when we came in the apartment and you . . . beat him. And later no explanation. Well, I . . ."

"It's okay."

"But I came here to make it right."

"It is right. Tell him, Drew."

"It was my idea not to tell," Drew says. "We didn't want you hating Maury."

"If I'd known. I mean, all these years. All the silence. Why wouldn't you see Drew?"

Billy looks at Drew as he talks. "I killed a cop. In prison that's a good thing, gives you a free pass. But if you talk to a cop, even your brother, it works just the opposite."

Drew clears his throat. "How about the game?"

"It should all be different," Alex says.

"Let's play." Billy picks up the deck again and shuffles.

"We're watching you," Drew says. "No tricks."

Billy offers up the deck for Drew to cut. He deals out the first cards and as he does, he recalls an incident in Panama. "This American charged into a squad of Panamanian soldiers, all of them armed and shooting. His gun jammed, but he kept running at them. When they saw a crazy guy charging them without firing, they tossed down their guns and surrendered."

"Really?" Alex peeks at his first card.

"It's true. I've never told that story to anyone."

Drew says, "Great story. Why not?"

"Because no one ever asked."

"What happened to the American?" Drew asks.

Billy deals the next round of cards. "Worst luck I ever saw. First whore he screwed in Panama gave him clap. It was also the first time he ever got laid."

Except for Billy, everyone laughs, including the guards.

Alex whistles. "That's some serious bad luck."

"True. I was the medic who jammed penicillin in the guy's butt." Billy imagines himself beside the helicopter, the whirling blades drowning out all other sound. The door gunner shook his head as Billy lifted the wounded girl into the chopper's belly. The gunner helped for an instant until she was safely aboard, then he fired over Billy's head as the helicopter rose. Billy turned away, and head down, charged back across the field through knee-high grass. The mud sucked at his boots. Tracers broke the air around him, but he heard nothing. When he again reached the irrigation ditch he threw himself down, next to the soldier, a Panamanian with a sucking chest wound. He saw the man's sweating face, smiling, hiding pain.

"You can blame it on luck or on bad judgment. Or say it's mostly random accident." I did something right once, Billy thinks, and wonders for the first time in years who has the medal.

"Threw down their weapons," Alex says, "because they figured the deck was stacked against them?"

Billy blinks. "What? Yeah, yeah," he says. "You're a quick study."

Billy pictures the Panamanian grimacing as he clamps a compress to the wound. The man shook his head and muttered, "*Mato.*" Billy told him, no, no. That soldier didn't want to be there any more than Billy did. In that queer time-event frequency they were two men precariously holding on to life while lying a foot below an erratic shower of machine-gun fire. If only, Billy thinks, he could have saved Riggs the way he saved that soldier. He begged him not to die.

"You okay?" Drew asks.

"Yeah. I'm okay. People like me, like us, well, we got a lot of bad shuffles. That's how I see it. You two made it okay. Good to have you two here."

"Are you scared?"

Billy set his gaze on Alex. "I don't want to talk about it."

"I do."

"Okay, if it'll keep the game going. Hell, I've been afraid most of my life. This is just one more thing to be afraid of. I figure when they press that plunger, they push all the fear out of you. I've always wondered what it was like not to be afraid. Now maybe I'll find out."

Memories circle him, hours spent at a kitchen table, a wobbly-legged thing that seated four, Maury jawing all the while, dealing at times from the top of the deck, sometimes from elsewhere. Billy was Maury's protégé, a boy who could roll a deck and deal deadwood like a deuce dealer. By age fourteen, he could imitate Maury, call a hand as it was dealt. His keen ear caught the subtle snap when Maury dealt seconds. "You're cheating," he would say. Maury would smile. "Billy's gonna be the one," he would say.

Billy turns his hand over and busts. "I lose. Let's try poker. What's the stakes? Hold 'Em. Two and five. Two bump limit."

"Jesus," Alex says, "just then, you sounded exactly like Maury. Drew, remember how he used to imitate him?"

"And cheat like him. That's why I don't trust the deal."

"Maury? You called him Maury."

"Yeah."

Billy grins and deals the hand. "Hateful words, Drew, hateful. If you want an honest deal, you have to deal with the devil. He's got the odds. You want to take a chance, you have to deal with God. Hope or odds? Take your pick."

"You've picked the devil?" Alex asks.

"I didn't pick anything. Let's play."

They raise and draw and raise again, the bets imaginary. Whenever it seems to deal with what's facing him, Billy steers the conversation away. He wants for a while to forget the things he remembers too well, the terror he experienced lying in that field while machine gunners fired at him, and the panic he felt as he sat on the dark highway crying and pleading for Trooper Riggs to live. Billy wants neither hope nor despair. He wants the middle ground that is life, the place where most people live, walking to the mailbox, heating a can of soup, listening to the calming sound of a dog chewing a bone, or playing a simple card game.

"You win again, Drew. Still think the game's rigged?" Alex says.

"It was rigged from the start." Billy looks at Drew. "Who has my medal?"

"Arden. At least I think she does."

"Uh-huh. Good. How about Texas Hold 'Em?" Billy asks.

"Don't care for it," Drew says.

Billy holds the deck. "I've wondered about something for a long while—Drew?"

"What's that? Why I don't like Hold 'Em?"

"No. I've wondered about our father. Haven't you?"

"Why wonder about a man who abandoned us? Never a card or a call. No child support. No, I don't wonder about him very much at all."

"No?"

Drew shakes his head. "The son of a bitch is dead. Died four years ago. Arden got a call from someone they both knew. He started another family after us. Stayed with them."

"No shit. Ever think it was her fault?"

"I used to think it was our fault. I grew out of that. Are we going to play or get morbid?"

"Let's play," Alex says.

"You deal, Drew." Billy passes the deck to Drew.

Drew shuffles, offers the deck to Alex to cut, and announces, "Five-card stud."

Billy sorts and fans his cards neatly and then lays them facedown on the table. "I ever tell you about the time I played out a seven-card-stud hand with only a king high? This guy across from me sitting with three kings says, 'All you got in the hole, son, is hope.'"

"Go ahead, tell us."

"I said, 'That's all I need.' And I turned over a king-high flush."

The door buzzer sounds. The brothers turn toward the door at the same instant the door opens. The warden enters with two guards. The brothers exchange looks. The warden nods to the guard nearest the door, who stands by the phone on the wall. Alex rubs his eyes and looks away.

Billy says, "And the guy says . . ." He pauses to acknowledge the warden, who's motioning to him. "'You have to play the cards you got.'"

For a moment the room is absolutely silent. Then Billy looks at the warden. "Well," he says, "time to pay up."

The brothers turn over their cards. Alex holds a pair of fours, queen high. Drew has a blank, ten high. Billy turns his over slowly and shows a club flush, jack high. Best stud hand of the night. The warden motions for Officer Cramer to open the bars. Drew and Alex stand. The table scrapes the floor as the guards move it. Everyone is silent and reverent.

Billy wishes he could think of something clever to say, something memorable, like a line delivered in a book or movie. He looks at the steel clamshell door awaiting him. Its closing will be the last metallic clang he will ever hear. Four straps to buckle, one for each limb, one for each guard. There's busy work ahead. He looks at Drew, who's crying, and his mouth goes dry. The last time he saw Drew cry was the final game of car tag when Billy broke a finger.

"Can we touch?" Drew asks.

The warden says it will be all right but then he and Alex must leave. Billy grapples for words to say, but can't find any. Where are the words in the poems? Have all of them been wasted? He reaches for Alex first as the brothers come together. Billy gathers both in. He closes his eyes and feels their breath, their heat. The warden lays a hand on his shoulder. Billy knows he must let go, but it will be the hardest thing he's ever done. The blood that flows through them flows through him, and there is time for this and only this. All the bluff and cheating are gone, and not a single word to offer. Is that his final punishment, he wonders? Is there more to come? He looks at the open door and his arms go limp.

Minimal Damage

A knock interrupted him as he was paying household bills on the computer. He figured Julie needed a hand with the baby or groceries, but when he opened the door, he confronted two men wearing wool overcoats and business suits. The white one, a large, stolid figure with a slouch, clutched papers that ruffled in the gusting wind. The second, a short black man, held in his open palm a leather case displaying a gold shield and an identification card.

The black officer smiled politely. "Rodney Jamison?"

"Yes."

The black officer pumped his thumb in the direction of his companion. "This is Detective Towers. I'm Detective Sergeant Blue."

The scene reminded Rodney of a television cop show, the kind he watched half interested when winding down from a day's work. He could not imagine two cops, not just cops but detectives, at his doorstep or even in his neighborhood, unless it was about the Bergmans, who had been burglarized in September.

"How can I help?"

The sergeant grimaced, then said, "We hate to inconvenience you, but we have a search warrant for these premises."

Rodney glanced at the document the white man handed him. It appeared official enough, stamped with a seal, dated and notarized. "There must be a mistake."

"No, sir. I'm afraid not. The warrant's for 1725 Mystic Place."

Rodney glanced at the document—a name, words about unspecified human remains. Exactly what that meant was unclear. "I don't understand. Who's Calvin Stops? I demand to know what you're looking for."

"We have to come in." The sergeant's voice was firm.

Rodney looked outside to see if anyone had noticed his visitors. The swirling autumn wind shifted islands of brown leaves, and the naked branches of elm and walnut trees whipped about, but the street was empty. Whatever brought them to his doorstep had nothing to do with him. To avoid any embarrassment, he stepped aside to let them in.

"It's too cold to stand in an open door."

His experience in finance had taught him that it is best to seek common ground whenever possible. He figured the sergeant, a black man like himself, was a professional who had exceeded society's expectations. Rodney felt certain they could resolve the matter before Julie returned. He pointed to the couch and asked them to take a seat, not out of a sense of propriety but because he reasoned that rudeness would merely exacerbate the situation.

"Thank you," Sergeant Blue said, but neither man sat.

"I'm branch manager of Union State Trust and Savings," Rodney said, establishing his position. "I can't imagine this being anything other than an error."

Sergeant Blue assured him that he was not a suspect and said there was no error, that the search was part of an ongoing investigation. Rodney asked for clarification, but the cop told him that he could not offer details as yet. Any leak might damage the case.

"Sir," Sergeant Blue said, "we do our best not to disturb things, but we have a job to do."

"I have rights. I'll have to call an attorney before I allow . . ."

Unruffled, the sergeant said. "Tell him the city will reimburse any damage to property."

As they spoke a black-and-white van parked in front, and four men wearing green jumpsuits embroidered with yellow badges stepped out and opened the rear doors. Three removed shovels, picks, and a wood-framed screen. The fourth carried a video camera, which he slung over his shoulder. He grabbed what looked like a camera case.

Rodney shook his head as the officers outside busied themselves packing tools down the walkway to the backyard. "What are they doing?"

"Like I said, you'll be reimbursed for any damage."

Rodney was baffled. One instant he was paying bills on the computer and the next his home was invaded by cops. "I think it's fair to tell me what all this is about."

"In time." The sergeant looked at Detective Towers, who nodded and backed away. "Mr. Jamison, please go about your business. We're not here to harm you."

"No. Well, you're damn sure troubling me."

"Yes, sir."

Rodney figured further discussion was pointless. Julie, who had likely stopped to buy groceries, was due home from her parents,' where she'd gone to pick up Abilene. Julie was enrolled at the university, working toward a master's in counseling. Three days a week she left the baby at her parent's. He had to call and warn her. No, he thought, not warn her, but prepare her. Then he could call Gary Mills from the bank's corporate legal arm. He knew him from staff meetings.

"Can I call my wife?" he asked.

"You're free to do whatever, but don't interfere with the search," the sergeant said. "Oh, Mr. Jamison, we may need to put you and your family up at a hotel. How many kids?"

"One. A baby girl. But that's jumping the gun. Our house suits us fine."

"One girl?" The sergeant smiled again. "I have four. Outnumbered from the time I get up until I go to work and then again when I get home."

Rodney said, "Just how far is this going to go?"

The sergeant dropped his smile. "We don't know."

Rodney's stomach churned as he picked up the phone. He could not fathom strangers barging into a house unannounced and disrupting life. He was not a suspect, could not be, unless in America being a black man was once again a crime, but he dismissed that notion as the rhetoric of bitterness and individual failure, a mantra for those who could not unfold a map to a better life for themselves.

Through hard work and determination Rodney had claimed that better life. This two-story white house of three thousand square feet on a quarter acre was proof. It was his along with the responsibility of paying its mortgage. During the Gulf War he had witnessed men, mostly scared and hungry, surrendering themselves for a meal and a chance to live, and from that he had finally understood not just the breadth of his mother's love but the depth of her fear. The memory of those men broken of hope was what he had brought home with him. He had returned determined to build something that those pathetic men were deprived of.

He dialed Julie's cell phone number and waited. A recorder answered. He pressed the disconnect button, called her parents, and got another answering machine. He dialed Gary Mills and left a message asking the attorney to call him at home as soon as possible.

When he returned to the living room, the detectives were outside. He decided to return to his computer, but just then a vehicle eased to a stop in front. He thought it might be Julie. He opened the door and saw instead an SUV painted black and white with a shield emblem on the door and lettering that said CANINE UNIT. An officer was stringing a barrier of yellow tape around the fence. Although a mere plastic ribbon, it seemed a wall of stone. Up and down the street blinds and drapes were open. A scattering of people, underdressed for the weather, gathered on the sidewalk across the street, chatting among themselves, arms wrapped across their chests to ward off the wind. Rodney felt besieged. The canine cop opened the rear car door. Out sprang a German shepherd, which landed on the island of grass by the sidewalk. Its fur bristled in the wind.

"It's a search dog," a voice from behind said.

Rodney wheeled about. Detective Towers stood behind him.

"Search dog?"

"Yes, sir. Do you have something to keep yourself occupied? People will be tromping in and out of here."

"I am occupied, Officer."

"May I use a toilet?"

"You didn't bring one with you?"

The cop stared, his face bland and patient.

"It's down the hallway."

He had anticipated Julie's arriving within minutes. She did not. Again he got recordings when he called the two numbers. The cops had been at the house almost an hour. He looked out the kitchen window. The canine officer held the dog's leash as it pawed a hole in the lawn near the barbecue Rodney had built last spring. He had not bought a dog for this very reason. As a latchkey child, the only son of a working mother, he had pined for a dog. But wants changed. A healthy lawn took precedence.

Upon first gazing out at the backyard of this house—lawn half dead, four neglected ash trees, gazebo in need of paint—he had imagined it transformed into the yard he had longed for as a boy. A brick patio, brick barbecue, lush lawn, white gazebo, shade trees. His mother had moved from her own mother's house to the suburb of Belcore when he was two, her openly expressed desire to rear him among whites. She wanted him far away from the drainpipes of the inner city that swallowed up boys, hoped to keep him from the random violence that had claimed his father. She had dreamed someday to live in a house such as the one he now owned, but had settled for a cottage on Tod Amber Street, the house where she had spent her last years, the one she died in. As he watched the dog dig up his work, his stomach turned for a second time.

At the other end of the yard two officers under the watchful eye of Detective Towers had busted out his brick walkway and were excavating a hole near the gazebo. He flung open the back door and screamed, "You're ruining my yard!"

Before Rodney was aware of it, Sergeant Blue gripped him by the arm. "Now, calm down. I said any damage would be taken care of."

Rodney blurted out, "I'm not some nigger you can come in here and do like this." As soon as it was out, he wished that he had held his tongue. He had given voice to the word that disgusted him, a ghetto word, a word of degradation and hate on the tongues of whites. He had profaned himself.

Sergeant Blue looked at him as one does when there is no hope for talking things through. It was a look Rodney had not seen for a long while. In giving in to rage, he had surrendered whatever power he had. He sensed the sergeant wanted to hit him as a parent might impulsively strike a child, but knew that he would not because he was a man well practiced in the art of self-control, the art the black man must master to earn respect and get along, an art Rodney himself had mastered.

"I'm gonna ask you to go inside and behave," Sergeant Blue said, his voice kindly, almost fatherly. "Or I'll have someone take you downtown."

"Am I a suspect in something?"

"No, Mr. Jamison, you're a bother right now."

One of the officers by the gazebo called to the sergeant. "We got something."

Sergeant Blue waved his hand to the officer, then turned to Rodney. "Excuse me."

Rodney returned to the kitchen and stared out the window again. The cops gathered around the hole by the gazebo screened his view. Two watched on hands and knees as the officer with the video camera aimed the lens at something. Rodney started to go upstairs to the master bedroom to view what was unfolding, but he glimpsed the sidewalk through the living room window.

Julie's gray Montero, his Christmas gift to her, sat parked behind the canine vehicle. Julie stood talking with a uniformed officer. She clutched the collar of her blue overcoat and balanced Abilene on her hip. Neighbors had gathered at the police barrier. Rodney hurried outside.

When she saw him, Julie hollered, "Thank God. What . . ."

She left her sentence hanging as a few spectators closed around. Rodney reached where the cop stood guard and informed him that Julie was his wife. He reached over the fence and gathered in his baby. He held Abilene in one arm and opened the gate for Julie. A young woman who lived a block north said, "See, I told you." He looked at her and said, "Told you what?" He got a blank stare as an answer.

"Rod, what's going on?" Julie asked.

"I tried to call and warn you." He kissed the baby's cheek and removed the pacifier from her mouth. He gave it to Julie and said, "Didn't the pediatrician tell us not to use a pacifier too much? We don't want her to have an overbite."

Julie brushed her bangs back and shook her head. "Don't do that, Rod. Never mind. Just tell me what's going on."

He turned and walked toward the house. Julie fell in beside him, asking again what the police were up to. If he didn't understand it himself, how could he explain the machinery that was in operation to her? At the stoop he paused and looked back at the neighbors' curious faces. He saw the judgmental look that he had seen in the eyes of people when as a student in college he first took Julie out to dinner, eyes that saw a black man with a white girl. He knew the equation—white women were girls if in the company of a black man. Without giving due thought to what he was about to do, he faced them and held Abilene overhead as if she were a talisman.

"What are you doing?" Julie asked. "She's a baby."

"They're tearing up my work," he said and then clutched his baby to his chest.

Inside, Julie kicked off her shoes, tossed her purse on the nearest end table, and slipped off her coat. He slumped down in a chair, brushed his hand over Abilene's hair, woolly like his, only reddish. He kissed where it was parted in the middle.

"Let me hold her and tell me what's going on," she said.

"They had a search warrant. They're digging in the back."

"What're they looking for? And give me Abilene."

It made no sense. All that was certain was that his world was out of kilter. He looked at his daughter, her copper eyes shining like waxy leaves. "You miss me?"

The baby pawed at his chin. Answer enough, he thought. Julie opened her arms to take Abilene. Rodney shook his head, but Julie nodded insistently. He surrendered. The baby settled into her mother's arms. Julie asked what the search warrant said. Rodney realized that he had not read the details.

He shrugged. "I laid it somewhere. I think the kitchen."

"For Christ's sake, let's read it."

He waited under the arch at the kitchen entrance and watched Julie walk to the counter. She said, "Nothing here," then looked out the window, gasped, and turned away. She ran to the passageway and said, "Here." She shoved Abilene into his arms and ran down the hall.

Rodney went to the sink and saw what she had seen. A body, mostly decomposed, lay half on the lawn, half in the hole. He covered his daughter's eyes to protect her, though she wouldn't know what she was seeing. He heard Julie vomiting in the hallway bathroom.

Julie decided to go to her parent's, said that she couldn't stay in the house. He agreed it was a better alternative to them staying in a strange hotel; besides, someone had to watch the house. Over the twenty minutes it took Julie to assemble clothes and items needed for a three-day stay, a half dozen more police officers arrived. They seemed to be all over the house now, two in the basement, a third tapping the wall beside the fireplace in the family room, another running some kind of electrical detector over walls.

He thought of the standard his mother had set for herself—be responsible, be safe, love those who love you and protect them. How, he wondered, do I protect them? Before he walked Julie and the baby outside, he said that the important thing to remember was that all of this would pass. He wanted to believe it, but the words seemed empty of truth, no more than a platitude. Julie nodded, he sensed, only because a response was called for. He picked up her suitcase.

"Was it a woman?" she asked.

He shrugged. She looked past him at the door, as if she could see through it and the walls and to the farthest horizon beyond the house. "Jesus, Rod." She shook her head.

The number of spectators had diminished. The cop standing watch at the gate pushed a wooden barricade aside for them. Rodney told him to leave it open, that he would be right back. At the car he told Julie he would call to check on her. She nodded, did not look at him. He strapped the baby in a carrier in the backseat and told Julie that he loved her. She said that she loved him too, but he detected a listlessness in her voice.

After the good-byes, he walked to the gate. The young woman who had made the earlier remark was still watching the house. Beside her was a young man who asked Rodney what was going on. Rodney did not answer him. Instead, he looked at the young woman and said loudly enough for all to hear, "If you're waiting for a black man to walk out in handcuffs, you'll be disappointed."

Gary Mills returned the call but had little to offer in the way of advice, said that a search warrant was a legal mandate from a judge and that criminal law was not his area of expertise.

"What should I do?"

"Stay out of their way. If you're not a suspect you have nothing to fear."

"But it's my house. There's a dead body in my yard."

"Rodney, you don't strike me as a murderer. Relax. If they make a mess of your house, I know a good attorney who'll sue the shit out of them."

Rodney managed a reluctant thanks and said good-bye.

His decision to stay had been easy. He felt uncomfortable at his in-law's, even on the shortest of visits, so staying with them overnight or longer was out of the question. He would rather sleep in a hotel room. Don and Alice had been pleasant enough when Julie had first invited him to her house for introductions. He and Julie had been part of a study group in a sociology class. What could be less threatening? But when they began to date, her parents had interceded, asking her to think what a future with a black man would mean. Rodney had tried to put himself in their place and had told Julie that he understood. She'd kissed him and said, "Well, I don't."

The paste had gone dry on the wallpaper, as his mother had liked to say. "Sometimes it's hung right, sometimes not." Now Don and Alice fawned over their granddaughter and tried their hardest to make Rodney feel at ease, but the more they tried, the worse it made matters. They had conceded that he was everything parents could ask for in a son-in-law. He had drive and common sense, was patient, gentle, and a good husband and father. All true, but they had wanted someone different, someone whiter.

A knock came at the back door. Rodney left the computer and opened the door. Sergeant Blue stood on the other side. Out back a dozen men and two women milled around, some talking, some taking photographs.

"You're knocking again," Rodney said.

"Yes. If you'd like, I've got a uniform car out front. The officers will drive you to the Regis. They're holding a room for you."

Rodney shook his head. "I'm not leaving in a police car."

"I can force the matter if necessary."

"No. This is my house. Those bricks you lifted, I put down. I seeded and weeded the lawn. A man's entitled to his house."

The sergeant pointed to the kitchen table. "Let's sit."

They sat at opposite ends of the small table. The sergeant held his hands together as if in prayer and rested his chin on the fingertips.

"Okay, I'm laying it out. You bought this house a year and a half ago. Sometime before you bought this house it was rented by Calvin Lewis Stops. He lived here three years and was evicted for not paying rent. He's in custody, no bail. Kidnapped a woman from a shopping center, tied her up, raped her, and was digging a grave when she managed to get away. We arrested him yesterday and have kept the lid on it for good reason."

Rodney's throat went dry. This was the junk news he turned off on television, the sick stuff that sold papers. He said the first thing that came to mind. "But the yard, the house are . . . look at them. Impeccable."

The sergeant continued without addressing Rodney's remark. "We unearthed two bodies out back, Mr. Jamison. We're taking the dog down to the basement. If we have to, we'll bring in jackhammers. You shouldn't be here. You won't be able to . . ."

"I'm staying. It's my house."

The sergeant took a breath and expelled it slowly. "Be reasonable."

He shook his head. "I'm a veteran of Desert Storm. I earned this house, bought on a GI loan, and I am not riding anywhere in a police car. Not so's my neighbors can draw conclusions."

The sergeant dropped his gaze. He stood up from the table, walked to the back door and opened it. He called for the others to bring the dog inside. The officer with the dog entered, followed by two detectives who looked at Rodney apologetically.

Rodney dragged himself up the stairs and spread the bedroom curtains. He stared down at his backyard bathed in a light so white it made the officers appear iridescent. The ash trees had shed their leaves. Their pale bark glowed. The cops had excavated two holes, both several feet deep. The second had also rendered up a body, the bones luminous white. He thought of the eerie sky over the Kuwaiti desert, the dull burning domes of light in the distance. It had happened. He closed the curtains and lay on the bed, held Julie's pillow and sniffed it, taking in the smell of her shampoo. He thought about the hundreds he had buried in that desolate place, the remains of Iraqis abandoned by their leaders, men bombed to death. There was nothing to do but sink the blade of the Caterpillar into the sand.

He lay there, for some reason thinking about a particular couple who had applied for a loan in Old Town. Both were young, the wife pregnant with a second child. The husband worked as an auto body repairman and wanted to open his own shop. He had photos of his work, shots of cars that glistened, but he also had two repossessed cars. Rodney believed the young man would have made good on the loan, but had to say no. Someone higher up would have stopped the loan from going through, and okaying it would have reflected negatively on Rodney. That was a tough no.

While in college he had interned in a loan department at a bank, and when he graduated, Union State recruited him to fill a position at the Old Town branch on Lyman Street, four blocks from the projects. The job came with a title and an office, not a cubicle as others started in. He had considered himself fortunate and deserving, anything but ordinary.

A constant stream of people applied for loans, couples, their eyes hopeful, nervous. Some asked for business loans. He looked to their needs, searched out federal assistance, set paperwork in order, made appointments. Within weeks he discovered how few applications cleared—bad credit, poor work history, insufficient skills to qualify for a particular business. Some reminded him of his mother, people with histories of long employment, years of paying bills on time, but no assets, no credit.

In time he realized he had been recruited and given a title mostly to put a black face on the word *no*. Then he initiated a program, went into the community, offered seminars at school gyms, community centers, and churches, instructed people on ways to manage debt, processes to improve their credit rating, methods to approach a business plan. In four years the number of successful loan applicants at the Old Town branch increased by 50 percent, and the success rate on loans improved proportionately.

When Julie became pregnant, she expressed concern that he would have to say no to the wrong person or that he might fall victim to some violent end. He had been more than diligent. He was assistant branch manager by then. She worried that his office was near a crime-infested neighborhood, insisted that he had earned the right to something better. Finally he requested a transfer. His initial request was denied, as was his second, so he applied for a position with a rival bank in the suburb of Del Visto and received an offer.

The day he proffered his resignation from Union State, he was offered branch manager at Old Town, but turned it down. He was cleaning out his desk when the district president called and said a manager's position had opened at the South Benson branch if he was interested. His mother's dream had been to move to the South Benson suburb. That day he knew exceptional things lay ahead because it was the day he had turned up Mystic Place and noticed the FOR SALE sign.

Although the house was only twelve years old, it had been rented out by an absentee owner for seven years and was in a state of general disrepair. The real estate agent had pointed out the finer features, the fireplace, the hardwood floors. She called it a property. He called it a house and countered with the things that needed repair and paint. She said that what it needed was mostly cosmetic. He maintained that it was mostly expensive. What he held back was that he intended do the work himself, wanted to. His training as a combat engineer had taught him the basics of construction. He had decided the best way to lay claim to the house was to invest himself in it. If need be, he could read books or seek advice from professionals. Now his hard work seemed perverted by events beyond his control.

He awoke an hour later to the grating sound of a jackhammer. He looked at his watch and called Julie. She asked what the noise in the background was.

"A jackhammer."

"Christ."

"How's Abilene?"

"Asleep. Rod, I . . . don't think I can come back to the house. And you shouldn't be there either."

"It's our house."

She went silent. He waited for her to speak, and when she didn't, he said that he was going to see what the cops were doing.

"Rod, who'd do such a thing?"

"Some man. Must have lived here before us. The sergeant said he'd kidnapped a woman who got away."

"I can't come back."

He looked at the window, the light on the outside so brilliant that the curtains appeared on fire. He swallowed and said, "We'll wait."

He told her to kiss the baby for him, hung up, and walked downstairs. A cop stood at the entrance to the basement. Rodney greeted him with a nod. "Would you tell Sergeant Blue that I'd like to take him up on his offer? I only ask that I drive myself to the hotel."

When Sergeant Blue emerged from the basement steps, he pointed to the table. He looked weary. He sat, fingers entwined, hands in front of him on the white tile tabletop. "Mr. Jamison, it's been a hard day. We're going to leave two officers on watch and return tomorrow." He looked around. "This is a nice house. It's a shame."

"I guess."

"We'll have to make a press release."

Rodney bowed his head. He remembered how the house was the first time he brought Julie to see it. Right away she had seen in it what he had. She entered the vacant living room and pirouetted several times as if neither he nor the real estate agent was present.

"Are there more?" Rodney asked, meaning bodies.

"Yes."

Rodney nodded.

The sergeant wrote a number on a business card. "This is the number of our community relations office." He handed it to Rodney. "It would have been better if you'd left."

"How would it have been better?"

The next morning he awoke in a strange room, a shaft of sunlight in his eyes. He fixed coffee in the coffeemaker provided by the hotel, called his assistant and left a message saying he would not be in. He lay on the bed sipping coffee and watching the news, the volume turned off. He wanted his home back, the sooner the better. He hated any separation from his family. He called the number the detective had scratched down on the business card. The department spokesman assured him that minimal damage had been done and a licensed contractor would repair everything to specifications. Bureaucratic talk. Pitiless talk, his talk.

The television broadcast an image of his house, followed by a mug shot of the killer. A roving reporter conducted spot interviews with citizens on the streets. A queasiness crept over him. He turned off the television. He lay on his back and thought about his mother's sacrifices to keep him in Eisenhower High, how she had insisted he study, not play football or basketball, didn't want him falling into the trap of being just a jock. So he had played baseball as a closing pitcher and competed on the debate and chess teams. He had often wondered if she was trying to whitewash him. No, he thought, she just wanted him safe.

For a time he paced the room. By ten o'clock he could stand it no longer. He called Julie, told her he was coming to pick her and Abilene up, and the three of them were going to lunch. She said that was crazy, that she had seen what she had, and it was on the news, and it made no sense them going out as if nothing were wrong.

"Yes, it does," he said.

He had brought three suits to the hotel, but decided to wear jeans and a sweatshirt. He picked her up at noon, intent on convincing her that they should not let events overwhelm them, that it did not have to affect them in the long term. It was their home and always would be. But the silence inside the car seemed to need the accompaniment of drum rolls. He drove them in the BMW to Piccardi's, her favorite Italian restaurant. They sat in a booth, where they took turns holding Abilene as they ate. They did not talk as he had planned. They did not talk at all.

Afterward, on the drive home they heard the newscaster on the radio say that the two women had been identified. Rodney turned up the volume. He looked at Julie, whose jaw clenched as she held Abilene. The women had names, he thought, had family and people who cared. The empty spaces they had left in other people's lives now filled his, his and Julie's, and the only defense against it seemed to be silence. Julie switched stations. He wanted to stop the car and hold her, but she was closed as a vault.

It was too cold to walk in the park, so they drove the shoreline from Tetum to Bradberg streets. The trees lining the parkway were stark. He parked facing the shore so the sun slanted through the windshield and warmed them. The baby began to fuss.

"She's hungry," Julie said.

He watched Julie nurse Abilene. He remembered the sad deprivation he had witnessed in Kuwait after the war, women nursing children under their robes as if it were something shameful.

"How are your parents?" he asked.

"They're worried about you," she said. "Will you burp her?"

He took Abilene and burped her as Julie wiped her nipple, slipped her breast into the cup and adjusted the strap. When Julie took Abilene back, she said, "I want to cry, but I can't figure out what or who to cry for. And I'm just too angry for tears."

He wanted to tell her that was what he was feeling, but he did not. It had always been difficult for him to speak of feelings. It was easier to speak of finances, of plans, those matters that life orbited around. He feared appearing weak, and had emulated his mother, who had always appeared venerable. He remembered how she had looked when coming home from work, frustrated, exhausted. He learned to cook dinner for her, did his homework, and worked for good grades so as not to add to her burden. His success was to be her final escape.

He looked at his wife and daughter, the women he loved as his mother had loved him, and felt that he had failed them somehow. But he could not talk about his fear of failure. From the beginning, when he and Julie had decided that something good floated between them, he took the responsibility to protect her from the stares and whispers. Now he felt assailable.

At her parents' house he walked her to the door but did not go inside. He lied and said that he had matters to take care of.

"What will we do, Rod?"

He was unsure what to say to restore her faith. He touched his forehead to hers, then smiled. "It's cold. Keep Abilene inside. I'll call."

He drove from her parents' house to the projects, drove without intention. He felt compelled to escape that other world, the safe one. These were the streets that had taken his own father's life the year that Rodney was born. The man who had killed his father had never been identified or arrested. There had been an argument, a knife drawn. The witnesses in the bar lost their memories, a convenient amnesia, not uncommon to those who live in the projects.

For a time he cruised the streets slowly and aimlessly, turned up alleys here and there. He thought of his determined mother, who worked to assure he did not have to live here. He left here as a toddler, though as an adolescent he had returned on occasion with his mother to visit cousins and friends. He recalled being disturbed by the poverty and frightened by the wiry boys who played boisterously in the streets. His duties while with the Old Town branch of the bank had brought him here infrequently, but he had never truly looked around. In fact, he had intentionally not looked unless he had to. What he saw now appeared remarkable.

People survive here, he thought, but none thrive. In an alley he came upon a man sitting with his back to a brick wall. As Rodney slowed the BMW, the man, wearing a black flannel coat and khaki trousers, stood and held out an open palm. His eyes were red. His dark face glistened as if lacquered. A step away, he began to shout and thrust himself toward the car. He hammered on Rodney's window with the heels of his hands and called him a pimp. Rodney pressed the gas pedal. The man tumbled away from the car and landed on his seat. Rodney exited the alley but did not quickly shake the image of the man's enraged face.

He was driving west on Emery Street, his hands shaking, when a thought struck him. He remembered the name—Baker, Jewett Baker—but not the address. It was Emery. That much he remembered. He parked the BMW curbside where it would be most conspicuous and took a business card from the console. He was thankful he had worn jeans and a sweatshirt.

He visited three buildings before he found someone who pointed him to a third-floor apartment. He topped the stairs and looked down at the gutter littered with bottles and shards of glass, noticed the brick walls up the alley tagged with colorful gang signs, saw what he had distanced himself from all his life, as an infant with his mother, later with the blinders of an adult. He knocked on the third door, which unlike the others wore a shiny coat of green paint.

The door cracked open, held by a chain. The house smelled of baked bread, his mother's bread. A woman exposed one eye and a cheek. She stared out at him but did not speak.

He questioned his motive for coming. Was he trying to set the world right? Ease his conscience? "You remember me?"

"You ain't from 'round here."

"I'm Mr. Jamison, from the Union State. Your husband applied for a loan."

"Uh-huh. That be biblical old. He ain't home. What you want?"

He held his card between two fingers and slipped it in the crack. "Tell him to call me in two or three days. Tell him I might be able to help now."

She eyed him suspiciously as she accepted the card. "Yeah. Why now?"

"Circumstances."

"Yeah."

He saw that she did not believe him.

She looked at the card. "That all?"

"Yes."

The door shut.

As he descended the steps, the door opened and she called to him. "He workin.' Ain't a day he don't."

"Have him call."

He slumped down in the seat of his BMW and turned the tuner to different stations. He suspected that Jewett Baker would not call, wondered why he himself had made the effort. He looked up and down the street, buildings in disrepair, potholes in the road. One tag on the side of an apartment said it all: FUCK THIS MUTHA FUCKA. He dismissed it as just another act by an angry kid. But then he reconsidered that, saw it as an act of desperation from a voice silenced for generations. He dialed in the news station. There was no fresh information, but the names of the women and details of Calvin Lewis Stops's incarceration were repeated.

He wondered why men who murder more than once are so often identified by three names. No one in the finance business went by three names, though some preferred using initials. Singers often go by one.

People in the hood are sometimes known by nicknames. The dead had lovely names—Angela Minghila, Doreen Asbe—all of them silenced now. He remembered how happy he and Julie had been when they named their daughter as soon as they knew the baby was to be a girl. Abilene Jamison. Pretty. Maybe, he thought, three names strung together creates an identity of the killers that distinguishes them from us.

With two choices ahead, either the house or the hotel, he drove to the hotel.

That evening he ate alone at the hotel, called Julie afterward to tell her he was exhausted. He thought for a time about his father, taken away from him by the hand of an unidentified man. No witnesses came forth. Another murder unsolved. He recalled the weeping at the funeral, the eruptions of wailing from family and friends that bounced off the walls of the church, his mother with her head bowed as she stoically listened to the preacher. How, Rodney wondered, could this happen to him after all he had done to . . . do what?

He walked to the mirror. He saw a man with weary eyes, a two-dimensional image, a man with dark skin, dark eyes, attractive but not handsome. He recognized his image, but saw it differently now. How often had he seen himself as handsome and powerful, a man in control, special? What he saw did not make him human any more than a photograph would. He realized his life had been largely illusory and ordinary. Calvin Lewis Stops had painted it. His was the kind of random act that affected ordinary people. This had not happened to the man in the mirror. It had only happened.

Rodney went to bed at seven o'clock in hopes of finding peace in sleep. In a dream he was buried alive. He awoke from it and knew what must be done.

Except for the unearthed backyard the house looked the same from the outside. For eight days he had watched his house flash on the tube, the immediate freak show for the media. He and Julie had been spared microphones shoved in their faces. Some neighbors were interviewed, not about Rodney or his family, the family that had been good neighbors, but about Calvin Lewis Stops.

He keyed the door and opened it slowly. Except for layers of dust everywhere the house was as he had left it. He remembered the feeling that had come upon him the day after Abilene's birth. He had experienced an inexplicable emptiness. Before he was aware of it, he had sat down on the wood floor in the foyer, his back to the door, thinking this was the house his mother would have wanted to visit. But she had died when he was nineteen and in the army and would never see his baby or his wife or his house. Then he had cried.

His heels struck the hardwood. The sound of his footsteps seemed different, hollow. He could not be certain of anything except that his house was empty. He peered into the room he had wallpapered for Abilene. She had never slept there. They had kept her with them in the master bedroom instead, thinking it best to wait until she was a year old. The room usually lifted his spirits. This time it failed to.

He descended the stairs slowly, listening for creaks and groans in the house. At the bottom landing he turned up the hallway, walked three steps, and stopped at the door to the basement. He hesitated before turning the knob. It smelled dank. When he flipped on the light, he saw that two sections of the floor had been jackhammered and holes dug.

He sat on the top step to survey the damage, which was considerable, his tools piled in boxes, his workbench unmoored. Dust floated up. He studied the rubble, then closed his eyes and imagined the house as he'd first laid eyes on it.

Rodney considered Sergeant Blue, a life spent dispassionately uncovering evil. Did he think he was doing good? Could he or anyone fix this damage? He thought about Jewett Baker, a decent man who repaints his door because he cannot repaint his world, a man who had brought his young hopes to Rodney. Perhaps all Baker wanted was a home for his family, a safe house in a fine neighborhood. Perhaps he could help the Bakers. If he tried, it might make a small difference. Perhaps. Thinking this dredged up a latent anger, as had the sight of the crowd watching his house from the police line. And he felt an even deeper anger toward the faceless man who had turned Rodney's father into a picture on a bookshelf.

There was one more funeral, that of Angela Minghila. Rodney would attend it as he had attended the others. It was what a human must do, and he would listen to the words of the minister and then offer feeble condolences to the family, a stranger, another human. He clenched his fists and trembled, wanted to shout. Then he looked through the dust again at the rubble and felt an unexpected calmness as he sank into a terrible silence.

He pictured the bodies in the trenches in Kuwait. His sergeant had told him not to look, but he had. Now, this. It was not, is not, my house, he thought, never could be. Theirs all along. He would abandon it. First he had to call Julie and tell her that she was right, assure her they would find another house. That would be a start, that and a FOR SALE sign in the front yard. He would get to it right away. That was what he would do as soon as he could stop staring at the damage he knew would follow him.

The First Hunger

The hard rain came suddenly and the flotilla hurried to the docks, where the crabbers sought shelter under the canvas on Halper's pier. The men spoke disparagingly of the weather, drank hot coffee from Styrofoam cups, and watched the horizon with vacant eyes. As they milled about on the pier waiting for the weather to break, out in the estuary Dan and Cal kept at it, casting crab pots, hauling in line, throttling the outboard to deeper waters, then back again to their markers to gather traps. Some men on the pier commented on the duo, muttering about crazy fools and wasting time.

Eventually the clouds lifted, the sun broke through, outboards churned again, and the hulls of small craft slapped against the choppy surface as the crabbers hurried into the estuary like dogs let loose from the kennel.

His hood dripping rainwater, Dan leaned into the gunwale as Cal, his half brother, swung the boat around to come alongside a float. He was thankful for the sun's return, though it did little to warm his numb hands, sore from reeling in nylon. Years before, Dan, his father, and Cal had spent innumerable weekends on Castor Bay, pulling in crab pots. That was long ago and gladly behind him now. A pediatrician by profession, he was unused to hard labor. He cringed at the thought of reaching into the icy water but refused to let on that his hands hurt. Nonetheless, he stretched out over the gunwale and kept an eye on the upcoming float. As the craft slowed, he grabbed the rope and scooped up the line.

Cal throttled the outboard to take up the slack and then eased off when the line grew taut. Dan disregarded the incipient blisters on his palms and reeled in the rope hand over hand, putting arms and back into the task. The pot, weighted with crabs, seemed to grow heavier with each pull.

Cal came up beside him, bent his knees for balance, and joined in pulling. As the trap neared the surface a crab, a nine-incher, clambered over the net and drifted off, followed by another not as big but a keeper just the same.

"Jesus, we lost 'em," Cal said.

The *lost* sounded like an accusation and the *we* seemed to imply Dan. He could not recall the last civil conversation the two of them had shared, though he did remember Cal's kindness and patience when they were boys. He wished he could see some evidence of it now.

The remaining crabs, a half dozen in all, came into the boat with the pot. They plucked those from the netting and tossed the small ones overboard. Cal measured five possible keepers. All but one were too small. Those he heaved into the bay.

They had not always tossed small crabs back. Under his father's direction, they would ice the legal ones and then gather driftwood to light a fire on the far shore of the estuary. The illegal ones went into the boiling bucket of water, to be eaten. Ralph Thayer was not one to abide trivial annoyances such as fishing laws. Dan had loved those times, watching the boiling pot, the anticipation, the passing of a bottle of brandy to warm the belly, the silent maleness of it all.

His sharpest memory sprang from a weekend outing at the bay. He was seven, and his father already in his late forties, when a pickup with three large men in the cab cut them off on the route home and ran them off the road. They had nearly struck a tree. His father took chase, honking and tailgating the pickup until the driver pulled over. "I got boys in here," his father had shouted. The men climbed out of the truck. The four of them exchanged heated insults. Cal, fifteen then, flew out of his side of the car and tackled one of the men as he approached Dan's father. Cal and the old man, bloodied and bruised, laughed as they climbed back into the car. Cops came the next week and told them that a man had lost the sight of one eye in the fight. From the porch Dan had watched his brother and father being handcuffed, charged with affray and mayhem.

"Not much like stickin' a thermometer up some baby's butt, is it?" Cal said.

Dan shook his head as if agreeing, but it was the undercurrent of rancor he was actually shaking off, a frost no number of warm seasons could thaw. The resentment had been fueled by a word here or a cold shoulder there, a condescending nod of the head, a scornful glare. In time the source of the acrimony had been obscured by the harsh, interminable silence that reigned over his family. The acrimony festered for nearly two decades, a wedge between brothers, between father and son and stepfather and stepson, even after the old man's death.

It had not always been this way, not for Dan, who at one time hero-worshiped his half brother and followed his lead in everything. Now he looked up at Cal, the older brother who had gotten him drunk on gradua-tion night and who had later walked into JC Penney in his Marine uniform and shoplifted an alarm clock as a graduation present. He was nearly fifty now, his eyes pewter-blue, framed in creases. Once those blue eyes had burned clear.

"Gets too cold for you, lemme know," Cal said and returned to the motor.

"I'm fine," Dan said. He resented Cal, mostly for his magnificent stubbornness.

Over the years Dan had made efforts to reconnect, calling when he began his internship in Salem, then later his residency in Portland, but Cal would not return Dan's messages. They had since remained estranged. For seventeen years they had not talked beyond what was absolutely neces-sary. Cal seemed determined to keep it that way. Last night Dan had attempted conversation, an effort to scrape at the layers of resentment. His was a sincere effort at a reconciliation, but Cal, who could growl with the best of bears, merely huffed, "We got one more day." Dan had told him to suit himself. Still, he fostered a faint hope that something similar to a rec-onciliation would come from this.

"Do you want to quit, Cal?"

"Do you?"

"I asked first."

"Your dad wouldn't quit."

Dan wanted to dock the boat and abandon the estuary as much as Cal likely did, but he would not quit even to avoid frostbite. He couldn't, not now, and not simply because it had been his father's wish. "I'm having me a hell of a time."

"Suit yourself."

They gathered up the next line of pots and were measuring crabs when another boat, the *Adriane*, passed by on the starboard side. One of the men called over, asking if they'd had any luck during the rain.

"Not much," Cal called out.

"Ah, too bad. Craziness deserves better results," the man shouted.

Dan huddled up in his raincoat and stared off. Water sloshed in the bow. He looked at his rubber boots, submerged in water to the instep. His toes were even colder than his hands. But not as cold as the silence that passed between his brother and him. He wished it were otherwise between them. Dan knew neither his nephew nor his niece. He had noted the family resemblance and wished he knew them. The niece had a daughter of her own, a pretty girl of three. All he knew of Cal was that his brother had built a profitable computer business that served mortgage companies. For his part, Cal did not know or care to know Dan's wife or daughter. He had not responded to the invitation to Dan's wedding. A family of strangers.

"Really think it's worth it?" Cal asked.

"Is what worth it?"

"What the hell are we doing? I'll tell you. Spending a miserable day in a stinking estuary, looking like fools."

Dan looked up. These three sentences were probably the most Cal had spoken to him in years. "It's what he wanted. It was in the will."

"Here," Cal said and handed Dan a beer from the ice chest. "Maybe if we drink enough beer we can put up with each other."

Dan took the offering. This was how it had been, beer no matter the weather, no matter how frozen the fingers. When had he started enjoying pain and deprivation? He held the beer between his legs and looked west. Several miles out another column of clouds had gathered. They had perhaps an hour of sunshine.

"Let's check the other pots," Cal said. "How're the hands?"

"Fine," Dan said.

Cal gave him the look, same disdainful one he had given him the night before, and off and on before their estrangement. As always, it made Dan feel inadequate.

"Yeah, look fine. You want, we can go in." His voice was softened, but the tone was no less sardonic.

"No," Dan said. He was determined. "We'll finish."

"Have it your way. He was your father."

Dan nodded. What was there to say? That was the case. Cal *was* a stepson, a distinction reinforced continually by Cal more than by Dan's father. With Cal it seemed a matter of pride and identity. After serving a year for assault in the state reformatory, he had returned to graduate high school and then enlisted in the Marines. Dan, on the other hand, had attended the University of Oregon after graduation. Sometime in his mid-twenties, Cal went to college at Portland State on the GI Bill. He had to do things his way.

Their mother, Anne Thayer, had died seven years ago. Now Ralph was in the ground, and that was that, except for the gathering of the family and the eating and drinking, which at the old man's behest was to take place this evening in the manner he had requested. He did not want to be mourned, but his wish was that "the boys," as he had continued to call them because he could not say *sons*, bring in fresh crab from the estuary for a final feast.

The boat was moving now. Dan gulped the beer down, mostly because the can was too cold to hold. As they neared the next float, the *Adriane* shot across their bow, dangerously close, and headed toward the pier. Cal cursed the pilot.

Dan watched the *Adriane* bounce over the waves. "Wonder what got into them?" He tossed his empty beer can into the trash bag and looked for the oncoming line.

"Can't handle booze," Cal said.

"You'd think . . ." The float came up suddenly, and Dan had to reach out at the last instant to catch it before it went under the bow. The rope felt like a limber icicle. He began hauling in line and trying to coil the slack by his feet in one motion, as his father had taught them. Cal watched. The pot got lighter as Dan pulled. As it neared the surface one small crab escaped. The bait had been picked to the bone. Cal nodded as Dan showed him the empty pot.

"If the others are like it, we'll go in for bait. 'Less you want to give it up," Cal said.

It was a challenge. "No."

"Have it your way."

Their other pots were picked clean, and the crabs that came up were too small.

Dan hunched over as they headed in. This was not worth it. Cal would never bend. Bitterness was part of his character. Dan had to face it. It was time to end the silliness. Someone had to stop being stubborn, he figured, at least about being out in the cold, following the dictates of a dead man. He would return to his father's house, pack this evening, and in the morning he and his wife would leave without a good-bye.

As they neared the dock, he looked over his shoulder. "All right," he said. "You win. We'll quit."

Cal feathered the engine. "Good. I'll get these pygmies boiled up."

A circle of men gathered on the pier beside the *Adriane*. Andy Halper, the owner, was not manning the boiling pots. Cal said he would find him. Dan walked toward the gathering. One was kneeling beside a man who lay on his back. Dan saw that the downed man was in distress. He brushed his way through the ring of spectators. The stricken man was the one who had called to them earlier. Blood trickled from a wound on the back of his head. It did not look serious, but he was twisting his head from side to side. His face was pale. The man kneeling looked up.

"I'm a doctor," Dan said. "Let me see."

The kneeling man said, "His name's Earl."

Dan tilted the man's head back, pressed his fingers and thumb against his cheeks, and pried his mouth open.

"Tell me what happened," Dan said as he ripped the man's shirt open to listen to his chest. He pressed the fingernails. They turned blue.

"Said he wasn't feeling good, was all, had to get to the bathroom right away. We came in and he slipped and fell when we docked. Hit his head."

"Is he diabetic?"

"Don't know."

"Has he been drinking or taking drugs? Is he epileptic?"

Dan did not wait for an answer. The man had suffered either a concussion or an aneurism. His heart was beating, but he had swallowed his tongue. Dan had to make an air hole. He stripped off his poncho, folded it and placed it under Earl's shoulders, then took a pen from his shirt pocket and separated the halves.

"He needs blankets. Someone give me a jackknife," Dan said.

Someone offered a pocketknife. Intent as he was on the stricken man, Dan didn't look up to see who gave it to him. There was no time to sterilize the blade. He opened the knife and pressed his fore- and middle fingers into the tracheal notch and probed around. He placed the tip to the skin and cut a small incision into which he inserted the hollow barrel of his ballpoint pen.

"Come on now," Dan said. "Try. Breathe."

Dan forced Earl's diaphragm in and released, again and again, and urged him with kind words. He was oblivious to the crowd of men who watched intently. Some natural color returned to Earl's flesh. Blankets came. When Earl was covered, Dan lifted both of his eyelids. One pupil was normal, the other constricted. Dan sat up. The crabber holding Earl's hand looked over and asked if his friend would be okay.

"I can't say. Is an ambulance on the way?"

Andy Halper, who had joined the ring of men, said he'd called for one. Dan held the knife up. "Whose is this?"

Cal spoke up outside the circle. "It's mine."

Dan stayed with the man until the ambulance arrived. The paramedics took vital signs and lifted Earl onto a gurney. One gave Dan a hapless smile. Although breathing, Earl might not live to see the hospital. Dan followed as they wheeled the gurney up the pier to the ambulance. He had witnessed miracles in emergency rooms, people coming back from the dead, similar events. He waited until the last instant to see if his help was further needed. The paramedic thanked him and closed the door. Only then did Dan realize that Cal had been beside him all the while.

They watched the ambulance climb the incline until it disappeared behind a curve.

Dan handed over the pocketknife. "Thanks."

Cal asked, "How's he going to be?"

Dan shook his head.

"Let's get some coffee," Cal said. "We got a long drive."

They sat sipping coffee and gazing at the bay. More seemed to be communicated in their silence than in all the strained conversation that had passed between them. It was a little past two in the afternoon. Another cloud bank had massed about four miles out and was heading in. Dan asked if Cal wanted to go home.

"Ah." Cal looked at his hands. "You know, the year Mom died the old man took on a guy half his age in a parking lot for insulting her. Ralph told the jerk to apologize for calling her an old bitch. The guy called Ralph an old man and said he was going to mess him up."

"No, I didn't know," Dan said.

"Yeah, Ralph looked at him and said, 'Now you've got to do it.'"

"Sounds like Dad."

"Yeah."

Dan detected a softening in the tone of Cal's voice. "He win?"

"You guess."

They smiled knowingly at one another.

"I wanted to be like him," Cal said. "All his faults, and that's how I wanted to be."

"You were. Remember the three guys you took on?"

"You mean him, not me," Cal said. "I got two licks in. Loved his beer and a fight now and then. I was the one went to the reform school. Just another name for prison, if you ask me."

"He was a fighter," Dan said.

Dan remembered other times when his father came home bruised and agitated. All in all, he had been a gentle father, though stern, sometimes terribly stern with Cal. "And raw oysters. Did you two ever get things right between you?"

"We were okay. That's all that it could ever be. When I came home with a few ribbons on my uniform, things changed. We were brother Marines. He fought in Iwo Jima and Guadalcanal both, you know. Though he'd tell you the real battles were out here, pullin' up crab."

Dan held his mug and smiled at a memory, a day on the estuary when his father and Cal decided it was time for him to have his first beer, an initiation of sorts. They laughed when the foam roiled up in his mouth and spewed out of his nose. He had felt humiliated at the time but later realized they were showing him respect.

"He loved us," Dan said.

"*Love's* a tricky word. He loved crab, too. Bet the family's going to be hungry," Cal said.

Those were the words Dan's father had invariably used as they loaded the crab on the truck. His father believed food on the table meant more if caught or grown. He had kept a garden for thirty-five years, spent spring and summer on his knees, grumbling about weeds and pests.

"You sounded like him when you said that," Dan said.

"Aah, I don't know about that."

"What kind of ribbons?"

Cal looked at his coffee mug. "Ah, nothing to speak of, nothing like the old man. You know, just kind of being there stuff."

"What was it like?"

"Grenada?"

"Yeah."

"Eighteen dead. Five from my platoon. Some casualties from the other units may have been friendly fire."

"I always wondered if I had it in me to do what you and the old man did. Be a Marine."

"Ah, you could have. What you did out there, that's what you were intended to be doing."

"What was it really like?" Dan asks. He doesn't want the conversation to die. He sees a bridge of words spanning the space between them.

"Like? Really like? Confusing. It was dark, tracers flying. We hit the airfield where the Cubans were. The place was a dot on a map, but on the ground it swelled up so's a man felt small and at the same time too big to hide himself. There was a guy, Dixon, a cutup, you know, took one in the knee right off. Ever hear a man scream like that, you don't forget."

Cal fell silent after that. Dan knew better than to push matters.

"Coffee ain't much." Cal held up his cup and looked in it. "Brandy wouldn't help it."

"We better come home with crab," Dan said. "Let's see what Andy has to sell."

Cal swallowed the last of his coffee and crushed the Styrofoam cup. "You did what you could for that guy."

"Sometimes nothing helps."

Cal slapped his thigh and stood. "Probably should stop along the way for some oysters too. Way you are with a knife, you can shuck 'em. I got a bottle of brandy to cut the cold."

They went to Cal's truck. He retrieved a bottle from behind the seat, uncapped it, and offered the first drink to Dan. "To the ol' man," Cal said.

"And to no more freezing our asses off." Dan smiled and took a swallow. A warmth spread from his belly to every extremity. His ears flushed.

"He kicked me out. You never knew that. That's why I joined the Marines. To show him. He did me a favor, all in all. Could be that was his intention." Cal took a sip and slipped the bottle in his coat pocket. "We'll be needing a little armor for the drive home."

How do you know a father's intentions, Dan wondered, especially a throwback like Ralph Thayer? Like many, he loved without knowing how to. Dan pictured a teenage Cal cuffed at the wrists, scowling as the cop pressed his head down and guided him into the patrol car. Had his insides begun to harden that day? Now Dan saw an aging brother, a man wounded in ways he himself would never be, and realized his own failings, his acts of pride, most especially the pride of successes. It was time to know this Cal. He could not risk letting the moment pass.

At the dock Andy Halper called to them. "That man's friends left these for you. I boiled 'em up." He opened a box with five crabs, three of them fine ten- and twelve-inch specimens, already boiled and on ice. Along with the three in the boat, there would be enough to feed the family. They stood under the tarp admiring the fine crab.

"That was thoughtful," Dan said. "But we catch our own." He caught his brother's eye.

Cal looked the crabs over. "Fine-lookin' crabs, I'd say. Sell 'em," he said.

"Sell 'em?" the dock owner asked.

Dan looked at his brother, who was now gazing out at the bay. He knew what Cal had in mind, and at that moment they were of one mind.

"It was nice of 'em," Cal said, looking back at Andy Halper, "but me and my brother just came in for bait when Dan here decided to be a hero. Though to look at him, you wouldn't think he was any kind of hero. But he's a bona fide doctor. Got a sheet of paper that says so."

"Sky's comin' in. Be like a lid real soon," Halper said. "Might get ugly."

Cal said, "Our ol' man would crab if it was raining knives. Ralph was the name. He was crazy for crabbing."

Halper nodded knowingly. Cal looked at Dan, who looked up to measure the sky, then back at his brother and nodded. Our ol' man, Dan thought.

"We'll need bait," Cal said. He glanced at the horizon. "Dan, you take the motor a while. Don't think your hands'll hold up pulling pots the whole day."

"My hands will do just fine."

"Take the motor just the same. I ain't puttin' up with no hardheadedness."

As they wired the bait to the pots, Cal said, "We ain't takin' any illegals." He pointed to a spot in the estuary where the men on the *Adriane* had cast their pots. "We'll start there."

Dan nicked a finger on the wire and held it up. Cal snorted and said it was nothing salt water and a good shot of brandy couldn't fix. Dan took the helm and idled the outboard. Cal slipped the bottle from a pocket in his slicker and passed it back. Dan took a sip and tapped Cal's shoulder. Cal palmed the bottle. A bead of water dripped from the tip of his nose. He wiped at it with the back of his hand, glanced back and smiled. Dan knew it would be wrong to attribute too much to that smile; years sat like ellipses connecting disparate sentences. Still, he felt something open like a cork coming out of a bottle, and for no good reason his hands felt better.

He throttled the engine and steered the boat toward the inlet. He recalled how it was when he first went crabbing with his father and Cal. Whenever the boat stopped, Cal would come to his side to help haul in line. He would laugh when Dan lost a crab and assure him that plenty were left. Those times seemed uncomplicated, jubilant, until the old man, sitting at the helm smoking as if it were an act of transubstantiation, would suddenly slap the coal of tobacco from the pipe bowl onto his palm and shout, "Cal, leave the boy alone. You're interfering." Cal would withdraw to the prow, where he sat watching for floats, his hands intermittently wiping at his eyes.

Rain came again as they dropped the first of the pots. It was not hard, but it was cold and steady and hard to ignore. Hunkered under rain gear, they prowled the estuary looking for the right spots, and when it came time to reel in the pots, Dan joined Cal and they pulled together with their hands and arms and backs. Wrapped in the warmth and silence of labor, they worked to fill empty stomachs, as men had since the first hunger.

Private

The morning we were to load into cattle trucks and head for basic training, Sergeant Wildafer gathered us around an unmade bunk, said he wished us the best and hoped not too many of us died in 'Nam. We were fine young men, he claimed, and capable of understanding fine treatment. "Ol' Wil'fer, he took care a' you boys, didn' he?" he said in an ingratiating way, then left the room, leaving us to Langsford's wise guidance. We were mostly draftees, and Langsford was a college grad and older by two years or more. Langsford said that Wildafer had been our usher through indoctrination week and had taken care of us. The college boy took a dollar from a shirt pocket, tossed it on the mattress, and his expression told us we should do the same.

With us was a kid named Wilson, who, to my knowledge, had never spoken to anyone. He was young, seventeen and days, pimply faced, blond. His shoulders stooped, and he had a forward-curving neck and pale eyes that seemed to take in everything but comprehend nothing. Following Langsford's lead, we dropped a dollar here, two quarters there, all but Wilson, who turned his pockets inside out, then left and climbed onto the appropriate cattle truck.

The sky was sunless, the clouds had dropped, and we were open to the wind. The damp air burned our cheeks and bit at our booted feet. We shivered. Wilson stood clutching the side rail, his body compressing and recoiling as the truck rocked over bumps and potholes. All of us looked a bit forlorn, but the lost stare in his pale eyes had the look of someone abandoned by everything, including gravity. The trucks pulled to a stop at Bravo Company, and the cadre flew at them, banging on side rails and tailgates, shouting for us to get our worthless asses down on Mother Earth. We were shitheads, each of us, and it was time we quit sucking Mommy's tit.

One recruit said, "At least Vietnam's warm."

By the time the NCO had us lined up according to height, we were genuinely appreciative of Wildafer. They ordered us to close ranks and stand at ease. First Sergeant Spencer mounted the steps in back of the mess hall. He told us to answer back with our first name and middle initial as he called our last names off a manifest. The wall of the mess, like the walls of the barracks and the headquarters, was a faded shade of yellow most often defined as baby-shit yellow. His salt-and-pepper hair was shorn close to the scalp. A formidable jaw-jutting, Kentucky Colonel type, he stood profiling like a down-home Mussolini, but taller and square-shouldered. He rang off names in alphabetical order, and we answered up, though sometimes not loud enough.

"Cain't hear you, Johnson. You got no balls?"

"Yes, sir."

"Yes, sergeant. Is that yes you have 'em or yes you ain't?"

"I got them, sergeant."

"Then sound off like you got a pair, private. Listen up. You're all a bunch of knuckleheads, and don't think otherwise. You don't even deserve those slick-sleeve uniforms you're goddamn wearin.' Now, talk up like your mama born you with some testicles. Johnson!"

"Anthony K.!"

All the while Sergeant Spencer called off the roll, other sergeants walked between the narrow ranks, telling us to square our shoulders and look straight ahead, no movement. Are you scared or cold? Both, sergeant. Well, don't shit your diaper. Spencer reached the last of the manifest.

"Wilson."

The sergeants quit harassing us.

"Wilson!"

We heard a response, something between a cough and a gag. Spencer narrowed his gaze on the rank from which the sound had emanated, and his brow thickened and his jaw extended as if he had transformed into a gargoyle. He descended the steps and strode slowly to where Wilson stood shivering. He smiled in a grandfatherly manner. "Wilson, it's okay if you speak up when spoken to. Do you understand?"

Wilson blinked, looked left, then right, then at the ground, anywhere but at Spencer. He squeaked something out that sound like a yes. Spencer leaned forward as if to whisper in Wilson's ear, then shouted, "I can't hear you, you goddamn girl!"

Wilson released something resembling a choking sound. Those nearest him heard him mutter, "Oh, Jesus." Spencer stepped back and looked down. Urine pooled at Wilson's feet and steamed up through the gravel into the nearly freezing air.

"That ain't gonna get you outta my army, Wilson. Around here our job is to turn pussies into soldiers. Understand?"

"Yes, sergeant," said Wilson, the sudden clarity of his voice startling us.

Spencer nodded a few times, turned, and as he walked back to the front of the formation, said, "And that goes for the rest of you worthless knuckleheads."

We stood in ranks twenty minutes more as the first sergeant explained that he was not our mother, that he could not care fucking less, that his sergeants' job was to make soldiers out of us, and they would accomplish this despite the pathetic material they had to work with. He turned us over to the platoon sergeants, who formed us into our respective platoons. Wilson was in mine.

■

The platoon sergeant, Abe Lester, a skeletal-faced Korean War vet from Virginia, lined us up by squads and assigned us to bunks. That first day we scrubbed floors, made bunks using military corners, and polished boots and brass. We watched Wilson carry his wet trousers to the latrine to rinse them. He looked at no one. No one spoke to him. We figured the platoon would soon catch army hell, and Wilson would bring it on us. In what form it would come, we did not know.

My bunkmate was a lanky black from Mississippi named Galvison. I asked which bunk he wanted, top or bottom.

"Both," he said.

"Can't have both," I said.

"You asked what did I want."

"I'll take the top, then."

He took in my name tag. "Carver, you take the bottom."

"It's settled, then."

He looked at me with a pained expression. "I don't want you keepin' me awake, playin' with yourself. Understand?"

I nodded.

Sergeant Lester walked in unnoticed and stood at the end of the bay. He glared until one of us finally noticed him. "Okay, girls, fall in at attention on the gravel by squad. Now!"

Some of us were still buttoning shirts and coats as we lined up. Wilson lined up directly behind me. Sergeant Lester paced back and forth until we were dressed evenly and lined up with the man in front. He walked to the head of each squad and checked the alignment. Satisfied, he stepped to the front and stood facing us. It was bone-cracking cold, so dark he was barely visible.

"When I come in the barracks, drop whatever you're doing and stand by your bunks, no exceptions. Understand?"

We shouted yes, sergeant, but it wasn't loud enough, nor was the next one, or any that followed. We shouted until our throats ached, until our lungs burned. He ordered us to face right and marched us out of the company area. He called cadence, said we were a sad bunch of recruits, that we couldn't march in a file if our lives depended on it. He halted us and started us over and over again. I whispered for Wilson to keep step, but he could not manage to skip into step or extend his stride. It was obvious Wilson wanted to keep pace, but he kept falling back.

Lester marched us to the PX and halted us in front of it. He strode back and forth, sizing us up. "See this? It's off-limits unless I bring you here. They sell beer and candy. You men will be tempted to come get some, but don't. If you do, I'll have your ass. Understand?"

The thought of something sweet and chocolate moistened our tongues. Thinking he was about to let us go purchase candy or soft drinks, we stared at the somber building as if its shelves were stacked with diamonds. Instead, Lester ordered us to about-face and jogged us back to the barracks double time.

Wilson was as bad at staying in step at a trot as he was while marching. Twice he broke ranks, and twice we stopped for push-ups on the icy asphalt. In the barracks we threw ourselves down on our bunks, unlaced our boots, and moaned. One and two at a time, we shuffled into the shower. We were too tired to notice that Wilson didn't.

■

After evening chow, if we had nothing pressing, we sat on our footlockers and polished boots and brass. The population was divided almost evenly in a mix of blacks and whites. For many it was their first experience with integration. Hormones were in our sweat. Torn from the comfort and routine of boyhood, we were alienated from one another and angry, mostly because there was no place to channel anger. Blacks tended to congregate into one group, disregarding squads, while white soldiers more or less paired up. Wilson was one exception. Galvison and I were the other. He and I had discovered a common love of fishing.

Galvison had fished lakes and slow rivers, bass and catfish. Being from the West, I'd dropped my lines in trout streams. By week's end we exhausted the subjects of lures, jigs, live bait, casting techniques, and our reluctant respect for fly-fishermen. The subject freed us from the immediacy of cleaning mud off boots and from the bitching. In the last moments before lights-out Galvison slipped between his sheets and opened a Bible, the only book allowed us.

Down the bay Odoms started up a song. He sounded like Sam Cook, sweet and sure on the high notes, smooth and melodious in the lower ranges. Some other black soldiers took up the harmony. We were without a radio, so the singing was rapture to listen to. I lay back on my bunk, hands behind my head, and became a civilian.

Ebbers and Lund, two whites, sat playing cards across the aisle. Ebbers asked if Odoms knew a Carl Perkins song.

"What's a Carl Perkins?"

"Best damned singer in the world, man."

"Yeah, how come I don't know his songs, then?"

It was impossible not to see something brewing between them. Ebbers studied his cards, trying to decide on a discard, then moved his index finger from one card to another. Finally he said, "Eeny, meeny, miney, moe . . ."

Odoms sprang up from his footlocker. "I know you're not gonna finish that."

Ebbers didn't look up. ". . . catch a pigeon by his toe." He dropped a card on the blanket.

Odoms gradually took his seat. The other blacks stared at him. Although Langsford and others had been appointed acting squad and platoon leaders by the cadre, that kind of leadership held no sway with the brothers. Odoms was their leader.

"Motherfucker," Odoms mumbled just loud enough to be heard.

Ebbers was a wiry farm boy from Arkansas. He could do pull-ups and push-ups with ease, but he was a full four inches shorter and twenty pounds lighter than Odoms. He grinned and in his backwoods voice said, "Ya'll say somethin'?"

"I called you a motherfucker."

"So you did. Jest checkin' to make sure my ears're workin.'"

"They're workin' just fine."

Ebbers watched Lund lay a card down. "Later. We'll get to it later." He didn't look at Odoms, but we knew that was who the words were intended for.

That night as I was walking fire watch, a duty we all shared, I heard sheets rustle and the distinct ting of bedsprings. Simultaneously Odoms and Ebbers stood from their bunks. Neither said a word, but Ebbers pointed for the far door, the one supposedly closed at night. They headed that direction, Ebbers leading the way. Passing me, Odoms said, "You didn't see nothing."

The bay filled with the sounds of snoring. Only Wilson sat up and watched the antagonists exit the back door. He noticed me looking at him and lay back, pulling the covers over his head.

At assembly in the morning Sergeant Lester noticed a bruise on Ebbers's cheek and a cut over Odoms's left eye. He didn't mention anything until after dinner. He called us into formation and ordered us to police the grounds behind the barracks.

"Leave one strip of paper, one cigarette butt, one goddamn pinecone," he said, "you'll spend the rest of basic policing up every square inch of Fort Polk."

With a half-moon as our only light, we started across the field, stooping here and there to gather up what scraps we could see and putting them in our covers. We knew the idea wasn't to police the grounds. Our fingers ached from the cold. Halfway across the field Galvison nudged me and said loud enough for Ebbers and Lund to hear, "Now you got a taste of what it's like bein' a black man."

Wilson walked into a low-hanging limb on a pine tree, banged his forehead, and dropped to the ground. He was too dizzy to stand. Sergeant Lester ordered Ebbers, Odoms, Galvison, and me over to carry Wilson to the barracks. We lifted him off the ground. Ebbers said Wilson smelled like vegetables gone bad. Odoms said we should just throw some dirt on him and leave.

Wilson came to his senses halfway back and asked us what we were doing to him.

"Calling your mama to tell her you don't take no baths," Odoms said. "I don't have a mother."

∎

We were doing calisthenics after breakfast when a deuce and a half rolled to a hissing stop across the street. Four soldiers with black armbands jumped off, each of them carrying a twelve-gauge pump shotgun. Sergeant Lester halted us.

"Chasers," he said. "After an AWOL."

We watched the soldiers disappear in the wood line. The driver put the truck in gear and drove off. In the back were eight more chasers with loaded shotguns. The message was not lost on us.

∎

Neither Ebbers nor Odoms spoke of what happened that night, but it became apparent that neither wanted a rematch. Nor did we want to spend the remaining six weeks picking up pinecones. A sort of unassuming civility settled over the bay. White soldiers began to talk to blacks and vice versa, not exactly an outpouring out of brotherly love but more a soft grasping for a common humanity. Wilson was excluded.

∎

Policing the field at night was just the beginning. Blame for that rested on Ebbers and Odoms. But soon after we were subjected to a series of punishments directed at us for events over which we had no control, a fact that mattered little to Sergeant Lester. Beck, a kid from a squad upstairs, went to sleep in the rain marching to the rifle range, then did the same during the instruction and fell through the bleachers, his M-14 rattling to the ground. He was sent for evaluation and discharged for suffering from narcolepsy, a disease most of us had never heard of. The week of rifle-range qualifying, Salazar, a kid from El Paso's El Segundo Barrio, went berserk and chased a range instructor with a loaded rifle, firing two rounds before he was tackled and subdued by trainees. Jessup got caught drinking beer in the EM club. Soon after that Silber, a draftee from Houston, went AWOL. Lester might have handled these incidents for what they were—outgrowths of an imperfect system. But he had Wilson to contend with. He took it all personally.

Wilson barely qualified on the rifle range. He couldn't field-strip a rifle. His footlocker was a disaster. While other platoons relaxed in the barracks, ours stood in ranks on the gravel or went on runs or prepared for inspection. Lester berated us in front of the company, said we were worse than worthless, the worst platoon he'd ever trained. Odoms quit singing. Card games stopped. We began to look askance at Wilson.

■

It began with Lund telling Wilson he smelled rancid. Wilson sat silent and motionless on the edge of his bunk, looking at his bare feet as if counting toes to make sure he had ten. Lund, who slept above Wilson, repeated himself. On occasion others among us were simply too tired for even a quick shower, but Wilson regularly failed to shower.

Lund looked across the bay at Odoms and Lawrence. "What'a you guys think?"

"Smells like compost to me," Odoms said.

The idea seemed to spread telepathically. Wilson sensed the mood. He slid off his bunk as unobtrusively as possible but too late to be inconspicuous. He was the center of attention. The next instant he was held aloft by a dozen arms and ferried overhead in the direction of the latrine. Others joined the parade. I stood ready to fall in as they passed by my bunk. Galvison grabbed my biceps. "Mind your own bidness," he said. I shook my arm free of his grip.

They turned on cold water and ripped off Wilson's T-shirt and shorts. He attempted to cover himself with his hands but they held his arms out to the sides and pushed his head under the faucet. They lathered soap and scrubbed his pale skin with brushes used to scour the urinals. He whimpered but offered no resistance. Someone handed me a brush and soap and said it was my turn. Wilson didn't protest in any way. I rubbed soap on his scalp and took my turn, then stepped back. Bar soap wasn't enough for some. They took cleanser to him and bleach.

Then, as spontaneously as it had started, it stopped. We dropped the brushes and took the bars of soap with us and left him crawling into a corner, the skin on his chest and back raw and oozing blood in spots. Galvison lay on his bunk, Bible open. I slipped between my sheets. He looked over the side of the bunk but didn't speak, just stared. Then he lay back, closed the Bible loud enough for me to hear it, and said, "Some men go fishin' with dynamite."

The charge of quarters came in a few minutes later for head count and stumbled right away upon Wilson. He stepped in the bay and announced lights were going out and for everyone in the latrine to get in the bay in fifteen minutes. Fitz, a PFC on temporary duty awaiting orders to permanent post, wanted no trouble. When Fitz turned the lights out, Galvison climbed down from his bunk and went to the latrine. A few minutes later he returned and stood beside my bunk. It did no good to feign sleep, so I asked what he wanted.

"Go on up to the orderly room and tell that Fitz boy we need a first-aid kit."

"It's after lights-out," I said.

"Think I don't know that? You sound dumber than Wilson. Go do what I say."

Fitz was reluctant but eventually conceded that it was to everyone's advantage for Wilson not to go on sick call. He handed me a first-aid kit but cautioned me to use only what was absolutely necessary.

Galvison had brought Wilson fresh underwear. They sat on the shower floor, neither talking. I opened the kit.

"Got alcohol?"

I handed him the bottle.

"Them brushes been used to clean shit. I mean, what was those boys thinkin'?" Galvison said to no one in particular.

Galvison, raised on a farm where he had learned to care for injured animals, was gentle and deliberate. I helped, following his instructions as he cleansed the scrapes. Then we applied gauze to the tender wounds. Wilson watched our progress, grimacing but never complaining.

"One thing I'd like to know, Wilson."

Wilson's lower lip trembled as he looked Galvison in the eye. "What?"

"Why'd you join the army. I mean, you bein' school age and all. Don't make sense. Least, I can't make much of it."

Wilson licked his lips and looked at the entrance to the latrine as if someone stood there, but we were alone. He took a deep breath, then let the air go from his lungs at once.

"My dad."

"Your dad?"

"Day I turned seventeen, he took me to the recruiter. In the post office back home."

"Why'd he do that?"

"He told the recruiter I wanted to join and gave his consent."

"Did you want to join?"

He shook his head. "I was happy when I passed the test. I didn't think I could."

"Your pa did that?"

"Said maybe the army could do something with me."

■

We lined up by squad, our shoulders weighted with backpacks, rifles cradled in our arms. When the whistle blew, we lay down and propelled ourselves forward using arms and legs. The pit was covered with a nylon tarp, but sand and pine needles made the surface abrasive. Sergeants walked beside us shouting a litany of words from their dictionary of contempt. Up and back, forty yards at a crawl, we gutted it out. By the halfway point, where we turned around, the veins in our temples throbbed; our chests seemed ready to explode. Wilson started out beside me but had covered less than half of the first leg by the time the rest of us had finished.

Sergeant Lester walked straddle-legged above Wilson and shouted, "Come on, you goddamn sissy, move it. Look ahead. Keep the rifle tucked."

Lester prodded him with a kick to the ankle. Wilson crawled on at his tortoise pace, panting, his cheeks glowing red. Lester kicked him again, asked how the hell he expected to survive in Vietnam. The other NCOs did not intercede.

Ebbers spoke up first, shouting, "Come on, Wilson! You can do it."

Lester looked in our direction and glared. It didn't have the effect he wanted, because a second voice called to Wilson, encouraging him, then a third. Many in the platoon joined in. The cadre let us continue. When Wilson made the turn, the volume increased. And when he paused, we urged him to keep going, shouted that he could make it. It took five minutes for him to reach the end and he didn't have strength enough to lift himself off the ground. Lester called him a mama's boy. Galvison offered him a hand. I gave him a lift up by grabbing his pack strap. When he was standing, others, Lund and Odoms included, patted his shoulders or gave him a friendly tap on the helmet. Wilson drifted to the side, leaned forward as if catching his breath, and vomited.

At lunch Galvison carried his tray to the corner table where Wilson sat. I joined them as the rest of the platoon took seats nearby. We didn't talk, just ate. When called into formation, we squared Wilson's hat and belt line, encouraged him to stand at attention and look ahead. He didn't seem to mind.

■

It was raining. The twenty-mile forced march was mandated no matter the weather. We marched out of the company compound with rifles and full field equipment on our backs, sixty pounds in all, our platoon in the rear. As the line stretched out, sergeants shouted for us to close ranks. Lester walked down the middle of the road between the files. Wilson was on one side of the road, and I was on the opposite. He was fine for perhaps two miles, but as the road got muddier, he began to falter. Every once in a while Lester's eyes would snap in Wilson's direction, but he didn't single him out when he shouted at us.

We hit a rise, and at the same time the clouds dropped. We wiped beads of water from our eyes with the backs of our gloves, which accomplished little. Our gloves were soaked, as were our boots. We locked our eyes on the man in front. Mud sucked against the soles of our boots.

The sergeant in the lead platoon began to sing cadence. Toward the rear we could barely hear his voice, but we took up the chorus nonetheless. Singing took our minds off the cold. When we hit the downslope, the clouds lifted and we could again see our surroundings. I noticed Lund step up and reach under Wilson's poncho, remove an item from his pack, and pass it behind him. Over the next two miles, whenever Lester seemed distracted, Lund would do the same with Wilson's pack. Ounce by ounce, the platoon lightened Wilson's load. An hour later Wilson carried an empty backpack. Ebbers toted two rifles.

We hit snow before reaching the bivouac area. We settled atop a knoll and dug trenches around where we staked our tents. Every man had a tent half. Lund carried two, one for Wilson. After we erected our tent, Galvison and I turned our attention to Lund and Wilson's tent. Lester came by, kicking tent stakes or slapping at the sides, checking each. One went down. Lester told the occupants he had warned them. He was disappointed to find Wilson's tent was secure.

■

The last snow of the season came in the night before we were to run the PT course. Wind shook the barracks. The coal furnaces barely warmed the old buildings. Outside, the pines swayed and shed cones. Lund said he couldn't take it and opened the back door to make a run to the PX for some chocolate. He earned a chorus of threats, shut the door, and crept to his bunk. The next morning we awoke reluctantly when the cadre charged in an hour before daybreak.

First Sergeant Spencer ordered us to stand at ease. The PT was coming up that afternoon. Any man who scored four hundred seventy or higher would get a weekend pass. Those scoring higher than four hundred twenty would be exempted from guard and KP duty for the remainder of the training cycle. He wanted our company to perform tops in the training regiment. He asked if we understood.

"Yes, sergeant."

Snow covered most of the black Louisiana dirt, but the army thought of that too. We and soldiers from four other companies cleared the course and the crawl pits with shovels and rakes. We began the course with a short figure-eight dash between four waist-high hurdles, from there we moved to the grenade toss at a ground target, then to a hand-over-hand ladder walk, followed by the forty-yard low crawl, and we ended the course with a mile run. The score on each segment of the course was recorded on a hundred-point scale gauged by relative degrees of possible excellence on each phase. It took Wilson sixteen minutes to finish the mile. High score or low, we collapsed on our bunks when we were dismissed.

From our platoon only Odoms and I earned a weekend pass. Wilson scored lowest in the competition and cost Bravo Company first place in the training regiment. Spencer was good to his word. The weekend came, and on Friday passes were waiting at the orderly room. The detail list was posted. Wilson was given two days of KP.

They told me later that there had been an incident in the kitchen. Waterham, a tall kid from the third platoon, had hit Wilson in an argument over who should use what garbage can. Both were called in front of the captain. Wilson had stood up to the bigger man, and the price had been extra duty and a mouse on his eye. He was given two more days of KP. When he came in from a third day of KP and saw me, he pointed to his black eye and grinned.

■

The last week of the cycle was devoted to preparing for and taking a proficiency test, part of it physical, part of it memory. After passing the test, we would advance to the next segment, some to infantry training or armor or artillery, others to noncombatant specialties. If a soldier failed to pass, he was recycled to another basic training company to start over.

Excellence wasn't demanded. The minimum required was accomplishment enough. The country wanted bodies, preferably young men, but boys would do, anyone who could pack a rifle and ammunition, so we hurried from practice station to practice station. The cadre that had humiliated and berated us for weeks became uncle-like, patient and encouraging. After a day and a half of preparation, we lined up to take the test.

Sergeant Spencer called the formation to attention for the last time. "Okay, knuckleheads. We got to run you outta here, so we can teach something to a new batch of knuckleheads. Don't expect no tears. You're mostly a worthless lot, but you learned enough to maybe stay alive."

Sergeant Spencer carried his clipboard about as he walked through the ranks, giving us our new assignments. Galvison would be going to missile school in El Paso, and I would be staying at Polk for advanced infantry training in light weapons. All but two in the company had passed. On down the ranks Spencer stepped, pausing in front of each of us. I heard him tell Wilson that he would be recycled. Orders would be cut that night.

Because of Wilson's failure, the celebration that afternoon in the barracks was subdued. He seemed despondent, but who could blame him? With an inspection and graduation parade ahead, we had more on our minds than worrying about Wilson. We packed our duffel bags and took off for the EM club. We drank beer or soft drinks, gobbled down hot dogs. I bought a book, Steinbeck's *Pastures of Heaven*. Wilson was curled up under his blanket when we returned.

That night during fire watch I sat on a footlocker reading in the beam of a flashlight. I heard Wilson's feet hit the floor and glanced up. He fumbled for something in his footlocker, then walked to the latrine, where he dawdled for an inordinately long time. We understood what it meant to be stripped of privacy. We let a man at night have his time in the latrine. What he did in there was his business. But whatever Wilson was up to, he had become a distraction to my reading. I set the book aside and walked the sixty feet to the latrine.

Wilson was buttoning his fatigue shirt. I startled him and he froze. Beneath the army shirt was a blue plaid shirt. Where he had gotten civilian clothes was a mystery, but he had them on. He looked at his open collar, then finished buttoning. I hadn't spoken. He looked at me and started toward the door.

"They'll find you," I said, extending my arm to stop him.

He didn't speak.

"Remember the chasers?"

He stepped back and looked at me. I wasn't sure what else to say, if it was my business or if making him stay was the best thing. Maybe a second attempt at basic would shove him over the edge. I wanted to do the right thing but didn't want the responsibility.

"Let 'im go," Galvison said. "Man's made up his own mind."

I stepped aside. The next instant Wilson bundled clothing under his blankets and was gone.

When the charge of quarters came through for a head count, he noted the peculiar lumps under Wilson's blanket. He turned on the lights and shouted. "Drop your socks and grab your cocks!"

Sergeant Lester locked us in formation in front of the barracks. He insisted that one of us had to have seen Wilson take off. If he found out who it was, nothing less than a court-martial was in order. Sergeant Spencer and the captain arrived sometime before dawn. We were still outside, shivering in our fatigues, no jackets, no gloves. The captain and the first sergeant looked no more pleased to be there than we were. The three leaders held a whispered conference. Then the captain and Spencer left, and Lester dismissed us to the barracks.

One by one, we were summoned to the first sergeant's office to be quizzed and coerced, alternately threatened with punishment and tempted with promises of rewards, told the army would hold up our orders, that there would be a criminal investigation. The CID would be called in. Foul play was suspected. No one from the platoon broke down. We were one against them.

At dawn we formed for chow along with the rest of the company. Lester stood in front of us, a scowl on his face. "You shitheads don't deserve even crappy army chow."

We paid him no mind. A figure stepped out of the shadows of the pines and distracted us as he walked calmly and steadily in our direction. He wore civilian clothes, a plaid shirt. I glanced at Galvison and grinned. He returned, I thought, driven back by the cold. Good for him.

"You think this is funny?" Lester shouted as he pushed through the ranks.

My smile disappeared, not because of Lester but because the figure walking our way was Fitz. "No, sergeant. I wish it were."

He glared at me momentarily and then shook his head and moved on. A jeep pulled up in front of company headquarters. We turned to see who was in it. Lester reminded us we were in formation. Two MPs got out and walked to the orderly room.

At breakfast we speculated about Wilson, where he'd gone and what he'd done. But that was to remain a mystery. Still, we guessed, mostly because he'd done something we were afraid to do, something extraordinary. After chow, transportation to take us to our destinations rumbled into the compound. I stood with Galvison as he lined up to board the bus taking him to a depot in Leesville. An uncertain future trembled before us, especially me.

"Vietnam," he said.

"Infantry. Sure looks like it."

"Well, don' be gettin' yourself killed."

I gazed off at the soot-blackened snow that still stuck to the ground and the pools of slush that lay on the shoulder of the roadway. "He beat them, didn't he?"

Galvison looked up at the sky and said, "Doesn't matter." He swung his duffel bag into the bus and followed it, pausing on the steps. "Let's do some fishing when all this is done."

"Trout?"

"Bass, boy. I think you might like to fish a black lake." He reached his hand down and shook mine. "That boy never had a chance."

"It's a promise," I said.

He hoisted his bag to his shoulder, moved down the aisle, and the door shut.

When my truck came, I tossed my duffel bag in the bed and climbed aboard. A string of cattle trucks with fresh recruits pulled into Bravo Company. The cadre began screaming at them. I watched the confused soldiers chaotically unloading. Across the drive a deuce and a half wheeled onto the gravel, sending up a cloud of dust. A jeep with two more MPs pulled in behind the deuce and a half. Four of the soldiers with black armbands jumped down and hurried toward the far pine trees. Each carried a shotgun.

I thought of what Galvison had said about it not mattering and wondered how it cannot. A soldier walks into a bullet that splits his breastbone in two, or he doesn't; a fishing lure works, or it fails; sunlight casts shadows through trees where a frightened boy, a private in no-man's army is hiding because he has no place to go, no home, no country. How can a kid who starts with nothing end up with less? All things matter. That's what I figured I might tell Galvison someday as we sat in a boat intent on our fishing lines, waiting in deep silence for the slightest ripple. The truck lurched forward and Bravo Company was behind me.

I barely heard the sounds of the sergeants' Bravo as they bellowed at the recruits, degrading them, terrorizing them. The wind swirled around me. It was warmer now, spring invading the Louisiana woodlands, but it still looked like winter, and that would be how I would always remember it, spotted with islands of soot-blackened ice and forested by thickets of lowly pines laden with slow-melting snow, a land hostile in its silence. The potential of life seemed diminished, while its harshness was amplified to degrees I never imagined. In the end I figured that Lester and the cadre were right all along. Wilson wouldn't have lasted in 'Nam, might have taken others with him. It was better this way, sad but better. I was ready to be a soldier, and that was part of everything that mattered. The front tire of the truck struck a pothole. I grabbed the rail and held on, held on tightly. There were more potholes ahead, and a knucklehead sat behind the wheel.

Groundwork

As soon as we met I knew I would somehow end up in a cell with Hard Wall. Not that I'm complaining about him or that I would dare. I would much rather share a cell with him than with one of the several wackos that reside in the county lockup. There's a guy named Pramby whose nose has been broken so many times he can turn his nostrils inside out, which, though distasteful in some circles, is viewed in here as a kind of quaint novelty. Another inmate barks at the jailers—not barks exactly but woofs and howls, which can get on your nerves at three in the morning. Once or twice a week he tries to take a bite out of a deputy's ankle and spends a day or two in the rubber room finger-painting vomit with the winos.

Hard Wall, a three-hundred-pound hard case who spends most of his time plotting revenge, just sits on his cot and broods over the fact that after all the crimes he committed he's incarcerated for looking out a window at a sidewalk sixteen floors below. He's not Hamlet torn by equivocation. If is not a consideration. He concerns himself with *when* and *how*, understands better than Hamlet the paradox of his fix because the charges came down on him after he'd decided to go straight. Well, almost straight, if you discount the drugs he consumed, which are, as I think about it in terms of quantity, pretty mind-boggling. But then Hard Wall never calculated an irony like Bussy when factoring the possibilities of a straight life.

I'm here for the very reason Hard Wall is. I went to the window and looked down at the same time he did. Sixteen stories below, a crowd agitated by the sight of blood and sinew and oleaginous matter looked up and pointed as if witnessing a witch crossing the moon on a bicycle. In the middle of the sidewalk, in worse than bad condition, lay what was once the great man Mr. K, the genius who pioneered reality television. To be precise, from where we stood he was a dark splotch, one that at a distance of sixteen floors resembled a beetle that had rendezvoused unexpectedly with the windshield of a speeding car. All in all, it was a sad ending for a great man. That was how the end, or the beginning of the end, began, for of course, the beginning began with Bussy, whom I mentioned before as the source of Hard Wall's agitation, and his novel idea.

Who would have guessed it would fly? Not me, the guy who spent twelve years scrubbing and polishing the image for the corporation, not the guy who did promo and on-location work for the "Miss-Heavenly-Ankles Beauty Pageant," the "New Orleans–to–Cincinnati Mississippi-River Jet-Ski Race" and the "Man-vs.-Great-White Fight." I picked winners and I recognized losers.

Mr. K trusted my judgment as much as he did anyone's. I submarined "The Nude Musketeers," a Bussy project that featured blurred images of naked men and women fencing in competitions. And I convinced Mr. K to scrub "Niagara Falls Kayak Team Jumping" because it was just too boring, not to mention profitless. Can't have fools dying like lemmings for fifty thousand, I explained, adding that the potential market didn't justify an increase in prize money. Didn't two die in the preliminaries? And no live audience draw or measurable TV ratings. Wasn't "Man Against the Elements" another of Bussy's brainstorms, a financial bust, even with one fatality (the guy in bikini briefs who sat on a snowbank during an arctic storm) and three serious injuries? We had hairy ideas that flew and a few that didn't, most of them his projects. So, when Mr. K called me into his office and told me to sit and listen to Bussy, I figured it was another gagger.

When something went up to Mr. K, it best be right. Being a POW in Korea who'd suffered some pretty terrible torture, he had a fierce and precise view of the world. Capitalism was good, and communism was evil. He'd suffered at its hands, bore scars from it. He'd built his enterprises against all odds, and everything he touched he saw as a tribute to the greenback. And he hated losers. People don't understand a man like him who started out in the promo biz as a kind of combination P. T. Barnum, Billy the Kid, and Marquis de Sade, and he kept the image up until he became an antacid and laxative junkie and stopped talking. He did manage to keep an edge on his fangs by preserving that fierce half-smiling sneer that turned the densest gray matter into pudding and the quickest talker into an icicle tongue. He'd been sneering a lot. In seven months we'd suffered a string of five flops, all but one of them Bussy's doing. Stockholders were pressuring Mr. K. All of us were sitting on a burner. In previous meetings

Bussy had earned that sneer and everyone knew he was out on the ledge. This idea had to fly.

Dressed in his usual Sherlock-Holmes-goes-to-college style—houndstooth jacket, blue jeans, and tennis shoes, pipe in his mouth—Bussy crossed his legs at the ankles and offered up a heartburn smile. He had a flair for melodrama and pitched his brainstorms as if each were the opus of a suffering genius. When he presented the kayak caper, his dark eyes were wet with genuine simulated sincerity—a finger-halfway-down-your-throat gagger that sent me into the hallway, where I pounded my head against the wall. Bussy clamped his long fingers together under his chin and bowed, an angelic expression in his eyes as if he were kneeling at the rail waiting for the wafer. "Danny Boy," he said, "it's bigger than five Super Bowls, one after another."

Then he started lining up the plays. "They kill each other anyhow, right?" he said. "Start with that premise." He looked at Mr. K, who winked and gestured back with both index fingers. Bussy was talking about street gangs, though I didn't see that right away. "They die every day and it's no big deal, nothing gained. Chumps, losers who live off drugs and crime, but—he offers the first plus—"they're organized." Mr. K, surrounded by all manner of laxatives and high-fiber bars, pointed one index finger in the air. "Two," Bussy said, raising his voice, "they have discipline." He added the kicker: "They're heavily armed." As Bussy made each point, Mr. K tallied it with a raised finger, and his smile broadened. Only one thing made Mr. K smile—money. Whenever he wrote the word, it was with a capital "M." I asked once why that was, and he looked at me as if I were as dumb as a quiz show host. He walked to his shelves, took down a Bible, and pointed out the first five references to God, all capitalized.

Getting impatient, I told Bussy I knew all that about gangs. I wasn't an easy turn. Part of my job was to punch away with an antithesis or two.

He grinned and said, "Think about it."

It sank in like lawn dew seeping through paper shoes.

"People won't settle for a fraud anymore. America's cable audience is too sophisticated for paint gun fights, roller derbies, or pro wrestling. They want death and they want it live. Danny, they want death live and in their living rooms."

He sprang to his feet, arched his ostrichlike body, aimed his index fingers, and shouted, "Ka-bang, ka-bang, ka-bang, bat-t-tit-ta, bat-t-tit-ta." Anything on Mr. K's walls that wasn't blue was a picture; there were photos of every imaginable event, from heavyweight bouts to beauty contests. Bussy simulated shooting them. Finished, he blew away imaginary gun smoke from his fingertips.

"Gangbanger Fight-Offs," he said. "It's orgasmic. It'll add an inch to every American male's manhood."

"The Gangbanger Grand Prix," I said. That's why I was worth three hundred G's a year and got called into Mr. K's office when the egg was first laid. I made the egg hatch, helped the bird grow feathers, and got it to fly on its own.

"Yep," Bussy said, "you got 'er. Glad to have you on board, Danny Boy."

His face stretched into an enormous dollar-sign smile, Mr. K raised all ten digits. When his face shriveled back to its customary expression of flatulent agony, he pointed his thumbs up, then higher up, asking for an opinion.

"Well, sir, what they do is pretty illegal," I said.

"I thought of that too," Bussy said.

Mr. K motioned for us to stop, staggered to his wet bar, and filled his hands with pills. After taking two antacids, a bromo, and a stomach relaxer, he half nodded, which meant he wanted to hear more. Bussy went on to name countries that would welcome the competition: Colombia, Argentina, Hong Kong, and Mexico, where bullfighting is still big, and said something about the Hemingway tradition. He was already calling the project competition.

"South America or Asia?" I said. Of course, I was thinking no way would this happen, too damned crazy. "No gate revenues in Third World countries," I said, laying down the first argument I could muster. "We gotta put it on here, and . . ." I paused to make certain I had Mr. K's attention. "Killing is just plain against the law."

Mr. K thought a moment, actually an instant, an immeasurable instant, about a micro-billionth of a nanosecond, and aimed a crooked index finger right at my chest, which meant start the groundwork.

That was me—groundwork—everything from bartering with agents to laying coin in the right palm. I was damned good at it too. Mr. K admired my morals, which are essentially not morals exactly, but I don't kill people or rob the elderly. No rape. I'm dead set against rape. So, when Bussy lit his curved pipe and suggested a sex scenario to include gangs going to war because one gang raped a girl who belonged to another, I said, "No, no way am I going to promote a rape."

Bussy said, "It was a passing goddamn thought, Dudley. You know sex sells anything."

He called me Dudley whenever I saw any small piece of beauty in the world. I could see by Mr. K's expression that I better get on board; the ship was going out to sea, and anyone trying to hold it to the dock was going to be pulled into the water and probably drowned.

"Well," I conceded, "we could say it was because of a rape without an actual rape."

After that the organization of the program consisted of Bussy and me in the conference room hashing out a format. Nothing too original—inner-city competitions, then state, followed by sectional meets, the regional fight-offs, then the final battle. Prize money maybe twenty thousand for the inner-city to one million for the winner of the final.

"Who's the winner?" I asked.

"Last ones standing," he said.

One quick look at Bussy told me he wasn't kidding.

"Okay. To the last gang members standing."

So where to start? Bussy said, "Hell's Angels," like you look in the phone book for "Dial-A-Biker" and say, "Hi, how do you feel about a gang war league?"

Bussy's an enormous freckle, by which I mean it's hard to find a part of him that isn't freckle, like Mr. K's wall if it were all pictures and no blue. He's got the muscle of a broomstraw, and his idea of working out is hooking paper clips to a proposal. Not the kind to get involved with a biker, not even over the phone. But he was right. If they vetoed the idea, it would tell us it was a huge mega-no. That was how I met Hard Wall.

To my surprise, Hell's Angels chapters were listed in the phone book, and some chapters had Web sites. In between murder and drug deals they seemed to have found time to mainstream their operation. The organization was officially recognized as a religion, its bible the *Harley-Davidson*

Repair Manual. When I walked into that smoke-hazed biker bar in Oakland, I figured Hard Wall, whose real name was Walt Smugnerson, would take the five hundred dollars and tell me if I ever showed up with another crazy scheme, he'd chain me to the rear fender and drag me through the back streets of Oakland behind his hog, which he called a scooter. There I was, forty bikers watching, and Hard Wall, a three-hundred-pound bearded blob of black leather, pushing a pitcher of warm beer across the tabletop while telling me the suds was a hundred dollars extra and I had to pay up.

Big Pig's Bar had the smell of a cat that had braved the interstate three days ago without making it across. The place even looked like it served road stew. I tell you emphatically, it was not a place where you would want to entertain a woman, at least not one with most of her teeth. I laid another hundred on the stack of bills. Before he would talk business, I had to chugalug the beer and snort a line of crystal meth, which cost another two hundred. Two bikers held my face down until the line of white granules was gone. I felt as if I'd vacuumed both a can of drain cleaner and a tube of Preparation H into my brain. I could feel the drug dissolving clots of gray matter while shrinking my mind.

"What's this deal?" he asked.

I slapped my cheeks with both palms until he came into focus. "We want to hold a gang tournament, nationwide. A warfare league, like pro football. Winners get a million dollars."

Walt looked at me without blinking, rubbed his beard, and slowly nodded his head, once, twice, three times. Near certain that he was ready to rip my head off and chew it like a chicken wing, I dug my heels into the hardwood floor, ready to run.

"Peanuts," he said. "Chump change. You want somethin' like this, make it five million. Make it more 'an one of those magazine giveaways. You dig what I'm sayin'? Make it big an' put me on the payroll an' I'll personally make it happen."

"You don't think it's a crazy idea?"

He looked at his fellow bikers, who'd gathered around the table. They laughed. "Yeah, it's crazy. Look around, tell me what you see. These are some crazy fuckers. There's plenty more."

"You actually like the idea?"

"No. But I like the money."

Hard Wall went on the payroll. The next line of crank was his treat. I don't know if I staggered out or flew out, but I ended up on the back of a hopped-up hog behind a string bean of a biker with a beard that flowed to his waist and two gray eyes that looked like they been tapped deep into his skull by a hammer. He practiced wheelies up and down the alley with me hanging from his bitch pad as a gauntlet of brother bikers sprayed us with beer foam.

Most of the West Coast contracts were negotiated on the back of a chopper in places no man in a gabardine suit had ever before seen. If you even think your heart beats too slow, take a ride into Watts on Hard Wall's bitch pad and listen to five hard-staring dudes decide whether to shoot you in the head or in the balls, all of them smiling and listening to gangsta rap on a ghetto blaster as they size you up. Usually negotiated at the barrel end of a Glock, the gun favored by the Crips and the Bloods, the contracts gave us, for a modest advance, exclusive rights to promote a war league.

In Norwalk, Madness, a skinny kid of seventeen, stood in front of two dozen armed brothers and quoted from *Macbeth* and *Atlas Shrugged*. He claimed capitalism had betrayed itself because America had turned into a corporate welfare state and that individual initiative had been reduced to being two meaningless words. He aimed a shotgun in the air and pulled the trigger.

"That is how America was born," he said. "We ain't takin' less 'an fifty big ones."

Hard Wall pulled out a .45 and held it to my head. "Forty thousand," he said, "or I blow his brains out."

Madness was stunned. I was stunned. The brothers were stunned.

"You think we care if you blow his brains out?" Madness asked.

"Yeah, man. That's what I think. Without him, no scratch."

Madness nodded and said they had to confer a moment. He huddled for several minutes with his comrades, on occasion turning around and looking over at us. All the while Hard Wall kept the gun to my head. About five minutes passed before Madness stepped out of the huddle and the brothers again formed up behind him.

"Forty-five thousand, no less. You think we're so much rhetoric?"

Hard Wall nodded. "Do you think I'm so much bluff? Forty."

Mindless circled us a half dozen times, each time getting closer until he was an arm's length away and facing us. He grinned. "Okay, man. Forty-two big ones and a microwave for my mama."

Hard Wall whispered for me to agree.

The cops nabbed us in Costa Mesa when we were negotiating a contract with some Vietnamese thugs. The police took us to the Federal Building in downtown L.A. That was it, I figured. Jail time. But at least the crazy idea would be exposed for what it was and Bussy would take his final fall from grace. I didn't mind so much. I'd had enough of back-alley deals hammered out with the cold steel of a barrel laid to the back of my neck. I figured I would regret the loss of the drugs. I was getting used to crystal-crank breakfasts and Walt's beer belches.

A guy in gray suit and wing-tip shoes flashed his ID and said he'd flown out from Washington, D.C. to hear our plan. He said for me not to waste his time. Racketeering, interstate commerce violations, conspiracy—I faced every federal crime he could think of at the moment. My life was ending. No three hundred thousand a year. No stock options. 401K gone. Gone. All gone. May as well go to prison. May as well take Bussy with me. I spilled everything.

Upon hearing the format, the agent shook my hand and said, "Ingenious. Why didn't we think of it?"

Mr. K granted Hard Wall the title and salary of junior vice president and advance man so he could lobby in state capitals. He went on the road with me, wore a tie, and used his given name. We flew to all the major cities and rented limos, dined with politicians in four-star restaurants. He proved to be a convincing orator as he showcased the practical side of the event, which was keeping the dangers of crime in the public eye while establishing a venue that would keep young hoodlums off the streets.

At his urging, legislators in states where gangs thrived quickly drafted and passed laws that allowed for pubic urban warfare for purposes of amusement—highly taxed, of course. California and New York lawmakers, their decisions spurred on by police and federal agents who willingly attested to the contest's general benefit to the public, convened and passed laws in a matter of hours. When I started recruiting in New York City, the FBI and New York's finest drove me to pickup points where gangs met us to escort me safely in and out.

A gang truce was declared nationwide. Gangs in every major city in the country went into training. Some were allowed use of police training facilities and pistol ranges. Those less well equipped received federal grants to purchase weapons. Gangs hired range instructors, military advisors, personal trainers, publicists. A group of former police officers started an urban war consulting firm. Law schools rushed to get a curriculum together to deal with gang war liability. An entirely new economy emerged.

By summer's end Mr. K and Hard Wall, who was a Vietnam vet, had formed a rather bizarre friendship. They would sit in the corner during strategy briefings and write notes on a pad, every once in a while breaking out in laughter. And there was reason to be happy. Sixty-four gangs in twenty-three cities were committed to our league, and all but six states—Alaska, Idaho, Wyoming, Montana, and the Dakotas—had passed laws legalizing gang war for entertainment and profit in a controlled environment. Though Idaho passed a similar law allowing for fast-draw competitions, it didn't spark much interest. I called Bussy to tell him we'd bagged every major street gang. That's when I found out about the first lawsuit, the one filed by the Mafioso Don Vito Rotelli, the Italian American Anti-Defamation League, and the ACLU, accusing the league of unfair business practices and ethnic bias, as we had contracted no Italian American gangs into the competition. This suit was followed in a week by three women's organizations charging us with gender bias. Our attorneys filed briefs explaining that we hadn't thought the Mob would be interested was all, but they were welcome to compete, even the women's organizations, and we'd supply them with weapons and training to prove our good intentions, this precipitating a run of suits.

The National Organization of Women announced a second suit complaining that gangs discriminate by refusing to promote females in their ranks at a pace equivalent to males. How many women, the suit demanded to know, will be in the trenches, earning the same wage as male gang members? In a television interview Mindless said women in gangs had no positions. He challenged Gloria Steinem to accompany him on a drive-by to see why.

After the suit was filed, A.M. talk shows attacked the reasoning, calling it frivolous. NOW filed for an injunction against all conservative broadcast coverage of the league, accusing the right-wing media of conflicts of interest and biased reporting of the issues, based on the fact that men were sports fans. Two representatives went on *Larry King Live* to argue that gangs everywhere should be disbanded because they practiced chauvinism and were another impediment to the progress of women, none of whom held executive positions in the league's management.

In response to the suit, we promoted three secretaries to positions as vice presidents of the league's PR, human resources, and blood donation departments and then proclaimed the suit moot. Carol Gilligan called a press conference in her Harvard office to proclaim the critical need for a study she wished to conduct on the oppression of girls' voices in inner-city cultures because of a lack of feminization of the males. She said that she would seek a federal grant to fund the project. The Democratic Liberal Caucus spoke up and demanded that the government intervene to stop the slaughter. All polls showed the public was in favor of the new league by a ratio of 70 to 26, and 4 percent of the population simply didn't care. Major television networks rebroadcast Mindless's challenge to Ms. Steinem, who refused the offer, dismissing his blatant misogyny as a by-product of rap culture, which NOW also wanted to see ended by congressional statute.

A committee elected Mr. K as league commissioner. At the press conference he stood before the cameras and clenched his fist in a gang salute, then turned the microphone over to me. I gave a pep talk praising the humanitarian aspects of the venture, the chance to share the American dream with those less fortunate. "Last year over twelve hundred died in gang-related slayings," I said. "Some innocent bystanders. By installing a profit motive, K Promotions International has found the most humane solution to inner-city turmoil. And bystanders will be protected from crossfire. This is the safest violence ever organized." I can dazzle when I have to. I asked my stunned audience for questions.

"What are the expected numbers in terms of casualties?"

"The high figures from our computers estimate two hundred dead, a dozen seriously wounded. Certainly more dead than wounded," I answered. "Although the finalist must go until one gang is . . . well, incapacitated to the extreme measure."

"You mean wiped out!" a reporter corrected, his voice laced with indignation.

"The winner must be clearly that. We don't want a bunch of revenge shootings. Hasn't enough unnecessary blood been shed already?"

"Those figures come out of how many competitors?"

"Two thousand fifty-six. And this isn't the NFL. No one sits on the bench. Everyone gets to participate."

"Can you defend those figures?"

"In terms of morality or accuracy?"

We had with us a gang member, a guy called Slash. I called him to the podium to field the question.

"Hey, man, what's with you? If we wasn't doin' this, we be doin' it anuder way. Dig it? You gotta problem with that? You wanna say somethin' 'bout my mama? My sister?"

I smiled at the trembling reporter, who melted into his seat.

We introduced Hard Wall. He and the Angels rode in on their scooters and lined up diagonally across the stage. They'd dropped out of the competition to become league referees. Someone had to enforce rules, had to frisk for body armor and hand grenades, both outlawed by the league. Who better fit the role? Hard Wall thunked over the stage in his motorcycle boots, stood beside me, and whispered that Bussy had quit the firm to organize a street warriors' union. Mr. K, on a stool at stage left, stuck both pinky fingers in his ears, which told me he'd heard the news before I did. He lit his cigarette lighter, which he carried despite his having quit smoking twenty years before. I nodded, indicating that he was right, that he should have fired Bussy.

Despite suits to shut down the league and because of the publicity they generated, the league made $40 million in advance from regular season ticket sales. TV broadcast rights were out for bid, and all the major players were scrambling to control the action. Ticket sales were enough to cover lease agreements, but not enough to pay for bulletproof screen installation and other modifications. Within a month product sales matched ticket sales. Finally broadcast bidding ended. Television contracts came in at $280 million, just for the first two rounds. We'd show a record profit by the final rounds. Then there was the toy market. All clouded by the threat of a season-ending strike led by Bussy, who maintained that the gangs wanted all the contracts renegotiated.

Opening day I sat next to Mr. K in the Orange Bowl at a contest featuring Los Pocos Locos from Miami and the Aryan Freaks from Denver. Mr. K gave a double thumbs-up overhead because Denver meeting Miami in the Orange Bowl was a natural. Britney Spears, dressed as the Statue of Liberty with her right breast exposed, sang the National Anthem, which spurred a rebuke from the fundamentalist right and the radical left. Denver won the coin toss and chose to do the first drive-by. Miami, the first turf defenders, flattened the tires on Denver's car and ambushed the occupants. Down four to nothing in the opening minutes, Denver had to face a Miami drive-by. The hometown fans went wild.

The season only got better. Television ratings for every event topped the Super Bowl and Oscar night, and much of the credit belonged to those scruffy little guys in the center of the stadiums giving their all to ensure the success of the league. The most exciting competition occurred in Baltimore, where fans hungry for a winner for years, rioted after the City Center Thugs from Baltimore upset the Parking Lot Looters from Atlantic City by a score of sixteen to fifteen. Both teams would be forced to use recruits in order to advance, for Atlantic City, according to *League Rules*, Section Seven, Sub B, could advance if Baltimore failed to field a full squad.

In New York a referee was downed by a stray bullet and the Hell's Kitchen Caballeros were penalized two drive-bys and lost in sudden-death overtime. A gang from South Chicago skunked the gang from Gary, Indiana, 20–0. The sports page of a New York paper called it "a fine slaughter that showcased the professional skills of the well-trained Chicago street gangs, which were second only to those of New York." Gangs in Los Angeles, Detroit, and Las Vegas claimed Easterners were punks and immediately issued winner-take-all challenges to any gang from New York. It was going to be a great season, and an even greater fight-off competition. We could hardly wait for the regional shoot-outs to begin. Then the week before the regionals, Bussy went on the *Today* show and said the league was exploiting its athletes and getting rich off of kids who really only wanted money for college tuition. The union, with a list of fresh demands, walked out.

Each gang member wanted a separate contract with the gang owner, which created a hell of a headache for us because no one owns a gang; gangs just

are. The gangs picketed the competition sites and made side money selling autographs and bullets etched with their initials. Mr. K began taking
double doses of the double doses of bromos and antacids that he was
already taking and tripled his intake of laxatives and prunes. He had sunk
his fortune into the league. More than twenty suits were filed against the
league, everyone from vendors to cheerleaders being involved in them.
Within five weeks the league and K Enterprises faced financial ruin. We
were doomed.

Then Hard Wall came into my office with the solution. Franchise
gangs, sell them to individuals. "Who?" I asked.

"Mob bosses, the cocaine cartels, the Israeli Mafia."

"Israel has a Mafia?" I asked—I, a Jew, unaware of the existence of
such an organization.

"Don't be a dumb shit. They operate outta Beverly Hills."

How was I to know? I'm a convert.

It seemed the only way to save the league. We took the proposal up to
Mr. K, who was standing on the ledge outside his window flipping the bird
at people on the sidewalk sixteen stories down, which he did from time to
time for amusement. Before I could get the solution out, he turned to us,
smiled, and for the first time in thirteen years, spoke. "If anyone's curious,
tell them it was the prunes. I hate prunes, can't swallow another one."

The papers called it a tragedy—two pedestrians injured, Mr. K's blood
and oily remains all over the sidewalk on Rodeo Drive. I said that the fall
probably cured his constipation. Hard Wall said that more likely the landing did. When the survivors looked up from what remained of him, they
saw Hard Wall and me leaning out of the window discussing those exact
points.

So Hard Wall and I were arrested and Bussy grabbed control of the league.
Our attorneys are asking permission for us to attend the finals in New
Orleans as relief from the terms of our bail release, if we get bailed.
Otherwise, we'll be restricted to Los Angeles and vicinity. Hard Wall wants
to get his hands on Bussy, just once. That's going to be tough, since Bussy
now lives in a New York penthouse under Mob watch day and night, but I
have faith in Hard Wall. You would too if you could hear the way he grinds
his teeth as he plots revenge.

Me, I'm sitting here wondering just how the hell all of this really came about. It's like a gutter ball popping back onto the lane at the last instant and hitting the pocket for a strike. Next year the league goes worldwide with new blood and fresh rules that allow terrorism into the competition. Imagine car bombing and kidnapping and beheading! The networks have been asked to bid the project, bidding to start at $5 billion. It was a crazy idea, plain crazy, that keeps getting crazier. If you have time to think about it. Who would have thought it? Not me, even though I did the groundwork.

A Pulling Thing

Keagler looks at Nora Paterson, who sits across the table. Her hair, beige business suit, and brown and white silk scarf speak of a fastidious woman, a raincoat-and-umbrella-in-a-rainstorm kind of female, neat, competent, thorough, hardly the type to commit murder. She calmly fondles the knot in her scarf as if waiting for an aperitif. He's seen people charged with simple assault more concerned, and he's heard the calm, boastful confessions of men, doctors and lawyers and even a cop who murdered, but never a woman. Just when you think all's predictable. Diane once said every woman wants to destroy at least one man for the transgressions of all men. He wonders if there is truth in what Diane said and decides that perhaps she was right. Perhaps.

He finds Nora Paterson attractive. Who wouldn't, her hair in a French plait, frosted lipstick freshly applied. But she is also unremarkable in the sense that upper-middle-class wives seem cut from a similar mold, the type who wear Bulgari jewelry and carry Gucci purses and lurk in the aisles of Saks, a woman spared the harshness of life owing to the fact that she was once beautiful—his opinion. But a cop has intuition. Yeah, he thinks, except in his own affairs.

In the stillness her breath and his seem to blend. Except for tables and chairs the room is bare and intimidating. The naked walls amplify every sound, a scraping of a chair leg, the clicking of a ballpoint. It has the peculiar effect of not only magnifying sound but also forcing submerged memories to the surface. Usually he's in command here, but today he finds the room disquieting. She taps her finger on the tabletop. He nods to assure her the delay will be short.

He has interviewed those who hear voices and those visited by angels, and he's watched the eyes of the disturbed turn inward and drift into galaxies deep in the mind. But his experience in interviewing women is limited mostly to victims—angry, distrustful, broken by the event—especially those raped or physically abused. Women who are suspects are usually addicts or lost souls dragged into crime by a husband or lover. Crime is a man's game, most especially murder. This one's enigmatic, fits no profile he's familiar with; still, he finds something about Nora Paterson familiar. He wonders if she's crazy or if that even applies. Too calm. Entirely.

"Were you . . . busy before I came?" she asks.

It's been a screwy day. Lost files. A detective twisted an ankle as he climbed the steps. Two daylight bar robberies. Now her.

"Yes, but not very." He smiles to maintain a sense of rapport. She smiles back. He wonders how many hearts she trampled in high school. She's the type, no doubt, he thinks, reflecting on his experience with women. Now she's traded her pink-lipstick-and-Volvo life for a new one.

The door opens. She looks up and smiles wanly as Harry enters.

"Would you like coffee . . . Ms. Paterson?" Keagler asks.

"Aren't cops supposed to have good memories? I gave my name, Miss Paterson. I'm not married."

Good memories? He finds the words ironic. What's a good memory? Diane lying in the hospital, the smells of Mogadishu, a rancid fruity smell blended with saltwater breeze? He wishes those parts of his memory would vanish. He pictures a dozen men in uniform seated in various positions by the wall, the captain approaching with the first sergeant, Hardaway puffing on a cigarette and Squiggles saying, "Shit, I hope the skinnies appreciate this."

"I'd like a cigarette," Nora Paterson says.

Keagler shakes off the memory. Cigarette? he thinks. She looks like she'd carry an anti-smoking banner in a protest march. Mothers against tobacco. Kills, smokes, chews tobacco—what surprise comes next? A lap dancer?

"What brand?"

She pauses before answering, "Anything with a filter . . . no, wait. No menthol."

He turns to Harry. "Harry, a pack for the lady . . . filters."

"No menthol. Got it, Lieutenant."

She chews at her lipstick, arches her eyebrows, and gazes up at Harry, who stands at the door. "Those slim ones," she says. "Though they're just as likely to give someone cancer."

Keagler locks his gaze on her as he speaks. "And see, Harry, what the holdup is with the stenographer."

"Yeah."

"Sometimes help's a little slow. And you took us by surprise." Keagler looks at her as if he's at a loss to understand, a technique he uses to make suspects drop their guard.

"I don't mean to be any trouble. I work," she says. "I know what you must go through. Would you like to begin?"

"I'd prefer the steno be here," he says. "Sorry. It's after normal working hours." She seems confused, so he adds, "Budget . . . Money keeps us at a skeleton crew after six."

Pointing at Officer Tishmin, she asks in a near whisper, "What's the woman's name?"

"That's Officer Tishmin."

The woman leans back in her chair. "Unusual name."

"Yes," he agrees.

She wets her lips and tilts her head in his direction as if flirting and says softly, "Is she . . . ah . . . gay?"

Concerned that Tishmin will overhear, Keagler leans forward and whispers, "It's none of my business."

"But she could be. You don't know," she says.

"Again, it's none of my business."

"I've heard things . . . you know, women in uniform and jails, that stuff. It's no secret."

"I guess it isn't," Keagler says, trying to be agreeable.

Clearing her throat, she addresses the woman cop in a full voice, "Officer Tishmin?"

"Yes," the uniformed woman answers.

"Are there a lot of gay women in your field?"

Tishmin stares, as much at the question as at the questioner. "There aren't a lot of women in my field."

"Yes. I didn't think of that. Are you gay?"

Tishmin looks to Keagler. "Lieutenant?"

"It's okay, Tishmin. I'll handle . . ." He starts to say it, but doesn't finish. "Ms. Paterson, I'll have to ask you not to be personal with us," he says.

"*Miss*. I work with men, but I do *not* want to be one."

She smiles as if they have shared a secret. He smiles back.

"No. Of course you don't." He wonders what kind of progress Harry is making with the stenographer. He thinks of Diane, their last conversation that echoed dozens of previous ones. She asked where he went when he tossed off the blankets at night and left. Was he having an affair? He assured her never, the truth of it. Never. Just out to think. No, out to forget. What? she asked. Nothing, something.

"He wasn't the first," Nora Paterson says.

Keagler moves his notepad close and picks up the pen. "Who?"

She draws a circle in the air with a forefinger. "That man, tonight."

Taken aback, Keagler asks, "Can this wait for the steno?"

"I don't think it can." She looks at the woman cop. "Did you hear that, Officer Tishmin?"

"Yes, I heard you."

"Good, I want to be heard. There were more than two."

He presses the tape recorder switch and says, "More than two, you say?"

"Yes." "I must remind you. You have the right to remain silent. You have the—"

"You already told me all that. I know you're being professional, but I'm not stupid. I want to talk."

"We need this for the record. You don't want to wait until Harry comes with cigarettes? Or for an attorney, maybe?"

She chews the last of her lipstick from her lip. "That's considerate, Lieutenant, but no."

"Okay, this is recorded and witnessed by Officer Angela Tishmin, P-number . . ." He squints to see her badge.

"Twelve forty-one," Tishmin says.

"And myself, Lieutenant Michael Keagler, P-number seven eighty-eight."

"Excuse me. May I talk now? Should I give my name? Nora Paterson?"

"Yes."

"I know you can do things with tape recorders, but I trust you. I bet you're very kind to your wife."

Yes, kind, he thinks, but Diane saw kindness as weakness, agreeableness as lack of interest. Perhaps that was why he couldn't tell her where he went or why, things he couldn't talk about. Men strapping on bandoliers of ammunition, looking at one another with their lips turned up in sardonic smiles, sweat beading down their foreheads. A comrade in arms apologizing for evacuating his bowels just before he takes a last gasp of air.

He points to the microphone. "Please, go on."

"As I said, there were more than two. To be exact, this was the fifth."

"Five?" Stunned, Keagler looks at Tishmin, who appears equally shocked. Murder's not usually an Olympic event for women.

"Yes, exactly five."

The door opens and Harry enters, holding a pack of cigarettes. From the hallway behind him comes a scraping noise, metal on linoleum. Harry shrugs and aims a thumb in the direction of the hallway. "Steno broke her heel. Can't walk fast."

"Help her in, so Ms. Paterson can get started."

"*Miss* Paterson," she corrects.

Keagler snaps a look at her. "You do know this is serious?"

She calmly smiles. "Absolutely."

Harry tosses the pack to Keagler, who opens it and offers her a cigarette. She holds the cigarette to her lips and stares. Keagler realizes she's waiting for a light and shrugs.

"No one smokes anymore," he says, sounding apologetic.

"It's not important," she says, but the cigarette remains dangling from her lips.

Keagler says, "Harry, did you bring matches?"

Harry fishes in his pockets, then tosses a packet on the table in front of Keagler, who lights the cigarette. She inhales luxuriously and holds the smoke in her lungs.

He remembers lighting Hardaway's cigarette with a Zippo, both saying they should quit as they exhaled. In the foreground the helicopter's turbine whined. Might be my last, Hardaway said and smiled. He flicked the cigarette from his fingers, spraying red cinders on the ground, then crossed the tarmac and climbed aboard the craft. Keagler crushed his own cigarette underfoot and watched the chopper carry Hardaway, his friend, and the others to their deaths. Tough way to quit, Keagler thinks.

"Smoking's not allowed inside," the steno says as she seats herself in the corner. "I don't feel I should be exposed to it." Ignoring the sharp looks she gets, she crosses her legs, adjusts the notepad on her knee, and nods, indicating she is ready.

"This may not be long," Keagler says to her. He shakes his head. "You may begin, Miss Paterson."

She looks at the three tables in the room, then at Keagler, but doesn't speak.

He smells the faint odor of hyacinth. "Is something the matter?"

She points at the tip of the cigarette. "Ashtray?"

He thinks this confession may never occur. "Is there an ashtray any-where, Harry?"

Harry rises from his seat. "You know, no one smokes."

"Okay, an empty coffee cup, Harry."

Nora Paterson flicks the ash on the floor. "I'll use this if it's okay."

Keagler nods. "Fine with me."

The steno glares at the ash.

Nora Paterson raises an eyebrow. "We're ready?"

Keagler says, "Please begin."

"You're very polite," she says. "Do you get a lot of confessions this way?"

"Please, Ms. Paterson."

"Miss. I was married, now I'm not. As I said, my name is Nora Jeanne Paterson—that's two 'n's and an 'e.' Not like Marilyn Monroe Norma Jean, though people have called me that." She keeps eye contact with Keagler. "I'm thirty-seven years of age, a rep with New Allied Industries, a junior vice president. I've killed five men. To my credit, I never notched my gun, which I had planned on saying if I were ever caught, which I have been. I suppose you want details?"

"Yes. But for the record: You did turn yourself in?"

"Yes. Will that help my case?"

"I can't say. That would be up to the DA. Go on." He looks at her, wait-ing for her confession to continue.

"Aren't you supposed to be asking questions? I mean, isn't that what you're paid to do?"

"Would you feel more comfortable if I asked questions?"

"I'm a taxpayer. I think you owe it to those of us who pay your wages."

Patience, Keagler tells himself. "All right. Ms. Paterson, would you give the details of your first murder?"

"That's not much of a question, but it's better. It wasn't murder exactly. None of them were—exactly. Killing and murder aren't the same, you know."

"Yes. Please go on."

"One of the reasons I never notched a gun was that I used a gun only once before tonight. So that makes tonight the second. One notch would be silly. Don't you agree?"

"I agree." Keagler looks at Harry, whose eyes telegraph Keagler's thoughts—sociopath.

She points to the microphone. "Can you fix this so I don't have to lean forward?"

Keagler adjusts the neck of the microphone so that she can sit straight.

"Thank you." She leans away from the microphone and tilts her head. "I ran over the first one. In a parking lot. I'd been to the movies—Mel Gibson. I always leave before the credits, and he followed me out." She smiles. "Not Mel Gibson. Told me I had great legs. My legs are nothing special. I was almost to my car when he asked me to go for a drink. I spun about and told him I was trained in the martial arts and could pulverize him. He used the c-word on me and just stood there. I started the car and backed out over him. He wouldn't move, after all. He went down so easily, almost no noise. Didn't even dent my car. Of course, that didn't kill him, just knocked him down. I ran over him twice and drove off. No one saw me. I read the next day in the paper that his name was Brando, like the actor. He was married. They said the only evidence was tire tracks, so I replaced my tires. Women can think of such things. We're not stupid, you know."

Harry leans over the table. "You killed him because he called you a cu—"

"Don't you say it!" she admonishes.

Keagler raises his hands. "Harry, please."

Harry trades glances with Tishmin.

Keagler smiles apologetically and motions for her to continue. "What about the second?"

"That one was different. I started carrying an ice pick. All women should." She stops and takes another drag off the cigarette, swallows the smoke, then looks about the room.

Keagler remembers when he and Diane tried to quit cigarettes, the torment bombarded on each other, hers from pent-up anger over the miscarriage. He was, she spat, always unavailable, even when home. The pressure got to them both. He quit. She didn't.

"The second one," he asks, "you used an ice pick on him?"

"Yes."

"Where was this?"

"Hollywood Plaza. Three years ago."

Another state, another jurisdiction. He would have to contact the other agencies. He blinks and notices a tautness in Nora Paterson's forehead.

"I'm not continuing unless you start interacting with me," she says.

Keagler notices that Tishmin's squirming. He clears his throat and sips water. "Would you explain the circumstances?"

"Much better. That's the way to question." She takes a last puff and stubs the cigarette out under her foot. "I was kind of restless, so I went window-shopping. He wasn't a handsome man, kind of plain. He stammered at first, like he didn't know how to talk to a woman."

Keagler pictures a faceless stranger, a construction worker or an accountant, an ordinary man in appearance but one who senses a woman's loneliness and knows the right words to lower her guard. He inhales and lets his breath out slowly.

"Lieutenant," she says, "you were doing very well."

He nods. "You were window-shopping, he approached you, and you killed him in broad daylight. Is that it?"

"No, it was around two in the morning. Sometimes I can't sleep. Something pulls me out of my bed."

Keagler understands what it is to be pulled out of bed and walk alone with your thoughts. What would have happened that night in Mogadishu had one decision been different? What if the captain had told him to harness up? He walks sidewalks replaying that moment, wondering whose life he's living. Hardaway's? Diane accused him of taking a lover. Each time he started to explain, words failed, and he closed himself off. He wonders, did he and Nora Paterson pass each other on their self-possessed searches?

"Two A.M. and you were window-shopping?" Harry asks.

"Yes? That's all, and he propositioned me like I was some kind of whore."

Keagler studies her blue eyes speckled with flecks of yellow. He wonders if loneliness is as powerful a motivator as hate. Can someone kill from loneliness? He sets the glass aside and says, "That's an unusual time to window-shop."

"No crowds," she says.

"No witnesses," Harry mumbles.

Keagler raises his eyebrow to silence Harry. "So, he approaches you and you kill him?"

"No, when I turned him down, he grabbed one arm and jammed his hand in my crotch. I gave it to him in the forehead with the ice pick four or five times, hit him until the blade broke off, but he was already dead. And don't insinuate I was at fault because I want to be on the streets at two in the morning. I have the right to be there."

"Yes. The man you shot tonight. What was . . . ?"

"Shouldn't you do this in some chronology?"

"Nora . . . Miss Paterson, this isn't a movie. This is very serious."

She gives him a bewildered look. "Serious? Of course it is. May I have another cigarette?"

He taps out a cigarette and lights it for her. He looks at the bare walls and the fluorescent-lighted ceiling, the squareness of the room, the sharp angles where the walls join. He takes a deep breath and exhales. "Would you like to think about this before you continue?"

Smoke drifts luxuriously from her mouth. "Isn't your job to take confessions?"

"That's part of it."

"Well, I want to confess. It's supposed to be so goddamn good for the soul. Let's see."

"How long ago were you divorced?"

"What kind of question is that? What does that have to do with confessing?" She sweeps a strand of hair away from her lips. "Don't be patronizing."

"A normal question." When she doesn't respond, he says, "Okay, tell me about the third."

She puffs on the cigarette, nervous, quick puffs. "A car again. A year ago, maybe more. I squeezed him against a wall at a shopping mall in the suburbs—Del Lorca, I think."

"Why?"

"I felt threatened is all. I just knew I had to do it, or else. What difference does it make? May I have that coffee now?"

"Do you want to quit?"

"No. I want all of you to earn your money. I want . . . coffee. I'll wait until the coffee."

Keagler doesn't want to stop. "How do you like it?"

"It's okay," she says. "You're asking better questions."

"No. I mean, how do you take your coffee?"

"With sugar."

"Harry, get the lady a cup. Two, black with sugar. How about you, Officer Tishmin?"

"Two-thirds full, cream, two teaspoons of sugar, and top it with water."

Keagler turned to the stenographer. "Ah, uh, Ms. . . . ."

"Kindleston. Lena Kindleston."

"Would you like something?"

"Oh, thank you. Hot tea with lemon and honey, if they have it."

"We'll get someone to fix your shoe. Got that, Harry?"

Harry leans close and whispers, "Can't Tishmin get the coffee and tea?"

Keagler looks up. "You know better."

Harry looks at Keagler, curls his upper lip, and leaves. The door clatters shut, echoing off the flat walls. Keagler recalls sidewalks, the hollow sound of his footsteps. Where was he that night, and did he leave the door unlocked? Those were Diane's questions. And his answers failed her. He failed her. When he looks back, Nora Paterson motions with her finger

"I shot the fourth. He had a moustache."

Keagler asks, "Where was that?"

"Is this on the record?"

"Everything you say is on the record."

"On his lip, like Officer Tishmin. I do not like Officer Tishmin." She smiles with her mouth closed, like the painted smile of a mannequin.

Tishmin glares at her. Keagler shakes his head at the female officer, who looks away.

"No?" Keagler says.

"Definitely not," she whispers.

"This isn't a game. I meant where did the shooting take place?"

"San Francisco. I was on vacation." Her voice swells with pride.

"On the street?"

She shakes her head.

"You have to speak your answers."

"No. Not on the street."

"When you shot this man, what were the circumstances?"

"He was in a room across the hall. He knocked on my door and asked to use the phone as he'd locked himself out. So he said. I told him to go down to the lobby and get a key. I wouldn't open the door."

She stops talking to suck down one last lungful of smoke, drops the butt on the floor next to the first, and crushes it. "I heard the door to his room open and slam. A half hour later, maybe forty minutes, he knocked again, said he'd ordered dinner for two and a bottle of champagne. I told him he had the wrong room. He said he'd be waiting in fourteen-twelve, that he thought I was beautiful and knew he loved me. He left and I heard the door slam.

"I waited ten minutes before I got my gun and a pillow and went to his room. When he saw me, he looked surprised. He smiled when he saw the pillow, then said there had been a mistake, that he'd thought I was someone else. I told him there was no mistake and placed the pillow to his chest and the barrel of the gun to the pillow. Afterward, I left the pillow from my room and took one from his bed. I slept well and checked out early in the morning. On a cruise to Alcatraz, I dumped the gun in the bay."

She leans back, eyes clear and remorseless, the eyes of a zealot or a crusader. Keagler senses something haywire at work but can't get a grasp on it. Is it hate? Loneliness? Greed and revenge, even killing over a block of gang turf, he understands. In Somalia weren't those the motives—turf, greed, revenge? Bearded men killing bearded men, women and children caught in the middle. He remembers the frail figures, stick thin, lips drawn back. Children black in life and blacker still in death. What motivated that?

"I have to ask. Why do you kill?"

"Why?"

"Yes. Why?"

She seems distracted by the question and doesn't answer at first. She looks anxiously at the door. "I could use that coffee. You know, this is making me feel better. You're not an unattractive man, do you know that?"

"Why?" he asks insistently.

"I don't know. It's a pulling thing. Once you do it, you can't stop."

"I see." He feels no closer to the truth of why. *Motivation* is the stuff of psychologists. Motive goes deeper.

She sets her gaze on the door. Keagler turns to see what she's looking at. Two shadows stand behind the milky pane, talking. One knocks on the door.

"Come in," Keagler says.

Nora Paterson glances at his left hand. "Are you married?"

Keagler turns away from her as the door opens.

"Are you?" she asks, her voice less composed.

Harry motions him outside.

Keagler pushes his chair back and stands. "No, I'm not."

He leaves the door ajar as he speaks in a hushed voice with Harry, who begins by saying that a team of detectives had called from the Paterson house. As Harry speaks, Keagler nods, raises his brows, shakes his head, and looks in the general direction where Nora Paterson sits. "And," Harry finishes, "the gun she brought in hasn't been fired in a long time." After reentering the room, Keagler closes the door, stuffs his hands in his pockets, and stands looking down at her.

"They went to the Fox Street address you gave us, the empty one down the block from where you actually live. Then the officers found your house."

Her lip quivers. She reverts to the meek-voiced woman who first handed a revolver to the sergeant at the desk and confessed to a murder.

Keagler thinks of the emergency room, Diane frail, trembling. Where had he been? she asked, her voice quavering. "I needed you," she said, then broke down in tears. He told her he was walking. Could he explain he'd been watching a medic take his place on a helicopter? That the helicopter woke him up?

Nora Paterson chews at her lip. "May I have another cigarette?"

He hands her a cigarette. She holds it to her lips.

He doesn't light it. "You know what they found?"

She looks down. "Yes."

"Two kids, both alive. Yours, and they're wondering where their mother is," he says loudly so that Tishmin will hear. "And a babysitter."

She starts to rise. Keagler motions for her to sit. She looks around the room before settling back in the chair.

"You have a pretty vivid imagination," he says.

"I'd like to speak off the record."

Keagler turns off the tape recorder and turns to the steno. "We're off the record."

Nora Paterson offers a smile, as if something intimate has passed between them.

"We've got important matters to handle here," Keagler says. "Real crime. Do you want to go to jail that bad?"

"I don't want to go to jail."

"Why? Why this?" Motive seems everything at the moment. He wants an explanation. He thinks of one dark predawn after he'd walked the streets for two hours. He ended up atop a high-rise garage, looking down six stories and wondering what pain he would feel at the last instant. That was after the night a stranger entered his house and raped his wife, entered when he was walking a sidewalk several miles away. He wants to understand Nora Paterson's sadness, and realizes he wants desperately to shed his own.

She shakes her head. "I had a husband. I don't know. I work hard, do my job well, very well. I go on vacations, but sometimes it's not enough. I'm afraid sometimes."

Keagler studies the expression on her face, different now, not beaten exactly but vulnerable. "No. Why?" He points to the tape recorder and the room.

"I drive by here. Do you ever wonder when you see a single light on in a house, do you wonder what happens in that lighted room?" She holds her hands together as if in prayer and stares at them. "I couldn't help it. The truth is I don't know. I was pulled in."

He sits. "Would you like the coffee?"

She nods without looking at him.

"Harry, the coffee. Bring it in."

Harry shuffles in, balancing a tray with four coffees, which he distributes—Nora Paterson first, the lieutenant second, then Officer Tishmin. With his index finger, he lowers the bridge of his glasses to the tip of his nose, looks at the stenographer, and hands her a cup.

"No tea," he says and turns his back.

Nora sips from her cup, then turns her lips up in something resembling a smile. She seems remote. This goes unnoticed by all except Keagler, who's reminded of his own repressed desire to kill the man Diane left him for, a man who ran a small insurance agency. Why? he wonders, and then remembers that in his profession *why*, unless it applies to motive, is meaningless. Still, it means everything to the rest of the world. She left because at least an insurance agent can sleep through the night. No, that wasn't why she left. And it wasn't Keagler's insomnia. She couldn't abide him living inside himself, couldn't forgive him being elsewhere when she needed him, couldn't forgive that night. Neither could he.

"Are you going to arrest me?" Nora Paterson asks.

"You come in here wasting our time, taxpayers' money. I can arrest you, you know, for making a false confession."

She nods. "I'm . . . not crazy."

Keagler dismisses her remark with a wave of his finger. "I should do that for the taxpayers—arrest you."

"We should do what we're paid to do. I know. I'm good at my work."

"I'm sure you are." He thinks of Diane, how his wife calmly asked for a divorce without a hint of regret. She'd told him he would be sorry, that when she left and he was alone he would understand why she needed a new life. He looks at Nora Paterson. "You're free to go."

Nora looks at him as if she recognizes herself in him, holds the cup to her lips, and pauses before drinking. "Sometimes, it's just too much. They ask too much of us," she says. "Every day, there's this . . . demand, someone demanding without saying, and I'm . . . expected to please. Do you know what it's like to want to mix salt in a cake batter, to sprinkle sugar on a steak?"

"No. I don't know." Keagler runs his fingers through his hair, then shakes his head at nothing in particular. "Your children are waiting," he says. "I don't want to see you here again."

She hesitates as if she doesn't understand, then reaches over and picks up his notepad and pen. She scratches something down and turns the notebook over.

"You may go," Keagler says.

"Do you think I'm crazy?"

He sees only her unhappiness, an isolation akin to his own. For months he thought that if only he could find the rapist Diane would return to him. But then what? Would it end his guilt? Only one guilt at a time. It seemed that living was measured by the quantity of guilt a man carried. Sometimes it was guilt brought on not by a man's action but by circumstances out of a man's control. They died, all of them who went in that night in Mogadishu. Hardaway, his friend, and Smits, the redheaded medic who took Keagler's place. But Keagler lived. Why did he feel guilt? Because he didn't die? That seems irrational, as crazy as her need for attention.

He shrugs. "I'm not sure what crazy is."

"So long as you're married, the women, the other wives accept you, but as soon as you're divorced, that changes. You're a threat, the one who wants to take another's husband. Do you see? Does anyone?" She sets the cup down and stares at him. "The world gets turned upside down."

That's it, Keagler thinks. The world upside down. There is no motive.

When he doesn't speak, she walks to the door. "Thank you for the cigarettes." She rests her hand on the doorknob and says, "I apologize, Officer Tishmin."

Officer Tishmin rubs her eyes and says, "Lieutenant, can I go?"

Nora Paterson says to Keagler, "Haven't you ever wanted not to be who you are?" When he doesn't answer, she says, "You believed me. Didn't you?"

"No," he says, lying. Too often he wishes he were someone else, someone who could sleep through the night. He takes the pack out of his pocket, crosses the room, and offers it to her.

She holds her palm up. "Thank you. I don't smoke." She turns to leave.

Keagler tells Harry to walk her out of the station. As he watches her pass through the door, he feels something tugging at him. Absentmindedly, he slips the pack in his pocket. Then aware of what he's done, he pulls it out, crushes it, and tosses it in the wastebasket. He rests his elbows on the table by the phone. The steno walks by, both shoes off.

"I'm going to report that there was smoking in here," she says and leaves.

Tishmin says it's been a long shift and asks if everything's all right with him, if he needs help. He shakes his head, says he's fine, and asks what she would have done.

"I suppose the same thing. She's more lonely than loony. She doesn't look the type, but loneliness can drive us to do strange things. Have you heard from your ex?"

He shakes his head.

"I've got a burglary report to finish," Tishmin says.

He turns the pad over and sees that Nora Paterson wrote down a telephone number with the message "Call me." He thinks of the empty space in his bed that Diane once occupied and imagines himself awakening in the middle of the night, perhaps to the sound of a helicopter. He looks at the phone number and thinks of Nora walking the streets. If he called, would she invite him over, offer him coffee, and sit ready to listen to his tale, or the one that he makes up? Would his story seem as crazy to her as hers was to him? He shakes the thought off. That, he decides, is a story authored by the kind of loneliness that kills, nothing more.

He pictures Diane on their first date, when he saw her reflection in a hall of mirrors at a carnival. She waved, and he touched the glass that captured an endless number of her images. He could not tell which was real. He stares at the number on the paper, tries to picture his ex-wife as he last saw her, cannot. What, he wonders, would go on between them if he passed Nora Paterson in the night? Would they lift their eyes and recognize one another or look away, not daring to see what unfinished creatures they were? Would they seek comfort? He crushes the paper and drops it in the wastebasket on the way out. He stops at the door to turn out the lights and stares back at the basket beside the table. Inside is a wadded paper. He feels it pulling at him.

Snake Boy

'd last seen that part of the country in 1970. Fifteen years later on a Friday I was near Auburn on my way to Reno with my wife and daughter when I saw his face on a billboard advertising Able Art's Car Lot. The picture showed him beardless, his hair gray, but I recognized him. Common sense said to go on, but impulse took over. I pulled the car off the highway between two signposts and stopped it.

Dust billowed up from beneath my car and spread slowly over the row of used cars facing the highway. Candace, who'd been napping, looked up at the listless red and yellow pennants hanging from wires and then at the line of used cars and pickups. She and I were on vacation, the day was dry and hot, typical of the foothills of the Sierras' western slope, and since the drive had begun, she and I had been getting on each other's nerves, the way couples sometimes do when both parties desperately need a break from ordinary life. She asked what I was doing.

"Nothing really," I said. "I'll be a minute." I leaned my shoulder into the stubborn door.

"It's hot, Pate," she said.

The office was a double-wide with faux wood siding. A sliding glass door opened with a grating sound. A white-sleeved arm emerged first and groped for the handrail. Bristol lumbered out, a cane in his free hand. He battled the stairs one at a time, his hand clutching the rail and his eyes fixed on the steps as he descended. His movements lacked the electric force they had once evidenced. He smiled and winked as he set his weight on the cane, then limped over, huffing and struggling with each step.

He wore white mesh sandals with black socks and gray gabardine trousers, and his untrimmed hair strayed over his shirt collar. His mottled jowls were mapped with tiny broken vessels. So, he had lived, I thought. I had always figured as much. It was apparent he did not recognize me, a thought that had not occurred when I'd decided to stop. I found that amusing. I guess he'd expected to never see me again, just as I'd expected to never see him. Now it had happened.

He sized up my car. "Fine car you got. A T-Bird. What can I do for you? A second car?"

"Maybe." I wondered how he could not remember.

A trace of the possessed look that had once dominated his face still sparked in his dark eyes. Had I not otherwise recognized him, I could have identified his voice. In earlier days he'd been a seducer, an orator well practiced in the mannered art of language, capable of adapting tone and dialect to fit his audience. He spoke in a spellbinding baritone that in an instant could shift from precise Midwestern speech to a careless Southern drawl, where he stretched his vowels out and let them hang like laundry on a clothesline.

"What kind you like? Got some fine cars here. Not like yours, mind you, but fine all the same. That Tempo, a good car, sixty-thousand-miler. Came from an estate sale. If you're looking for Chevys, well, confidentially, I bought the three I got at the auction. Can't vouch for 'em. Don't know anything about them really."

Candace glared at me as she rolled down the window. Angie had climbed into the front seat and was sitting behind the steering wheel.

"Fine-lookin' family," he said. "You from these parts?"

"Thank you. I'm a lucky guy." He still had the knack for small talk and disarming people with small compliments. How could he not remember? I stared into his eyes, hoping to spark his memory. "No. We're on our way to Truckee, then Tahoe."

"Nice country." He squinted. "You look sort of familiar."

It seemed he wanted to talk as much as he wanted to sell a car. Of course, that was part of his art. "I get that a lot. Guess I'm pretty ordinary."

He looked at Candace. "Well, don't sell yourself short; you're a good-lookin' fella with a real pretty wife."

Candace leaned across the seat and sounded the horn. Her expression said that I'd best drop what I was doing.

"I've got to go," I said, waving to her to indicate I was coming.

"Have her and the daughter come in the trailer. There's water. It isn't much, but the place is air-conditioned. This is a nice place to be spring and fall, but summers are hell."

"Thanks just the same. Better go."

"I understand. Ever want a car, stop back by. Can't guarantee that

Tempo'll be here." He looked at my family sitting impatiently in the car, Candace fanning herself with a magazine.

He squinted at me again. "You sure look like someone I should know."

I backed toward the car. "Don't think so."

"Too bad. You seem like a nice young fella."

I walked to our car and looked over the roof of it getting in. He stood in the same spot, staring. I told Angie to climb into the back. She said she wanted to drive.

"Not at age twelve," I said.

"Hey," he called, "you spend any time in Arizona and New Mexico?"

I nodded slowly. He might remember soon enough. He wouldn't need good eyes, just a moment of reflection. "Passed through is all."

I slid behind the wheel. Candace's cheeks were red, and she stared out of the window, refusing to acknowledge me. When we were on the highway several miles east of Auburn, she asked what was so important that I had to stop there. "Nothing. I thought I knew him," I told her. I imagined him sitting in the sales office, rummaging through a long-ago history and then remembering.

Angie complained that it was hot and asked if we were ever going to eat. The expression on Candace's face told me that my answer was unsatisfactory. I turned up the air conditioner. When we hit the climb to the Sierras, I pressed the accelerator and drifted into myself.

II

I stumbled into Bristol in an alley in Albuquerque in 1970, the spring after I had been discharged from 'Nam. At the time I had fallen in among the social detritus that accumulated around Central Avenue. I was a thief, but a sad one. In the daytime I earned minimum wage washing dishes and pans. At night I ransacked doctors' offices for money and drugs or small businesses for whatever I thought I could fence for a few dollars. Looking back, I'm sure I wanted to get caught, even did once, but it wasn't enough to stop me.

I had picked up a habit after getting shot in 'Nam while pulling a dead squad mate to cover during a battle at a place called Hamburger Hill. I used the wound as an excuse to snort China white. Truth is, I was just reckless. I had brought the jones home with me, and a year later eleven bucks a day for scraping grease from pans could not pay even a tiny percentage of what I was shooting. That particular night I was desperate. I decided to take off the pawnshop on Central Avenue where I often hocked stolen merchandise, mostly cameras and tools. The broker knew he was loaning money on stolen goods, and he burned me on the transactions. I knew the layout. His dishonesty seemed reason enough to justify ripping off his business.

The area was frequented by panhandlers, whores, and bewildered souls such as Case Man, who claimed he had been kidnapped by aliens and used as a stud to impregnate their women, all of whom looked like Ursula Andress. My plan was to hit the place and rather than run off, stash the merchandise and then blend into the neighborhood, merely find a vacant spot in a nearby alley, roll up in a ball like one of the several winos who begged coins off passersby, and appear intoxicated and dumbfounded if the cops pulled up to question me. I climbed a drainpipe to the roof, pushed the swamp cooler on its side, and dropped down through the vent without setting off the alarm.

I was feeling confident. After all, I knew the layout. I felt my way to the display cases. But it was dark and the valuables—expensive watches and anything with diamonds in it normally on display in daylight—were secured in the safe. Two dozen or so gold wedding bands remained in the display case. That was all that held any promise. Mechanics' tools hung conveniently from a rack over the case. I grabbed a drill, used it to shatter the glass, and promptly activated an alarm.

The bell was a primitive dinger, small, inexpensive, the kind you would expect a chiseling pawnbroker to install. Still, the pulsing sound it emitted came loud enough to spark a seizure, which I nearly suffered. As part of my plan I'd figured on setting off the alarm on the way out, so triggering the bell now threw my game off. Left with no alternative, I grabbed what I could, stuffed the gold bands in my pocket, and hoofed it in the direction of the back door.

Along the way I knocked over a stand of string guitars. One clattered to the aisle in front of me. As I kicked it aside, my foot got trapped in the sound box. I stumbled forward, stomping my trapped foot in hopes that might free me. Instead, I tumbled forward. I reached out and grabbed the nearest thing for balance and in the process knocked over a second display case. I managed to stay upright, but this time I stomped on the guitar with my free foot until the instrument lay in shards. Then I scrambled for the alley. It took precious seconds to lift the two-by-four that barred the door, and more to throw the latch. A few more ticked off before I broke the lock.

I was pouring sweat by the time I hit the alley. The blare of sirens echoed down the narrow passage, seemingly from every direction. I imagined cops descending on the pawnshop, spotlights trained on me, nowhere to go, the glare of headlights, bullhorns blaring commands. The alley was vacant except for a blue tanklike '59 Buick parked by the garbage cans at the north end. Without giving it much thought, I ran north toward Central Avenue.

I was three strides from the sidewalk and feeling assured of my escape when the driver's door of the Buick flew open and something hooked my ankle. The asphalt rushed at me; my left hand and elbow seemed to catch fire. My head snapped back, then my face came to rest on an oil stain, the smell of road grease being the last thing I noticed before passing out.

I came to inside the Buick, my ribs and head aching. A trickle of blood ran down my jaw from a wound on my head. I tried to move, but my hair, long and straight in the counterculture style of the day, was tied in knots and rolled up in the window, and my wrists were manacled behind me. The driver looked over, held up a blue-steel revolver for me to see, and said, "Stay calm." That was all—"Stay calm." I turned away and leaned against the armrest, appearing as calm, at least on the outside, as a saint on Judgment Day.

The car sped down a dark highway. The driver kept one hand on the steering wheel, the other clutching the revolver. Once he looked in my direction and said, "I knew I'd find you." I asked what kind of nutcase he was and said that he'd best let me go, that I was a war veteran and not some pushover. He snorted and then trained his eyes on the road, his raptorlike profile occasionally illuminated by oncoming headlights.

Eventually he slowed the car and searched the edge of the roadway. He drove looking to the side for several minutes, then suddenly slammed on the brakes. I vaulted forward as far as my hair would allow and came to an abrupt stop.

"Take it easy!" I shouted.

He jammed the gun inside his waistband and calmly steered down a washboard road. The car bucked and swayed and jerked me back and forth as gravel pelted the undercarriage. My left elbow, raw from the fall, rubbed against the seat and began to bleed. A fine dust filled my nostrils. Because my nose had clogged with blood, I was forced to breathe through my mouth. I coughed from time to time. He drove on, using both hands, never speaking or showing me any concern.

We arrived at a site consisting of a dozen tents, one the size of a circus tent. He reached across to open my door, and motioned for me to get out. When he saw I couldn't, he came around and jerked the door open. My hair was rolled up in the window, so I hung between the door and the seat until he rolled the window down. I fell to the ground and lay still. I heard a popping sound and the whine of a gasoline generator. Several floodlights snapped on at once. I looked away from the blinding glare. Overhead a drooping sign hung suspended by a lanyard. Two shadowy figures approached out of the brilliant lights and took positions on either side of me.

I looked up at the driver. "Where am I?"

He didn't answer. The three of them hefted me to my feet.

"Why hasn't someone taken the sign down?" the driver asked.

"Where are you taking me?" I asked.

He scratched at his beard. "To salvation, son."

Blood rushed from my head, my knees buckled, and the men and the tents evaporated.

I lay naked, tied to a cot, only a white cotton sheet covering me, and unable to distinguish between delirium and reality. I felt as if I were being pulled apart at the joints. I remembered trying to move and being restrained, a voice telling me, "Don't struggle." I heard myself in a dream saying, "Give me a fix!" I begged for someone to kill me. At one point a hand clamped down on my mouth so forcefully I thought my jaw might break. Then the temperature dropped, and I was freezing. I seemed to shrink inside myself until I became a dot.

In the fog of my withdrawal my senses would temporarily connect me with my other circumstances—the fact that I was a prisoner, that I was helpless, that people were nearby. He would be there, sometimes beside me, sometimes holding me, wiping sweat off my forehead, sometimes attempting to feed me, his words low and soothing—*here, take some; you'll be fine; rest now*. But it could have just as easily been a dream, a whimsical counterpoint to the black nightmares.

In my dreams nitrates and phosphorus permeated the air. I heard the rattle of helicopter blades, saw tall grass flattened below the struts. A voice shouted, "Go." I fought my restraints to follow but could not free myself. The men around me scurried out. A featureless woman told me, "No," and as I was about to enter her, her pale face cracked apart like the shell of a hard-boiled egg. At times I was aware of my own screams and would tell myself to stop. Had my hands been free, I might have smothered myself. More than once I imagined I was buried in ice.

The day I regained my senses, he was there, sitting on the edge of the cot, occupied with a rug he was hooking. Attired in black from head to toe, he smiled, his teeth glistening white against his dark beard. He held the rug up for inspection and said, "It relaxes the mind. You should try it."

He set the rug aside and took a small leather-bound Bible from his coat pocket. Clutching it to his chest, he began to pray. I was too weak to speak, much less protest. He kissed the book and placed it on my chest.

That night my shakes returned. I screamed and kicked, but this time I was cognizant of everything I did and all that happened around me. The next time he came in, two men accompanied him. They carried me to a trailer. I spent the next long hours strapped naked and helpless to a bunk inside the trailer, as it was ferried to some destination unknown to me. When we arrived the next day, the door of the trailer flew open and he entered.

"Are you hungry, Pate?" he asked.

I carried no identification, ever. But somehow he knew my name.

"You got the wrong guy," I said.

He shook his head patiently. "You'll do until I get the right one."

I ached. A fix would do me fine. I jerked at the restraints. "Look, I'm feeling a lot better now. How about you untie me and I'll leave? I appreciate what you've done. I could send you—"

"I'll have them move you as soon as the tents are up."

Move me? Who was he? Where was I? More important, what was he up to, and what was his interest in me? Had I survived the lunacy of war just to fall into the hands of a band of tent-dwelling lunatics? Then too, the world seemed composed of lunacy and lunatics. No matter; I wasn't about to remain his prisoner, or whatever my status was. I began to recollect the near past, remembered the burglar alarm, tumbling onto the asphalt, and the strange ride. The gun—I remembered him with a gun.

"You can't keep me here."

"You'll be needing soup." He backed out the door and slammed it behind him.

The same silent men moved me to a tent that night, where I was again tied to a cot. A generator whirred nearby, and a bare bulb swung back and forth above the entrance to the tent, the walls of which were raised. A breeze cooled the evening. I wanted to step into fresh air, see the sunset and feel the wind blow over me. For the first time in months I thought about my parents, what they must have suffered wondering where I was and why I had disappeared mysteriously after being discharged. It was the first time since we'd been overrun at Hamburger Hill that I felt homesick.

A woman fed me that night. Stout though not fat, she was in her late thirties and smelled of laundry detergent and lilac. She said her name was Anna. I asked her last name. "M" was all she offered. There was a busyness in her expression as she cooled the sausage soup with her lips and spooned it into my mouth. She spoke in motherly fashion about how everyone in camp was concerned about my progress, assuring me that many said prayers on my behalf.

"I don't want prayers," I said.

"Don't be foolish," she said. "Prayer works miracles."

"Untie me," I insisted.

"You're not ready, and he wouldn't have it. If you'd only seen yourself!"

"Who?"

She shook her head. "Eat. I have to go."

"Don't you understand?"

She kept at her task till the bowl was empty. When she left, I tried to slip my restraints but had no success. Outside, a crowd milled about. I heard organ music, singing, then later, shouts and screams of joy. I listened, trying to take cues from the noise. The hubbub came to a head several hours after dark. Finally the commotion subsided, and exhausted from it, I slept.

When I awoke the next morning, my wrists had been untied, and the sheet pulled down. I felt something cold and heavy on my chest. I started to rise.

"I wouldn't." He was standing at the foot of the cot, his eyes wide open and filled with humor. "His name's Peter. He's lazy. But if you startle him, he'll bite."

I tilted my head enough to see the wide diamond-shaped head and plated snout of a snake resting on my chest four inches from my chin. Its red eyes gazed at me with indifference. The rest of its length was stretched out between my legs. I was fortunately too weak to make any quick moves. "Oh, God," I muttered and closed my eyes, not daring to breathe.

"I'm the Reverend Marion Arthur Armstrong Bristol."

He rested his weight on the hickory branch he used for a cane. He smiled. "They sense emotion. One long sensory beast, he sees, smells, feels the most minute vibrations, hears the sound of a mouse's footsteps and has membranes that detect heat."

The snake undulated, and I gasped. The next instant the weight of it was gone from me. I opened my eyes. Bristol held it at arm's length, gently gripping its neck at the base of its triangular head. It dangled, its lateral muscles flexing in a frenzied dance. Its tail reached the ground.

"You're a crazy man!" I said.

He kept smiling calmly. "I had to know. Now I do." He turned to leave.

I sat up and untied the rope from my ankles. I stood to follow him, but my knees buckled and the tent swirled. I sat back down until my wits returned.

"Do that again, I'll kill you," I said.

He looked over his shoulder at me. "You're a guest, Pate. Don't be unkind."

One hand carrying the snake, the other clutching his cane, he spread the canvas flap open with a shoulder and stepped outside. He spoke in a hushed voice to someone. I heard my name mentioned, and wondered again how he knew it.

I didn't see Bristol for two days. After the cramps ceased and the shakes ebbed, the same men who'd carried me first to the trailer and then to the tent, walked me to a latrine, then to a tent where a tub filled with hot water awaited me. Other than soup, the bath was the first pleasure I'd enjoyed in days. My joints felt better. I craved a fix, but the withdrawal symptoms had passed, and I no longer ached for one. When I climbed out of the tub, I turned to the larger of the two men, a redhead with a salt-and-pepper beard, and said, "It's against the law, what you're doing."

"You're alive. Best leave it at that."

His shirtsleeves were rolled up to the elbows, exposing his forearms, tanned and sinuous. On one was a tattoo of a parachute and the word AIR-

BORNE. Being a veteran of the 101st in 'Nam, I figured I might make some headway with him—the brotherhood and all.

I pointed to the tattoo. "What unit?"

"Don't ask questions," he said. "No one here has a past."

They walked me to the tent, where the other, a stout Polynesian, spread the canvas entry. The two of them shoved me inside and tied me up. I didn't bother asking why.

For three nights the crowds came, and the human din continued past dark. Drained as I was, I slept through most of it. On the third day the crowd noises lasted deep into the night. This time I could not sleep. After the crowds departed, some men began pounding. One shouted about the apron. Then the night was quiet. I fell asleep listening to the whir of the generator.

III

The camp pulled up stakes and caravanned down a back stretch of highway. Again I lay bound to a cot, listening to the stirrings of life outside the tent, or at night to the flapping tent walls and the distant howls of coyotes. I stared at the canvas top and cataloged ifs . . . If Barger had not been blown in two by an RPG, if I had made this choice or not that one, if I had stayed away from the bar where everyone went to score. Asian white, we called it. *Schuss*, ah. Up the nose, and the war went away. Ifs. I thought about the reason I had been running down a darkened alley in Albuquerque.

At Oakland Army Terminal they checked us for AK-47s and grenades and gonorrhea, stuck fingers up our butts, dry sticks down our throats. I had trembled and sweated during my discharge physical. The examining physician asked questions off a chart, checked the appropriate boxes, and conveniently overlooked the constant flow of mucus from my nose. Army doctors were trained that way. Kick them loose. They're someone else's problem now. Two blocks from the main gate, I scored a balloon of Mexican brown. It did not bring the same bang as Vietnamese dope. When snorting failed to get me off, I started mainlining, soon had a hundred-a-day habit.

I recalled clearly the evening Barger had whipped three Marines for selling me smack. He had lifted me on his shoulders and carried me back to camp, sweat pouring from his forehead, mosquitoes buzzing. He had set me down. Then I had crawled on my knees through my own puke, him telling me what a fool I was. My sins went on.

I had missed my sister's wedding, a ceremony delayed for months so that I would be able to attend. How were they, my family, safely tucked away on eighteen acres of asparagus rows and peach orchards in Sunnyside? I pictured Dad grafting saplings, as intent on his experiments as any scientist in a lab; thought of him with Mom at the Yakima State Fair, arm in arm, standing over a hog display, arguing details of some obscure event in family history, Dad holding a cupped hand to his nearly deaf ear and saying, "I can't hear you." Though I was concerned as to what end I was being held prisoner, foremost in my mind was the past. I decided that those who loved me deserved someone better.

Bristol entered. He stopped a step from the cot and rested his weight on his long cane. He seemed in pain as he studied me. Finally, he untied me. I covered myself with the sheet as I sat up.

"A little late for dignity." He took a seat next to me.

"Can I go now?" I tried to stand, but was forced to sit back down.

"You have a purpose here."

"But I feel fine."

"Good, good. That's how the Lord wants it."

I shook my head. "That's how I want it."

He stood and stepped over to a wooden footlocker and raised the lid. He took out a shirt, undershorts, trousers, and a pair of socks, which he placed on the cot next to me.

"Took us a while to find enough for a week's change of clothes. We launder once a week. Cleanliness is important. Use the latrine, have your clothes ready on time for laundry day."

I stared up at him. "You must be crazy."

"All things under the sun. Your days are starting. Get dressed."

My legs wobbled, but I managed to stand. I turned my back to him and slipped into the trousers, then the shirt. The clothes fit loosely. I rolled up the sleeves.

Bristol was staring at me when I turned around. "Are you afraid of snakes?"

"When it's on my chest."

"Under other circumstances."

"Tell you the truth, I never thought about it."

"Think about it."

"I'll tell you what I think. This shit is too weird, and I'm about to put it behind me."

He pulled a familiar piece of paper out of his pocket. I looked down at my ankles and realized that my bail receipt had been in my old socks.

He waved the paper with all my vital information on it. "One count of burglary."

"Why didn't you turn me in?"

He folded the paper and stuffed it in his pocket. "They're interested in your corporeal body, Pate. I'm interested in you."

"Me? Go find another boy. I don't go for any funny shit."

He turned, his thick frame resting on his good leg, and motioned for me to follow. He bobbed up and down like a hydraulic device, his lame leg swinging rapidly to meet the ground as his good leg propelled him forward. I stepped outside into what seemed the most brilliant day of my life. My eyes watered. I squinted and used my hand as a visor to shield them from the sun. The camp was being dismantled, all the tents already broken down except for a white pavilion with a red cross painted atop it and a tent beside it. People bustled about carrying bundles of this and boxes of that. They paused and looked up long enough to smile at Bristol and get a close look at me, then lowered their heads and continued their activity.

Bristol led me to the tent and tossed back the flap. A noxious odor rushed out. I hesitated. He grabbed my sleeve and yanked me inside. His strength surprised me. The tent was unlit. A moment passed before my eyes adjusted to the interior. When I could again see, he guided me to the edge of a pit, its nylon walls, waist high, supported by a frame made of angle iron.

A tangle of serpents slithered over one another. The stench was horrible. My forehead beaded with sweat. I backpedaled from the sight, fought a sudden urge to vomit. He pushed me back to the pit, said I needed to get used to them. I shrugged him off and reluctantly inched forward. I held my breath and looked.

"You'll have to clean cages." He stepped up beside me. "They've been neglected."

I looked at him, then at the boxes stacked like apple crates.

"While they're out," he said, intent upon the snakes, "of their cages."

"Listen, pal, if it's all the same, I don't plan on hanging around to clean cages."

"Bristol. I'm Bristol, and it's not all the same to me. You take them out of the cages and place them in the pit—one at a time."

"Pick them up?"

He looked me in the eyes. "They'll get used to your touch."

I shook my head. "Are you not hearing? I'm a fart in the wind, see?"

"It'll take a while to learn how to extract venom and distill it."

"Venom yourself. Look, I'm a veteran of a goddamn war. This is kid stuff."

He smiled condescendingly. "I've taken most of them out. Clean those cages first. There's a noose you can use for now. When you get confident, you can use the hook. Act naturally, no sudden moves. Let them get used to you. Later your hands. We'll work on handling them later."

"Hey, Jack, don't you get the message? I'm saying no."

"You're doing the Lord's work, Pate. Think about that."

I aimed a finger at him. "I don't want to think about it."

"The thing I like most about you is that you have no choice. Me, or the nearest sheriff. We've gone to a lot of trouble for you."

"I didn't ask." I sensed that if I demonstrated fear, my problems would multiply.

He was looking at the snakes and spoke almost absentmindedly. "Some sheriff might be happy to take your complaint. Now, matters need my attention, and I imagine you wish to eat. Around here we earn our bread."

I studied his face. "Where are my rings?"

"Rings?"

"Yeah, I had them in my pocket and twenty-six dollars when you kidnapped me."

"And now you don't." He slapped his hands on the edge of the pit wall, just hard enough to punctuate his irritation, then turned, limped out through the flap.

I waited several minutes and stepped outside. The men who had tied me down sat on the fender of a truck opposite the tent. They glanced in my direction. I went back inside. I'd forgotten what it meant to have an appetite for anything other than heroin. I was hungry, could escape later— at least that was how I figured it. A clean cage or two might just pacify my host. I didn't know what constituted cleaning a cage. Nonetheless, I went to one that appeared empty and opened the door. Before I realized it, the sand stirred, a snake emerged and, jaws agape, thrust itself at me. I slammed the door on its head.

"Judas, a red Mojave. Treacherous. Mojaves, particularly the greens, are territorial rattlers. They'll actually crawl out to challenge an intruder. It's best to start with a more passive snake, like Peter."

The snake's unfortunate head was trapped in the frame. I held the door secure and looked over my shoulder. Bristol smirked. He wore a hat now, black with a wide brim, and was squeezing the bridge of his nose as if he had a headache.

"Judas hides at the worst times and invariably tries to bite."

That was how I thought he talked at first, educated, precise. I found it peculiar that he should be in this line of work, which I surmised had to do with snakes and salvation.

"He must coil to strike." He approached the cage, placed his hand on the door, and eased it open. The snake retreated inside, and Bristol shut the door. "All of them do except sidewinders. Be extra careful of sidewinders."

"Do you have any?"

He shook his head. "Too much bother."

He pointed to an empty cage and led me through the process of cleaning, which amounted to throwing away the old sand and replacing it with new. Afterward he told me to follow and led me to a table with folding legs that was set up in the shade of a cottonwood. He introduced me around as the new snake boy. I recognized only Anna M., the woman who had fed me soup. She sat next to a stout black woman, who went by Simone. Before I could back away, Anna stood and engulfed me in her arms. She said everyone's prayers had been answered. All but mine, I thought.

Bristol chatted with one person or another, talking in a homey drawl, an octave lower than earlier. The people seemed to adore him, referring to him as "Brother Bristol" and listening intently as he syruped out homey praises in appreciation of some favor or undertaking. A lot of "Praise the Lords" threaded the conversations together. We ate black-eyed peas and corn bread, I and a bunch of angel-whacked believers whose dull smiles bore an uncanny resemblance to those on rubber baby dolls. I watched, listened, and thought, Jesus freaks and rattlers. From my observation, I concluded one thing: I had to heel-toe it out of there, and soon.

After the meal Bristol took a snake from its cage and with his cane pinned it to the floor of the pit. He bent down, grabbed it behind its neck and swooped it up. He held it close to my face and pressed down on its neck with a thumb. The jaw opened, exposing the needlelike fangs. He smiled and tossed the snake at my feet. It hit the ground with a rude thud and rolled, twisting as it reoriented itself. It coiled and hissed. I froze.

Bristol moved to my right and, using the staff, pushed the snake sideways. He handed me the cane and bent forward, circling his hand in the air. The snake lunged. It was a blur of brown and orange scales. Bristol jerked his hand back, and when the snake was extended and about to recoil, he snatched it with the ease of an infielder scooping up a grounder.

"If you're too afraid, you'll make mistakes. If you're not sufficiently scared, you'll make mistakes." The snake dangled before my eyes. He measured my reaction, looking for fear, then offered a self-amused smile. "This is what you do to render them harmless. Pay attention."

He carted the snake to a work counter and from a drawer retrieved a glass with a thin rubber diaphragm stretched over the rim. He set it on the countertop, waved his free hand in front of the snake, then forced its head to the diaphragm until the serpent bit. An oily amber liquid drained into the glass, rapidly at first, then in glistening drips.

"Don't worry if a fang breaks off. They grow new ones. This one I'll need tonight. Do you know how to use a needle on someone else?"

I'd watched junkies fix each other but had not shot up anyone but myself. "No."

"You'll learn. Better start thinking about yourself. Small doses of venom over time will give you immunity to the effects of bites. They still hurt, of course. You may get sick, but nothing serious."

He lifted the hinged top on a two-foot-wide black box and dumped the snake in. Smiling, he closed the lid. "Carry it to the stage tonight, drop the snake, and back away."

He limped back to the counter and picked up the glass containing the venom. He told me the trunk with my belongings and the cot I slept on would be moved to the snake tent, that this was where I would sleep from now on. I asked where and when I would be bringing the snake. He didn't answer, just limped toward the entrance.

"Where'd you get the limp?"

He looked over his shoulder. "I don't limp." He twirled the staff and stabbed the narrow end into the ground. "We'll be leaving in the morning. After the service, you'll need to load the cages in the bed of the red Ford. Be ready to ride."

The same two men showed up with a cot but no bedding. They introduced themselves, Henry and Gabe, propped the cot next to the entrance, left, and soon returned with a trunk. Henry said my changes of clothing were in it. They left me staring at the cages. I considered making a run for it, but didn't know where I was. Besides which I was too weak to get very far. My situation consisted of no place to run to or any means to get me there, so figuring to bide my time for the present, I walked to the closest cage to clean it. To be safe, I shook it before opening the door.

The simple task of changing sand in the cages left me exhausted. I quit at a half dozen and sat until it was time for dinner. At the fade of day, the generator came on and lit the camp. Cars and trucks began to arrive. I listened to the grumble of the horde that milled outside. Soon after cars stopped coming, organ music flowed out of the main tent and across the campsite. The organ went silent, and Simone sang "There Is a Balm in Gilead" as Bristol in a booming voice urged the crowd to join in.

Around nine o'clock Henry and Gabe stepped inside and motioned for me to follow. I gathered up the box that Bristol had instructed me to bring and marched between them to a set of crude steps at the side of the stage, a platform assembled of plywood sections bolted to two-by-four trusses.

Bristol, dressed in black from the neck down, paced back and forth as a brilliant light created by overlapping spotlights followed him across the stage. In his hand a microphone glowed as if it were a torch. He picked up the pace with each pass until he bounded across the stage like a lopsided ball. On the far side of the stage, Anna M. reeled the speaker wire in and out. Finally he slowed and approached the steps that led to the audience. He spread his arms, rendered a string of praise the Lords, and bowed his head. A flood of blue and green lit the apron of the stage.

The spotlights went off. "Jesus," he shouted, "went'a into the wilde'-ness." He elongated each vowel until it sounded like two or three. He even added a vowel here and there where none existed and softened consonants, even dropped a few.

"He'a went to face down temp-a-ta-shun, met the, ah, Devil, who poein-ted to all the riches of the Earth. These the, ah, Dea-mon off'ed to the Lah'd Jesus, sweet Lah'd Jesus. The consternation on the Lah'd's face, oh, he'p that may I not see it." His voice trailed off. "It's the beginning of sufferin'."

When the lights came on he stood at midstage. He angled an ear to the crowd and cupped a hand over it. "Jesus listened and was temp-a-ted. The Son of God was flesh. The Son of Man born of womb listened and was temp-a-ted. But he, ah, resisted! Resisted all!"

He raised a finger as if to speak but said nothing, just thumped back and forth across the stage, and at each pass quickened his pace. Anna M.'s face was red from the exertion of letting out and reeling in the cord. He shouted to the crowd, asked if they were ready. Then he stood, his toes over the front edge of the stage, and said softly, "Let us pray in silence."

Again the lights went out. It was warm, the middle of the spring. The heat was palpable. I sweated, as did the crowd, but for a different reason. The snake stirred in the box. Silence settled over the audience as if the entire body had been struck dumb. Then a few murmurs rose from the crowd. I heard weeping. A single light flashed on and beamed down on Bristol's mop of a head. He kneeled, eyes closed, hands across his chest. He held the pose as, one at a time, a string of red lights flared below the stage.

He rose to his feet as if lifted by an invisible hand, an impressive feat for a large man with a lame leg. Extending an arm overhead, he shouted about the fury and wrath of God and the treachery of Satan. The spotlight died. The crawl space below the stage glowed red. Simone sang "The Old Rugged Cross" as Bristol turned and signaled me forward. A hand nudged me, but I could not move.

His forehead furrowed as if in pain and his thick body trembled. "Satan," he said into the microphone, "came in the guise of a serpent to, ah, tempt man. Robbed us of, ah, paradise and opened the door'ah to Hell. But He faced down temp-a-ta-shun, defeated the Devil! Defeated sin."

He limped toward me and motioned discreetly with one hand. "Bah-ring fora'th the serpent. Bah-ring the Dea-mon fora'th that I may by the pow-ah of Jesus defeat him!"

Henry shoved me, this time hard. I stumbled on the first step, caught my balance and ascended. I lowered the box, fumbled with the latch for an instant before opening the lid. Bristol glared and aimed his finger as if it were a weapon.

"Behold the spoiler, Satan, the low one. Come to earth to ruin mankind!" He bent down, picked up his staff, and twirled it. "Devil, I shall, ah, beat thee tonight, beat thee in the name of the Lah'd, in the name of sweet Jees-uss!"

I left the box on its side and backed away. I missed the steps and ended up at the edge of the platform. Henry pulled me off. On the way down I banged my head on the edge of the stage and blacked out. When I opened my eyes, a woman named Esperanza was bent over me, holding a bottle and sprinkling water on my cheeks. In the background Bristol screamed at the snake.

The woman helped me to my feet and whispered that I was supposed to dump the snake on the stage, that sometimes they were shy and wouldn't come out. She said that I had to wait until Bristol returned the snake to the box, then go fetch the box as inconspicuously as possible. I positioned myself out of sight at the base of the steps.

The crowd gasped when the snake's head emerged. It tasted the air with its tongue, then gradually it slithered out, effortlessly. It coiled its way toward the front of the stage, where Bristol cut off its path. It gathered itself into a whorl and rattled. Bristol pointed with his staff and nudged it. The snake struck at the stick, then tried to escape.

Bristol moved swiftly for a man with one bad leg, fronting the snake, keeping its attention on him. He turned his back, inviting the reptile to strike. The snake attempted a second rush for freedom toward the steps at the front of the stage. Bristol barehanded it and held it overhead. He pirouetted across the stage once and then wrapped it around his neck. Except for Bristol's heels pounding the plywood, silence ruled the tent. He stopped and spread his arms wide as the three lights flooded the stage in a blinding glow that distorted all sense of reality.

When Bristol placed the snake back in the black box, Henry gave me another shove and told me to go retrieve it. I rushed onstage, gathered up the box, and retreated without pause.

After the baptizing, after the collections, Bristol showed up at the tent, where I lay on the cot devising a plan of escape.

He rested his weight against the wall of the snake pit. "What do you think, Pate?"

"I think you're liable to break that wall."

He shook his head. "You'll understand in time. Some take longer than others."

"How do you expect me to sleep in here? The smell."

"Smell?"

"Yeah, damn things stink."

"You have to pack it to go, all of it." He stared at me.

I matched his stare.

He snorted and said, "Tourists pay to see Indians dance with rattlesnakes in their mouths. It's impressive. I've seen it. I can't turn water into wine or feed the multitudes off a loaf of bread. That's why I need you. That's why you're here."

No sooner did Bristol leave than Henry and Gabe entered the tent. Gabe said I would have to be less clumsy, that my job was simple. They closed on me from two sides. Henry struck first, a blow to the abdomen. I bent over and stiffened. Gabe told me to relax, said that they wouldn't break any bones and that it was okay for me to puke. I did.

We drove for a day to the next campsite, in a dry wash off a highway. Bristol left in his Buick to, in his words, "prepare the way." When I asked if that wasn't John the Baptist's job, he grinned and told me my humor was wearing thin. The camp population rested for seven days, awaiting his return. Wherever I turned, Gabe or Henry or both were nearby. I spent most of my time in the tent with the snakes, who, all things considered, were better company.

During that stay, I made an ally in Esperanza, the camp cook, who was seventy. Although toothless and bent with arthritis, she had eyes that glowed with the sheen of youth, and her mind belonged to her. She was warm and effusive, and her *rellenos*, stuffed with two types of goat cheese, made my captivity nearly worth it.

On idle days I sat outside the kitchen tent and listened as she prepared meals. She was equally patient whether cooking or telling stories. Her stories came from faraway days, and her English was accented, but she never had to search for a memory or for words. She'd been reared in south El Paso, in El Segundo Barrio, and was a girl at the time Pancho Villa invaded the United States. The one sad story she told was about the El Paso riot.

She was seven when men on horseback rode down on her uncles and killed them. A wall collapsed in the corner of her room and set off a chain reaction and her family's house caved in, roof and walls crumbling around her. When the last adobe brick settled, she sat untouched by the devastation. She talked and at the same time mixed flour tortillas, flattening them in the palms of her hands, then rolling them before she laid them on the grill. She looked to see if I was listening. But I was seeing something similar—in 'Nam, a village, mud houses crumbling, women huddled together, children in their arms, old men and women spitting betel nut juice.

"Mamacita was a small woman, until her eighth child, my sister Luisa—small, but determined. Mama cleaned house for a rich woman on Magoffin Street. My cousin carried me there after the house collapsed. The family let us sleep in a carriage, under blankets, outside because it was too hot to sleep in the stable. At night in the dark Papa rebuilt the house with adobe bricks. He could not see so well, so the walls leaned with love.

"You want?" She wrapped a hot tortilla in a napkin and handed it to me, then took one for herself. She ground the food in her toothless mouth, winking and nodding at me, me nodding and winking back in approval.

There was little to do but care for snakes, think of escape, and talk with her. I asked why was she with Bristol?

"I am an old woman. They called me Tia, Aunt. I had no children. I married young, he died young. Then one day I was an old aunt. I moved to Clovis to live with my sister Luisa, the one who made my mother fat. I didn't like it, taking in laundry. Bristol came two years ago." As child she'd seen a circus and had since fantasized a life like that, riding from town to town. She explained how her sister went to the revival because of the snakes, but she did not go herself until the third day. Bristol's caravan seemed the closest she would ever come to realizing her fantasy.

"I took food to him like we did for the priest. Bristol said come with me, cook for us. I'm Catholic I tell to him. He smiles, says he's a Buddhist. I laugh and tell him no. But that night I tell my sister I am going. She looks at me like I am crazy, but I pack my things. No one ever offered me a job. And he promised me these." She took a pair of false teeth from her pocket and displayed them proudly in her palm.

"Why don't you eat with them?"

She placed them in her mouth. "I only need them to smile with." She handed me a tamale. "You will never taste a tamale like mine."

"No?"

"No." She forked out a tamale for herself.

"Are you happy here?" I asked.

"I am an old woman."

I asked what ingredients she used to make her meals so special.

She turned her back to me and spread oil and chopped garlic on the grill, her thick arms shaking salt and spice in as she stirred the mix. "Ask about the men I have loved. I may tell. But the food is my business."

When Bristol's Buick arrived, his followers displayed the energy of an army on the offense as they dismantled tents and loaded equipment. No one complained, no one doubted. I transferred the snakes from the pit to the cages. Henry and Gabe carried the snakes to the back of the red pickup. Then Henry got behind the wheel as Gabe pushed me inside the cab, where I sat sandwiched between them.

"Just the way I like to travel," I said.

We drove in the predawn dark. I sat between Henry and Gabe in the cab. Neither spoke the whole distance. Near dusk we pitched camp somewhere outside Las Vegas, New Mexico. My tent was raised first. I ate and then lay on the cot smelling the visceral odors. I imagined snakes crawling over one another, imagined I could hear them talking, telling me to escape for them. I walked to the pit and said I would escape for my sake, not theirs.

When not dogging me, Henry was in charge of the roustabouts who set up and dismantled camp and served as Bristol's police. I figured either he or Gabe would be assigned to cover the front of my tent, leaving the possibility of escape from the back side. I decided to test my theory after the generator fell silent and the camp went dark. I lay an added hour before I sat up. I listened for another hour or so until I was certain the camp had settled in for the night. I heard nothing unusual, just the howl of a coyote or two in the distance, the occasional stirring of the snakes. Satisfied that the camp slept, I went to the back of the tent near the cages, lay on the ground, and cautiously raised the canvas skirt. A few snakes buzzed. I paused until their noise stopped and then eased out slowly. When I had squirmed myself halfway out, I looked around.

"Bit early for a walk." Bristol sat on a milking stool at the outside corner of the tent, the revolver on his lap. Henry stood beside him.

I nodded and squirmed back inside, then curled up on the cot.

Gabe and Henry did not pay a visit until just before dinner the next evening. They went easy because Bristol was preaching that night and I was essential.

Having no resources at my disposal, I had to improvise if I expected to escape. Two days after the first attempt I tried leaving in the truck that ferried in supplies. I was hidden under a blanket in the bed when Henry dropped an intake manifold on my hip.

"Shit, damn. Watch what you're doing," I said and climbed over the side of the truck. I limped back to the snake tent. Bristol watched from the steps of his trailer.

That night they introduced me to the effect of a car battery and copper wires wrapped around my ankles.

A week later, in a new camp, I crawled out from under the latrine tent and walked north, which seemed as good a direction as any. I covered about two miles before they overtook me. I was hiding in a wash when Bristol and Henry walked up on me.

"What are you doing, Pate?" Bristol said.

I looked at the purple bluffs to the north and the faded gray peaks to the far west. "Just checking out the wilderness for temptation, Bristol. I understand it's out here somewhere."

Henry slammed a fist into the fold below my ribs and pointed me in the direction of camp.

Bristol limped alongside. "You're a snake boy, Pate, and don't belong wandering in the wilderness. I'm losing patience."

I stopped. "Then why not give back what you stole from me and I'll cruise on?"

This time a blow landed to my kidneys. On my way to the ground, a foot to my butt sent me facedown on the hardpan. Bristol planted his staff on the back of my neck.

"What we have, Pate, is for all. To share is the Lord's way."

We played escape off and on for two months, until I quit because running became just a game. I couldn't win anyhow because freedom didn't exist, not so long as I was penniless. Then when I was ready to surrender to despair, an idea took seed. Bristol brought in plenty of money and seemed to spend little, and I was a thief, although a lame one. I could make a score, flee to Mexico, and go straight, whatever straight was. Be patient, I told myself, and find out where the money is stashed. I never mentioned that I wasn't playing the running game anymore. I just stopped. He seemed to sense it. Outwardly, I accepted my role. I became Snake Boy, and Bristol stopped waiting beside the tent.

IV

Once I put myself to the task, I learned much about the snakes. Peter was docile, not all territorial. Still, I could not shake the memory of him stretched out placidly on my chest, his snout aimed at my chin. Judas was a grenade with the pin pulled. John actually liked to be handled and would crawl toward an outstretched hand as if he were a dog. Nonetheless, I did not relish sharing a tent with snakes, not even one that had the temperament of a cocker spaniel.

Gradually my strength returned, and I began to master my duties, which were not too difficult but demanded absolute attention. During that same time I came to get a sense of camp life among these Jesus Gypsies, who called themselves the Disciples or the Following. On the surface nothing was ever amiss—no jealousies, no intrigues. Their tongues were lubricated with the oil of the blessed, and their eyes filled with a doglike desire to please. Except for run-ins with Henry or Gabe when I attempted escape, nobody harmed me in any way. In fact, they were, in general, a friendly bunch, eager to perform some small kindness or another for me, while never passing up an opportunity to praise this act of God or that of Bristol's, which often overlapped in their minds. I, on the other hand, was not so kind.

"Good morning, Pate," one might say, the greeting including a smile.

To provoke a response, I might say, "Eat shit" or "Did you get fucked last night? Is that why you're smiling?"

My victim would invariably respond with a shake of the head or say, "Now that's not nice."

I was Pate, the snake boy, while they, nineteen in all, were Brother or Sister somebody. Soon enough the paradox of my situation became apparent. They regarded me as they did not out of saintliness but because I spared them the horror of having to handle snakes, and everyone in camp knew the snakes were indispensable to Bristol, and thus to those dependent on him. I claimed this as my power.

I used my station as the snake boy to torment Brother Clyde Flowers, a simple, red-cheeked blond who was the largest of the roustabouts and the friendliest. Early on I discovered he was terrified of snakes and found one excuse or another to lure him into the tent—something too heavy for me to carry, a pole that was unstable. Others went along with the gag.

"Over there," I would say, pointing to a box I'd planted in the midst of the snake cages.

He would press his hands together, beads forming on his balding head. "Can't do it by yourself, Pate?"

"No way, Clyde. Might put my back out."

"Couldn't find nobody else?"

"Looked all over."

Once I resorted to actually hiding a snake in a box I asked him to move. Bristol's orders were clear on the subject of doing what the snake boy wanted. Clyde picked up the box and the rattle went off. His knees buckled, and each painful step he took seemed one toward his own grave. When he set the box where I instructed, he turned and faced me. He stood for a seemingly endless time, his normally red cheeks paper white, staring as his ball-bearing eyes moistened. I saw that he'd peed on himself. Slowly the words crawled up his throat and out his mouth. "Pate, I'd like it if you didn't do this to me anymore."

I stopped tormenting him, but life in camp got duller.

Of the seven women in camp, five were married and two single, one of whom was Sister Anna M., the woman who'd fed me soup during my withdrawal. She slept with Bristol, which the Following pretended was not the case. When she went to Bristol's trailer, the Following averted their eyes and looked for some small busyness to occupy themselves with.

Part of the problem with being straight again was that memories began to haunt me, along with a powerful sense of guilt. I was like the snakes, which spent their days futilely slithering toward an impossible exit. I was in bondage, which was an extension of earlier imprisonments. The military. Heroin. Bristol's camp. Memories. I had exchanged the prison of heroin for a site where everyone thought freedom was spiritual, where praise for the divine assured a life beyond and a joy denied them in this one. I saw their version of hope as another prison, salvation as a myth. I thought of buddies who had taken the worst of it at Hamburger Hill and Hue, of the Vietnamese slaughtered by the thousands and heaved into the Perfume River by Vietcong during the Tet offensive. I saw in my dreams the five bodies we pulled out of an eddy where they might have swirled endlessly, one a pregnant woman no more than twenty. Had they found peace in nothingness?

I missed home. I wanted to contact my parents and explain why I did not come home after my discharge, tell them about the drugs and that I was okay now, but had to find my own way. I wanted to shake Dad's hand and put my arms around my mother. Out of desperation I wrote a letter, addressed it to Mother, and gave it to Ham Hardy to mail. He promised to keep the secret, but something in his eyes told me that I'd made a mistake. I hid behind a pickup and saw him hand the letter to Bristol, who came straight to the snake tent, where he shredded the letter and left the pieces on my cot. Again Henry or Gabe posted himself outside my tent at night.

Besides Henry and Gabe, who never talked, Esperanza and Bristol were the only two in camp who did not attempt to save my soul. I suspected Esperanza was at heart a nonbeliever who was merely learning a new story. The others took time to tell me how well I was doing, how good I looked, and how it must be the Lord's doing. They were quick to mention Bristol's hand in my good health. He had helped many. He could help me. They all told stories of how he had helped them.

Anna M. told me, in confidence, punctuated by whispers and an occasional squeeze on my arm, that Bristol had found her in a "house" outside Tonopah, Nevada. "I was whorin' and plain lost. I went there to make fun of him with a bunch from the house. Before the day was over, he had bathed away my sins." I didn't bring up any of her current sins. She squeezed my arm a little tighter and leaned close. Her breath aroused me. Lately I'd been thinking about sex, a sure sign the worst of the addiction was behind.

Her skin had the appearance of bleached leather. Her eyes, a flat brown, looked patiently at my face, then gazed at my crotch, which evidenced a nascent erection. "You'll find out someday, Pate. Your soul will be reborn."

I looked at her hand on my arm, her fingertips crooked as she kneaded my muscle. I wondered if she knew where Bristol kept the money. I gazed openly at her breasts. "What else comes with being saved?"

She pulled her hand away. "Eternity."

"Eternity comes anyhow." I stood so that she could clearly see the bulge in my pants.

The snakes had ways of ruining my rest. Some were nocturnal and hissed and rattled in the dark, interrupting my sleep. I often awoke panicked, as though I were still in 'Nam being hit with a barrage incoming. Once the situation seemed so real that I cupped my groin and rolled off the cot. I found myself face-to-face with John the Happy Rattler, as I called him. After having somehow managed to escape his cage, he lay submissively as if waiting to be petted. "Thank God you're not Judas," I said and carried him to his cage. After that I double-checked the cages before I retired.

As the days got hotter and the snakes became more active, I dragged the cot outside and slept in the open air. Once on an unusually cool summer morning Esperanza awakened me and said that I could sleep in her tent. Her expression hinted of a sin I wasn't prepared to commit.

Nobody in camp wanted my job. That made me inexpendable and brought me privileges. I washed no clothes, cleaned no portable toilets, and although constantly encouraged to do so, I attended no prayer services. Bristol was only slightly more subtle about proselytizing than he was about kidnapping. He had his followers work on me through sundry acts of kindness. They brought me fresh fruit and gave me, among other gifts, a patched-up cotton windbreaker, a monaural phonograph, and a pair of leather work boots. Once a week one shining face or another would show up at the tent and offer to do my laundry or hand me a jar of pickles or marmalade and ask if I intended to come to the prayer service. I would accept the offering with a smile and ask, "Will Satan or God be frying up souls tonight?" or some such question.

Ham Hardy, who played the organ, worked on me harder than anyone. He was a kind man, devoid of subtlety and insight, who happened to be gifted with perfect pitch and blinded with perfect stupidity. I never let his proselytizing bother me, not like the others' anyhow, the ones who acted like they got bonus points from God if I signed up with Jesus.

Ham was sincere and open about his past.

"Bristol pulled me out of a bar," he explained. "I played the piano for tips. Mostly my tips were drinks. I didn't get this red nose from the sun." He pointed to the mark of his repentance, his bulbous nose, as if proud to have such a protuberance on his face.

"So, how much does he pay you?"

"Pay?"

"Yeah, money. You hanging around because you love him?"

"I owe my life to him. Him and the Lord. So do you."

"Listen, buddy, I know you mean well, but the truth is I owe my life to an M-16 and some pimply-faced kids."

"You'll feel better when you find the way."

"Ham, except for being imprisoned here, I feel fine."

I sat thinking I needed a fix, not for my body but for my head.

Although Bristol was absolute law, he let me get by with running off at the mouth, even in front of others. It was the one freedom I enjoyed. The first time I told him to take a leap into the snake pit, that I was only there because he had the nuts on me, he seemed amused. "You're our guest, Pate. We want to keep you happy," he said and walked over to the pit, where he stood on a chair and pretended he was going to jump in.

I sometimes forced him to repeat an order before I would do his bidding.

"Pick up something from Esperanza to feed to the rats," Bristol said.

I was holding a snake over the pit, amazed at how little it resisted. I ignored him.

"Did you hear me, Pate?"

"Excuse me?" I answered.

"Food for the rats. You've been neglecting them."

The rats were fed to the snakes. "They're going to die anyhow."

"Do as you're told."

"I'm the snake boy. That's me. Why don't you kidnap yourself a rat boy?"

His face seemed to darken. He pulled at his collar. "Take care of it."

On one occasion he told me to get Peter out of his cage and feed him and I said, "I don't get paid. You do it."

He told me again to get Peter out of the cage and put him in the pit, then bring a rat. I shook my head. His hand slipped inside the breast of his coat, where he kept the revolver.

"Pate, I should have shot you."

"That would be un-Christian," I said.

"That's a matter of perception."

Peter was a timber rattler with the heft of a tree limb, but predictable in his behavior. I lifted him gently from his cage and set him loose in the pit. The rats scurried away as I reached in to snatch one. I carried it by the tail to the pit and was about to release it when Bristol told me to bring it to him. He took it in his palm and stroked it.

"Go find Anna M. Tell her to come here."

She was playing Crazy Eights with Ham Hardy. They smiled that dullard's smile that infected the camp.

"Bristol wants you in the snake tent," I said.

She dropped her smile and obeyed as if Bristol himself had spoken.

He was still petting the rat when we entered. He glanced in our direction. "Pate, I'll feed the snake. You wait outside until I come out. Don't come in and don't let anyone else enter."

I stationed myself by the entrance and shifted my weight from foot to foot until curiosity got to me. I went to a pinhole in the tent where I shaded my eye with my hands and looked see in. Bristol sat in a chair facing the pit, his pants folded at his ankles. Anna M. kneeled between him and the pit. I could see only the back of her head on his lap. Bristol stroked her hair until suddenly he thrust his head back and released a guttural sound and then looked down at her and lifted her chin. I rushed to the front of the tent just before she stepped out.

As he left, Bristol said, "Ever spy on me again, you'll sleep in the pit with the snakes."

That afternoon Ham Hardy told me the story of an usher who had pilfered money from the collection plate. Bristol had him tied to two poles and suspended over the snake pit. "Never heard a word from that boy since," he said, shaking his head sympathetically.

My days revolved around the cycle of the snakes and the schedule of the evangelist. Witless creatures with no more concept of freedom than they had of religion, they nonetheless jabbed their heads against the cage door to escape just as if freedom were as significant to them as it was to an ACLU lawyer. Seeing the reptiles every day banging at the screens, seeking escape, worked on my mind. Judas was the most persistent. His desperation gained my sympathy, and his determination my admiration. Once I was on the verge of releasing him, but as I opened the door, he struck at me, and I slammed the cover shut and tossed his cage on the floor.

There were twelve snakes in all, and Bristol had named each one after a disciple.

"Twelve is powerful, Pate," he said once. "Twelve apostles, twelve jurors, twelve to a dozen, twelve snakes. Makes you think, doesn't it?"

"Makes me think this is all nuts."

It made me think a little more about getting out of there. But the way I saw it was that if I were to leave, I would likely end up shooting smack and running down alleys in the dark. For the present, living with snakes was not all that bad. In ways it was even better than living with people, and a far cry from crawling under mortar fire or seeing Barger take a hit from an RPG. Still, I could see the day nearing when I would be strong enough not to return to drugs, and when that time came, I would flee with Bristol's bankroll and fat-cat it south of the border.

With little to occupy me, I studied the snakes, their cycles of rest and activity, how certain vibrations or sounds startled them while others did not. They had their own peculiar personalities. Some preferred night, and some day. I milked and distilled venom on a rotating schedule after a snake was fed. I kept records of that and feedings as well. I did not watch feedings, not then, although often Bristol tried to coax me into it. I had seen enough death in 'Nam to resolve that it was not a spectator sport, even the death of a rat. Like sex, death deserved privacy.

Instinct drove a rattlesnake to kill its prey; the venom was its digestive enzyme. There was nothing sexual about a snake's eating habits, and it was certainly nothing to prompt a human to orgasm. But for Bristol, feeding was an event. When he showed up to watch and sent me for Anna M., it upset me. It seemed not just quirky but indecent, in some aspect disrespectful of nature. Once I told him that he was showing disrespect to the apostles. He laughed and told me to keep remarks like that between us.

Some days I would set up the pit outside and let them bask in sunlight. I handled some, always remembering they tolerated very little. The Jesus Gypsies would see me holding a snake and talking to it and would shake their heads and whisper. They thought of snakes as descendants of the devil and so saw me as a communicant with Satan's kin. If the brothers and sisters thought I was a bit touched, it was fine with me. As far as I knew, none of them had arrived in the dark of night with his hair wrenched in the window of a car door. The fact that each of them was here of his own volition was all the evidence I needed to know I was not the crazy one.

Esperanza was the only one besides Bristol who was unintimidated by the reptiles. More than once she came by to look the pit over. Each time she asked me to bring the fat one, meaning Peter, over for dinner. Each time I responded that no matter how good her cooking was it would not suit him; he ate only live rats.

She would laugh and say, "No problem. With jalapeño, he'll taste like a lover's kiss."

I would say to her that under no circumstances was one of my snakes going to go through the stinking guts of some "glassy-eyed true goddamn believer."

And she would laugh.

Several evenings every week Anna M. knocked on Bristol's trailer and the door opened for her. Although the arrangement was obvious, they displayed no signs of affection in public. In the morning she returned to her tent and emerged later, rubbing her eyes as if she had just awakened.

Bristol was not so tolerant of other people's behavior. In Tucumcari a woman named Marlene joined the camp. An ordinary-looking woman of forty, she took on the jobs of washing laundry and singing backup to Simone. A month after joining the following, she was caught with the camp mechanic making love beneath a pickup. Bristol had them taken to the main tent, where he called a meeting of the congregation. I attended only because Gabe yanked me off a chair after I'd refused the summons. When all were seated, Bristol raised his hands for silence.

"Marlene, do you love this man?"

The woman nodded.

"Enough to leave us?"

"Oh, no."

"But you love him?"

"Yes."

He turned his gaze to the man. "Carl, do you love this woman?"

The mechanic hesitated.

"Carl?"

The man nodded.

"Then it's settled. You'll be married."

The mechanic raised his hand. "Do I get some time to think about this?"

The congregation laughed. Bristol was laughing too as he walked over to the man. Carl by then had turned toward the crowd and was laughing. Bristol struck him in the jaw and knocked him to the ground.

"Pack his clothing and put him out of here. Marlene may stay."

How was a mystery, but at the next revival Bristol recruited a new mechanic from among those he baptized, some seventy in all.

Another time Ham Hardy and a roustabout smuggled in two bottles of whiskey and got drunk off one of them. Bristol had the two drunk men carried to the main tent and again called a meeting. He preached about the evils of liquor, ranted about saving them from themselves too many times already, then he took the bottle the men had not yet drunk, and uncapped it. He held it over them and anointed them with the contents.

"You want the putrid smell on you, have it."

He carried the empty bottle to the stage, raised it over his head, and slammed it down. With the broken neck in hand, he returned to the men and grabbed Ham Hardy by the collar. Bristol shoved the jagged edge at Ham's fleshy throat.

"How 'bout I let this bottle do fast what it will do slow otherwise?"

Ham's eyes protruded like golf balls in a sand trap. He said nothing. Bristol let go of the organist and tossed the broken bottle aside. It hit a bench and tinkled harmlessly to the dirt floor. Bristol threw his arms around Ham and embraced him, then the other man. He told the congregation to do the same. Bristol went up onstage and offered a prayer of thanks. I snuck out of the tent, unnoticed. Later, Bristol came to me and warned me not to walk out of meetings, that my behavior was being judged.

What he said was true. Worse, I was on the threshold of losing myself to his authority as the others had. Ironically, I saw my salvation in refusing to be baptized. I preferred damnation over submission. If only I could get my hands on Bristol's money, which I was determined to find, I would be saved. But when I thought about how I would spend it, I realized I had no needs. Camp life provided me the means to survive. It offered everything— except the freedom to leave it.

By October the snakes had become lethargic and began to burrow under the sand. It was time for them to hibernate and too cool to save souls by dunking them in an open tub. We drove south and wintered on an isolated ranch outside of Las Cruces, where I was constantly under watch. Bristol forced me to attend prayer sessions and got serious about having the waters purge my sins. I insisted that I did not want to become one of the Following, mentioned that I was pretty attached to most of my sins.

"Religion's just a waste on me. I'm not spiritual."

"There's no connection between religion and spirituality, Pate, and you're wrong in confusing two vastly different concepts."

When alone with me, he left off with his syrupy talk. He argued that faith is a discovery that often needs a little prompting and baptism makes for good appearances. Then he patted me on the shoulder. I told him I would have to work on the idea of religion a little longer, maybe a long time, and he would likely be dead by then. He laughed.

"If you force me to be baptized, I'll go kicking and screaming."

He nodded and said, "You're getting boring, and the Following is getting anxious."

When not harping on baptism, Bristol badgered me about injecting myself with doses of snake venom to ward off the effects of a bite. He said it was best to start soon because when the snakes came out of hibernation, they were most dangerous. Although I'd gotten hooked, I had taken no pleasure in jabbing myself with a needle. It seemed unnatural, like watching the death of a rat. So I had avoided injecting the venom; instead I survived by respecting the snakes for what they were—God's creatures.

"I don't know what kind of high you get off of it, but I shot up too much other poison. I'm not about to fix snake venom, diluted, pasteurized, or otherwise."

He paced for a while, gathering his patience. "I can't afford to lose you."

"Tough spot for you," I said.

"I can have them hold you down and force you."

"You can."

He said that the Philistines in central New Mexico needed a touch of salvation, so he had decided when spring came to start the circuit around Alamogordo, Cloudcroft, and Ruidoso.

"You better be ready," he said. "We can't be taking time off because you were careless and got bit."

I took it as a warning and wondered just what had happened to the previous snake boy. It occurred to me that no one in camp had ever mentioned one.

"Did the last one get careless?"

"There was no last one."

It was April before we headed north. The last night in Alamogordo we had to raise the side flaps of the big top to accommodate the overflowing crowd. Later Bristol came smiling inside the snake tent. He grabbed me by the waist and tried to dance with me. When he saw that his behavior merely confounded me, he let go and ran his fingers through his black hair.

"You're a magical charm, Pate—on the snakes, I mean. They're going to get me to Pyramid, I tell you," Bristol said, slumping down on a stool and looking in the pit. "Let's feed one, Pate, a mean one. Let's feed Judas, and I'll think about Pyramid."

I had no clue what Pyramid meant, but I nodded as if I understood what he was talking about. I was getting stronger, rarely thought of heroin. I knew the time had arrived to think seriously about hoofing it. I had to find the money and ditch this traveling asylum.

"Judas isn't ready to be fed."

"Put him in anyhow. With a couple who are ready to be fed. You can pull up a chair and watch."

"You watch all you want," I said. "Not me."

As I placed the snakes in the pit, I formulated a plan, decided to wait until we left Ruidoso, then steal the money and escape. The money and my rings had to be in Bristol's trailer. I would hitchhike southwest to Alamogordo, buy a bus ticket to El Paso, and then cross the border to Juárez. I could hide for a few weeks before contacting my parents. It seemed like a good scheme, and it would have been, for someone with guts enough to follow through, and if the Following had not taken on a new member.

V

We were a circus without elephants and tigers, a moment in people's lives when they could share in something unique. The troupe pitched camp for two or three nights in one spot and then moved on to the next. Bristol gained popularity with each performance, and as word spread, it carried over to the next revival, especially on those rare occasions when he was bitten. He would take the fangs on the wrist or the hand, occasionally a forearm, then stand facing the crowd and show the wounds as proof that Satan couldn't hurt him because the Lord was on his side. It was apparent, at least to me, that more people came wishing to see a man bitten by a snake than wishing to get closer to heaven.

Three or four times a week he pandered salvation for a "small piece of someone's food budget or vacation savings." After returning the snake used in the performance to its cage, I would steal into the back of the main tent and watch the ushers pass the silver offering trays. In my head I counted the piles of money that Bristol ran through his fingers at night in his trailer. I imagined him and Anna M. making love on a pile of money, imagined myself sneaking into the trailer, and as he lay in a snoring embrace with her, pilfering his ill-gotten treasure. That was my goal—until Eva strolled into the picture.

She arrived for a Sunday-afternoon revival, and when she surfaced out of the baptismal water, Bristol took one look and dropped her back in. When she popped up the second time, she opened her wide-set brown eyes, and Bristol asked her to stay around for supper. She sat at the dining table, chewing on a pork rib, her long black hair, still wet, clinging to her throat. She was Apache, a Mescalero, and the smooth skin on her face was the color of a walnut. Three silver half-moons hung from one ear, and on the other a miniature kachina dangled on a silver wire. She wore a Beatles T-shirt rolled up from the waist and tucked under her breasts. Her hard abdomen, tattooed with a red dot the size of a quarter, was burnished copper.

Bristol whispered something to her. She smiled, then laughed, her unfettered breasts rising and falling as she did. I chewed the last of the meat off my pork rib as I furtively watched her. When she noticed me, she stopped laughing and I looked away, dropped the bone on my plate, and went for the ear of corn. Bristol pointed me out and said, "That's Pate on the far end. He's the snake boy."

Avoiding her gaze, I nodded and lifted a hand. From then on, I stared at my plate. A short time later I left hurriedly. As I walked past Esperanza, she shook her head.

"What?" I asked.

She motioned with her head in the direction of Bristol and Eva.

"Don't be an old woman," I said.

That night as sleep came, I thought of little but Eva, imagined her in my cot, her hands kneading my hips as she thrust her hips to me. I awoke on the floor staring into a cage full of panicked rodents, an erection pressing urgently against my shorts. I tried to think of my parents, then Barger and his mother, whom I had promised to visit. Where was it? Asheville, North Carolina. How far? I closed my eyes. As I did, I pictured Eva.

I rose to my feet. It was late, but the generator still hummed. I stepped outside. The camp lights were off except for Bristol's trailer, where a lamp glowed orange as a harvest moon. I imagined him counting his money and playing with gold rings, pictured him placing the rings on her outstretched fingers one at a time until every finger on one hand was covered. Then she smiled at him as his hands lifted off that Beatles T-shirt. I hated the pictures I imagined.

After that Eva seemed to be everywhere. If we approached from opposite directions, I would nod and look away. She did not. Her gaze was like iron, her eyes dusky and impenetrable. I thought to speak, but whenever I did my forehead leaked sweat and my feet went cold.

At first I lied to myself about her power over me, but eventually I begrudgingly surrendered to it. I spied on her from shadows or sat at an angle where I could watch her during meals.

When we left Ruidoso, Bristol decided to travel east, first to Roswell and then south to Carlsbad. A farmer outside of Roswell offered his unplanted cotton field as a campsite. One of Bristol's tactics to draw crowds was to pay money to a needy farmer with a bonus for inviting friends and relatives to the services, as he called them. A wind from the northwest hit at dusk when the camp was only half raised. The sand-darkened sky drove us to the safety of the vehicles. I found shelter in the red pickup. My tent, the first up, foundered. Wind began to drag it across the field. The stacked cages collapsed and were dragged along with the canvas by the heavy wind.

Sand swept across the field in flurries. It was difficult to see or breathe, and I shunned the idea of braving the storm. But the snakes, I thought, the snakes. I planted my shoulder against the door, cranked the handle down with a shouted curse, shoved the door open, and stepped into a screen of blistering sand. I pulled up my collar, tucked my chin to my chest, and turned away from the wind. With the worst of it to my back, I charged off in pursuit of the tent.

I nearly had hold of my tent at one stage, but another canvas whipped across my path and a loose rope looped around my ankle. I landed on hands and knees. I pulled myself upright, but the wind shifted direction. The tarp flew up violently and swallowed me as if it were a predator and I its prey. I grabbed what cloth I could and tried to free myself, but the force of the wind against the canvas drove me to my knees. Grappling to free myself from the heavy tarp was like wrestling a wave. I felt a sharp pain in the tip of my index finger as the canvas swept me along. I traveled helplessly for a rough few yards, stopping only because the wind had again shifted. A seam in the canvas had torn my fingernail, and I couldn't use that hand effectively.

Then an unexpected force grasped the flapping canvas and freed me. Only Clyde had the strength to hold on to it by himself. I crawled to my feet and oriented myself. Clyde dropped the canvas and motioned for me to help him. Between the two of us we managed to overcome the wind enough to keep the tent flat and fold it. We dragged it to the truck and secured it underneath the bed. Cages were scattered over the field, some on their sides, some upside down. Clyde, despite his phobia, helped me gather up the undamaged cages, seven in all, and carry them to the bed of the pickup. He left me to deal with the broken cages by myself. Three were empty. Two contained snakes. Those, I secured with duct tape that I found in the truck. I loaded them onto the pickup bed, then climbed in the cab beside Clyde to weather the storm.

I held up my injured finger, which bled where the nail had been, and tried to see how bad it was. But it was too dark. I had to trust the pain to tell me the fingernail was gone. Clyde sat silently, his eyes fixed on the windshield as the wind buffeted the truck. I rummaged through a box behind the seat and found a rag, oil-stained, but otherwise fine. I blew my nose in it until I could breathe and then handed it to Clyde. He cleared his nose and leaned his head back. After the horror he had just endured, using a soiled rag did not much bother him.

"Clyde," I said, "I've got one of the snakes inside my shirt."

He looked at me. "You know, Pate, like some others around here, I'm tryin' real hard not to pinch your head off."

A while later he went to sleep, and a thunderstorm erupted. He snored through the rain. When the storm abated, I shook him awake. The desert was dead still, and the moon floated high in the western sky, an eerie diffused orange. Everything smelled of dirt. Here and there came sounds of doors opening and slamming. The Followers stepped slowly into the field and milled about, surveying the damage. Esperanza seemed to come from nowhere to hand out wet cloths. She instructed us to cover our mouths. "Breathe quick," she said to me, then disappeared.

The new mechanic cranked up the generator, and work began. The men, and I among them, organized themselves, flattening tents, realigning poles, driving stakes. They shook out the heavy canvas, strained their backs. No one complained.

When my tent was up, Clyde went on his way. I found a flashlight and searched for the missing snakes. Two were gone. The third, Peter, had been crushed, if not by a tumbling cage, by a human foot, most likely mine or Clyde's, since we were the only ones who'd gone out during the storm. I placed the dead snake in a broken cage, then sat on a crate nearby.

"How're the snakes?" Bristol asked.

I looked up but didn't answer. He repeated himself. I turned my back to him.

The first blow struck me on the shoulder. The next on the back of the legs. As I rolled away, he planted the tip of his staff on the base of my throat.

"I asked a question."

I pushed the stick away. "Peter was killed."

"That's all?"

"Two got away."

"Replace them," he said and walked away.

I spent three hours looking in the dark and found one snake, which actually found me as I stood urinating into an irrigation ditch.

Bristol canceled the revival until the lost snakes could be replaced. He claimed that it was necessary to have twelve disciples at all times. I said that sounded a little superstitious. He promptly corrected me, said that it was crazy, but it was his craziness. He sent Gabe and Henry into the desert with gunnysacks and snake nooses, then shut himself up in his trailer with Eva. An hour after night set in, Anna M. walked to the steps of the trailer and knocked. There was no answer. She stood there for a long while, torn over what to do next. Several times it appeared she was going to knock again, but finally she gave up and went to her bed.

In the morning Bristol was in a foul mood because Gabe and Henry when hunting for replacements for the missing snakes had blanked the day before. He said I was crazy for insisting that Peter be buried. He told me it was a waste of time, that I should be out scouring the desert for rattlers.

"I'm not asking you to pray over the damn thing. Just give me a shovel," I said. Clyde showed up, shovel in hand and a smile on his lips. He said he enjoyed the idea of putting a snake in a hole and covering it with dirt.

After Peter was properly disposed of, Esperanza told me it was a waste to bury a good meal.

"Put your teeth in and smile," I said. "He was a good snake."

She pointed a finger to her temple and called me loco.

I thought of the old women in Vietnam, how they squatted in a circle and traded banter, smoking hand-rolled cigarettes and chewing betel nuts, their lips red as blood. They had seemed impervious to the world, as if there was no pain in it too great for them. That was how Esperanza seemed.

"I need two snakes," I said.

"Do I keep snakes?" she asked.

"I've never caught a snake."

"Nor I, *pobre*, but we can learn," she said. She put a kerchief over her head and a straw Stetson atop that and smiled her toothless smile. "Vámonos a buscar por las culebras." Let's go look for the snakes. She headed toward a mesquite clump as if she knew what she was doing.

Anna M., cast aside by Bristol, was relegated to camp chores and spent much time alone. At meals she sat at the first open chair at the table and lodged a list of complaints to anyone who would listen. She hinted of having information that would hurt Bristol, matters that he would prefer to remain unknown. Her sullenness upset the harmony of the camp. I thought to use her to my own ends. Surely she knew where Bristol hid his money.

At Bristol's bidding she began taking evening meals to Ham Hardy's tent, under Henry's watchful eye. Anna M. was a passionate woman who needed to feel worthy. Though convinced that she knew where Bristol kept the money, I never had a chance to exploit that possibility. She and Ham Hardy were married in two weeks in a ceremony presided over by Bristol. Harmony was restored, I was not one bit closer to the money or to freedom, and Bristol had the woman I wanted.

One afternoon Bristol dragged Eva by the hand into the snake tent and ordered me to get him a snake and a chick. I stood at the entrance and stared at Bristol's trailer. I tried not to think of what was happening in the tent, tried to concentrate on where the money might be. It was my money now. I claimed it though I'd never seen it. Sweat rolled down my neck. Pretend you hate her, I thought. Better still, hate her. Then the flap flew back and Eva stormed past me. Bristol followed seconds later, shrugging and pointing at the air as he limped to his trailer. All eyes in camp turned away.

He knocked, but the door did not open. He looked about. Ham Hardy stroked the air with his fingers as if practicing on a piano. Bristol tilted his chin, sniffed the air, and walked to the dining tent, where he took a seat facing the trailer. Esperanza tossed a few more briquettes on the grill and fanned the fire. I figured the snake was swallowing its meal about then and went inside the tent to bring out a few to bask in the sun. When I came out, Bristol was gone, as was the Buick.

Esperanza watched me so much that I occasionally doubted her motives, wondered if she was a spy for Bristol. Two days after Bristol took off, I was sunning a few of the snakes. She took a seat on an empty cage and rolled a cigarette. She exhaled and passed the cigarette to me.

"You know how some people think God keeps score?"

"I don't think He does," I answered.

"What you think maybe doesn't matter," she said, taking the cigarette back. "Some people think that way. Some think they are like God Himself."

She had heard something, I was certain, and was trying to warn me.

"So?"

"So nothing. Perhaps you should just think about this." She extended the cigarette. "If you like, tonight I will make a habañero sauce."

I nodded and returned the cigarette. So few things in camp escaped her watchful eyes that I figured she probably knew where the money was kept. But I did not dare ask.

Bristol returned that night, but we didn't see Eva for several more, not even at the dining table. Anna M. carried trays of food to Bristol's trailer, but Bristol himself ate in the dining tent, where he banged on tables and demanded silence during meals. He slept in the supply tent and went about the business of salvation as if nothing out of the ordinary were taking place. The revivals didn't fare well, but he blamed the farmer and not himself. The camp whispered. An usher and a roustabout left after dark that week. I worried for a while that they had absconded with the money, but then figured otherwise when Bristol did not send anyone to pursue them.

A week after she went in the trailer, Eva emerged. Holding Bristol's elbow, she walked with him to breakfast. We packed up that day and headed east, our destination the Texas Panhandle.

The deeper we journeyed into the Panhandle, the thinner the crowds got. In one town the Followers were stopped from posting handbills. In another Bristol performed to an assembly of six. He was bucking all manner of Bible Belt fundamentalists: Baptists, Church of Christ, Assembly of God, and Pentecostal ministries dominated every county. Sheriffs in two counties visited the campsite and brought along health inspectors and a suggestion that we move along.

"Campbellists, Calvinists," Bristol complained, adding that he would rather wrestle a battalion of Mormons for the soul of a skunk than compete with a single Baptist for a nickel in an offering plate.

Eighteen miles north of Amarillo we were visited by two deputies who cornered Bristol and drove away with him. Two hours later he returned with the same sheriff's deputies and two more squad cars. The deputies searched the camp, took names, checked sanitation facilities, and probed the interiors of the tents with flashlights. Two came into the snake tent and set off a dozen rattles. They did not bother taking my name, merely excused themselves and let go of the tent flap. I stepped outside. Bristol was shaking his head and furrowing his brow while talking into the reflective sunglasses of one stern-faced deputy. They left again.

The next afternoon uniforms were everywhere. The whole sheriff's department arrived and surrounded the tent where the roustabouts bunked. The flap flew open and Clyde charged out, headed for one of the pickups. The cops surrounded the truck and pointed shotguns and pistols at him. He threw the truck door open and challenged them to take him without weapons. It took most of them to wrestle him to the ground. Once they had him cuffed they took turns sitting with him in the backseat of a patrol car. I started for the patrol car, but Bristol used his cane to block me.

"You want to be in prison?" he asked, never taking his eyes off the scene in the patrol car.

Clyde looked pretty harmless by the time that cop car started down the road.

Bristol said, "You're all impulse, Pate. That's good with the snakes, but not with people. Clyde will be a hard man to replace."

Bristol left camp for the remainder of the day, returning in time for the evening meal. He seemed truly troubled by Clyde's misfortune and claimed he had offered to post bail. He called the Following to the big tent for a service. The assembly offered up a prayer for the lost brother. After the prayer, Bristol ordered us to sit.

"I'll do ever'thin' in my a powa' to see that Brother Clyde gets fair treatment. But I think this part of Texas is the land of Cain, and we are lost in it. I see no good for us here, no good. It is a heathen land that preys upon good brothers and sisters. We must go where the Word'll be welcomed—Arizona, the Promised Land."

Afterward, Bristol visited me in the snake tent. He watched the snakes crawling over one another. "Imagine," he said, "a killer in our midst. Imagine."

I wondered how old Eva was. Seventeen? Younger, perhaps.

That night I changed my plans. A miracle had taken place inside me as I watched Clyde being beaten in the back of the cop car. I realized that I had to leave. It was no longer freedom or the desire to see my parents that prompted me. Though Bristol was the one who limped, we, all the rest of us, were the cripples. I did not want that. I felt ready to rejoin the world. But I could not simply walk away. He would not let that happen. Moreover, how far would I get without money? I could not pack in the middle of the night and leave without transportation, or land in the nearest strange town and pull off a burglary. Where could I hide without crowds of people? Besides, stealing was all but behind me. I would commit one more crime, just one.

I lay awake much of the night, thinking and listening to roustabouts load the trucks. I decided that Arizona *was* the Promised Land. About two A.M. I went to sleep.

I awoke with a surprising sense of resolve. Serious matters often seem amusing in the morning, and the humor of ripping off Bristol's stash lifted my spirits. I calculated that, stacked up high, Bristol's bankroll had to be thicker than the Chicago phone directory. I reminded myself that I had worked a year with no pay and that Bristol had converted my gold bands to his use. The dilemma confronting me was where he hid it. I figured he kept it close, which left only his trailer. Hanging was the question of how much time I would need inside to find where it was hidden.

Tearing down camp tired us, and driving long distances further fatigued us, and setting up camp after hundreds of miles of travel left us thoroughly depleted of energy. That was when I would strike. But not when Bristol was present. If, I decided, he chose to leave in the Buick, I would take a chance the first night we reached Arizona. And if not then, some-time when all those circumstances came together.

Bristol turned the caravan west. He asked me to ride with him on the first leg of the journey. Eva rode behind us in a pickup with Ham Hardy and Anna M. During the drive Bristol didn't once mention baptism. He spoke vaguely about loyalty and about me being reliable and how he was glad he could depend on me. I nodded solicitously and wondered if he could look inside my mind.

"You were an addict when I found you."

"Yeah."

"Look at you." He glanced at me, his eyes gleaming. "You're healthy now, Pate. In your prime. I envy that."

"Isn't that one of the seven deadly sins?"

"We were tested." His lips tightened, his voice dropped an octave. "We went into the wilderness, like Jesus, and confronted the Philistines."

As ignorant as I was of the Bible, I still saw that those two ideas some-how did not fit together. "Tested?"

"Yes. There are people who need what we've got. Sometimes we have to make a sacrifice we don't want to. You, you're indispensable. You do the devil's work. I'll do the Lord's."

Something was implied that I did not grasp right away, but he had set me to thinking. I understood at one level what he was saying. I had long realized that the reason the Following was so gracious toward me was that none of them wanted my job. If not me, then no one. He would have to find another who was down and out. I told him the devil's work suited me best and asked if he wanted me to drive.

He shook his head. "Pate, the people of Texas are not chosen."

"You know, I've been thinking it would be a lot easier on me and the snakes if we fed them chicks. I got bit by a rat."

He looked over at me. "Chicks?" He returned his attention to the road. "Chicks. Of course. Brilliant."

We drove without further conversation and listened to music on AM radio stations fade into static. At the first rest stop the caravan made, Bristol told me to take Eva's place in the pickup and send her to him. She stepped down slowly, looked me in the eyes as she did, and brushed against my shoulder as she headed to the car.

The next night we pitched tents in a field at the foothills to the Sangre de Cristos, and Bristol left with Henry. I had thought about what he meant by an undesirable sacrifice. Then it came to me. Bristol had known about Clyde all along, just as he knew about me and probably others. He had surrendered him either for a reward or to avoid arrest himself.

I waited until an hour after the camp went dark before I left my tent. I circled the perimeter twice. Assured that no one had seen me, I crawled under Bristol's trailer, figuring that he might have a drop box welded under the floor. I found nothing. I crawled to the edge of the trailer and looked both ways, then pulled myself out.

"What are you doing?"

Eva stood a few feet away, one arm folded under her breasts and the elbow of the other propped on the fender of a truck.

I brushed off my shirt and trousers and pointed beneath the trailer. "I was looking for a snake."

She stepped away from the pickup and walked to the trailer door, pausing long enough before entering to look at me. I returned to my tent.

An hour or so later the Buick pulled in. I waited for Bristol to come for me sometime before dawn. He did not.

VI

Bristol stopped in Santa Fe, he alleged, to telephone an attorney about the well-being of Brother Clyde. When he came back to the trucks strung out beside the highway, he told us he was called away to Albuquerque for two days. He sent us on our way and put Ham Hardy in charge of the caravan. The troupe set up outside of Gallup. Still scared over what had happened the night before, I busied myself with the snakes and tried not to appear guilty.

I had moved seven snakes to the pit while I changed dirt in the cages. Suddenly the snakes came to life. I heard nothing prior to their rattlers going off. She stood by the pit, watching me.

"You want something?"

"Do you know me?" she asked.

"No."

"Then why do you watch like you know me?"

"I don't."

"You do."

I turned my back to her and finished with a cage. She came up beside me.

"He told me about you. You're a junkie and a thief."

"Was and was." I brushed past her, went to the pit, and with the hook caught one of the rattlers. I lifted the snake out and carried it to its cage. She followed.

"You don't know me?" she asked.

I shook my head.

"From anywhere?"

She inched closer until I could feel her breath on my neck. I broke out in a sweat. "Lady, I got work to do."

She walked to my cot and sat, angling herself to face me whenever I changed position. I thought of asking her to leave, wanted her to and did not want her to at the same time.

"My name is Eva. Call me by my name. He said you're afraid of the snakes. Are you?"

"I've got respect for them. He has none."

"What he does with them onstage, that's why I'm here. He'll teach me."

"That's crazy."

She said nothing more, just watched as I took the last five from the pit and caged them, each struggling. They rarely went easily into the cages.

As I was about to hook the last one, she raised her hand. "No, I want you to feed it."

"It's not time. I keep schedules. This one doesn't . . ."

As I turned to look at her, she unbuttoned the straps that held her dress up. She held the top across her breasts with a forearm, studying my reaction, then dropped her arm to her side. The dress fell to her ankles, and she stood naked. She said, "Feed it."

I refused. She stood that way for several seconds, her eyes implacable, then bent down and pulled up the dress, buttoned the straps, and left. I had to sit down.

The next day we passed several times. She stared but did not speak; I looked at the ground and mumbled to myself. That evening at the meal, she sat opposite me, chewing slowly on her food, studying me. When I was finished, I stood to leave.

"You're part Indian?"

I shrugged. I knew only of my mother's side of the family, all Dutch. My father never spoke about his roots.

"You are. I know it."

"Then you know more than I do, lady."

"Eva. Call me Eva. You sweat all the time." It was a statement. "You have dreams."

I bit down on the potato. One of the Following, an usher and carpenter, sat down beside her. She looked away. I finished my meal and went to the snakes. That night, as usual, I sweated and had dreams.

After Bristol returned, we drove south, then turned west into Arizona. Bristol seemed preoccupied most of the time, not just with Eva but with the reception he'd gotten in Texas. I do not know what spurred it, but one afternoon he demanded that I stay and watch while a snake was being fed a chick.

"That's okay, I've got things to do." Under normal circumstances, I felt uncomfortable around him, but knowing his peculiar interest in snake feeding and Eva's recent demand, I became suspicious. Had she told him about seeing me scouting under the trailer? Or concocted some story about me in case I mentioned the episode in the tent?

"I insist."

"I don't like to."

"Stay, or I'll have you tied."

I sat down on my cot so as not to witness the drama and looked at the ground to avoid seeing his excitement.

"If things go right I can get us to Pyramid," he said.

Pyramid still meant nothing to me. "Good, I guess. What's Pyramid?"

"A lake, Pate. Just a lake. But the Pyramid Lake Revival is the biggest in the West. It's the Olympics of the gospel. One week of slinging God's word to up to fifty thousand people per day. You understand what that means?" He dropped the chick in the pit.

I had no more interest in a gospel Olympics than I did in a revival held for an audience of five. "I guess."

"Do you like Eva, Pate?"

I swallowed and stayed as calm as possible. The rattler buzzed and the panicked chick chittered. "She's okay."

"Okay?"

I looked up. He was bent over, resting his weight on the wall and staring into the pit, his eyes wide.

"I got things to do," I said and stood.

He looked at me over his shoulder. "No, you don't."

He looked back at the pit. "Fifty, sixty thousand will come looking to heal their bodies and souls. Do you see what that means?"

I envisioned it. "I see." He was seeing money; I was seeing money and Eva.

Outside of Ash Fork we lost two snakes. They somehow escaped the cages. I told Bristol. He said to go find some and replace them. I said ten were enough.

He flipped over a table and screamed. "You're not paying attention to work! We need twelve! You know that." His hands were doubled up, trembling. He opened them and stretched his fingers. "Replace them, Pate. Two before tonight's service," he said, his voice softening.

Although I had been granted many new freedoms, he did not yet trust me with a vehicle. I tried to recruit Esperanza, who refused to go, said I was the snake boy and should be able to find my own snakes. I took a canvas sack and a long hook and left camp on foot heading north, where the stonecutters quarried flagstone. I had hiked about a mile when a pickup came bounding over the rough ground, spraying dust. The horn blared. I turned and saw her face leaning out of the window, her long black hair pulled behind her head in a single braid.

"He told me to help you."

Because I wanted her and because he had her, I resented her. "I don't need help."

She pulled the truck forward, honked, and leaned across the seat to open the passenger door. She said I better get in or we would both be in trouble. I shrugged and tossed the snake gear in the bed, then climbed in the cab.

I pointed to a ravine about a mile off to the northwest. "We may find some sunning themselves on the rocks."

We reached the western slope of the bluffs fifteen minutes later and stopped on a rocky wash dotted with barrel cactus and creosote. It was quiet as only the desert can be, and the sound of the doors slamming sent a lizard scurrying through a bush. Eva kept to herself as we walked up the arroyo. I stopped in the shade beneath a ledge.

Although she made no sound, I sensed her approach from behind me and looked over my shoulder. She reached over and grazed the back of my hand with her fingertips. She had seemed tall whenever I had seen her, but it was an illusion. I was surprised at how short she was. I took her hand and led her to a flat boulder. We did not speak. As if in anger, we grasped one another in a desperate embrace and kissed, our mouths urgent and demanding. When we pulled apart, we ripped at each other's clothing, fumbling with buttons and zippers, groping each other wildly. When we were both naked, I sat her atop the rock. She leaned back, her weight resting on her arms, and opened her thighs to accommodate me.

Afterward, I lay beside her on the boulder as she stroked my scalp with her fingernails.

"We have to find two snakes," I reminded her.

"No." She smiled and placed two fingers on my lips. "In a sack in the bed of the pickup. I took them while you ate yesterday."

Still naked, we sat cross-legged on a flat rock as she told me about Gallup, where she had been sent to Indian school, which she called away school, where proselytizers had tried to de-Indianize her. She told of preachers whose wives and daughters laid out cookies and pastries on tablecloths on Sunday morning. She and her friends went from the Methodist Church to the Baptist to the Lutheran to the Assembly of God to the Catholic, "eating our way through Christianity." She looked away and wiped her eyes with the back of her hand, then said, "They wanted to baptize us even if we had been baptized already. All of them thought their baptism was better than the next guy's. I think they just wanted to wash the brown away."

She said the children, the Jo Boys and Jo Girls, as they were called, kept their Indian names secret and used Christian names. There were conflicts between the Navajo and the Pueblo boys. The Apache were outsiders, except for the girls, who were prized. "Always liquor and boys and girls to drink it."

We made love again, her sitting on my lap staring into my face.

She became my new heroin. I lived for the moments with her, but we had to be cautious. I had not yet mentioned Bristol's money, but I was sure she would go along with stealing it. I began to think about Pyramid and the fifty thousand souls with five bucks apiece to drop in an offering plate. At night she went to Bristol's trailer. And I would go to sleep thinking of her and would wake up drenched and feel around for her, knowing all the while that she was in his trailer. I wanted him dead, but knew I would not kill him. Now that I had something besides my freedom at risk, I feared him all the more. I was even more afraid of myself.

We were cold, even antagonistic toward one another in front of people. But when alone, it—whatever it was, passion, lust—had us. We would find moments, our trysts quick, almost brutal, with little foreplay, full of racing heartbeats and violent spasms as we repressed the sounds natural to the love act. Seldom did we fully undress. She would wear a skirt with nothing underneath. Her fingernails would scrape the canvas wall and I would crawl beneath the apron of the tent. We would find concealment under a parked truck, in a shadow somewhere. Her skirt would come up as I kissed sweat from her throat, her long hair brushing over my bare chest.

During one revival, while Bristol was dunking converts, I took her by the wrist and pulled her to his trailer, where we made love on his bed. "Scream now," I said, begging. "Please scream for me." Another time we crawled under the stage with only the canvas aprons to shield us. I heard him overhead, thumping on the plywood, the heel of his crippled leg marking each step like an exclamation point at the end of a sentence. I had to hold my hand over her mouth at the critical moment.

Sometimes I no longer felt like me, but like someone who was watching me, both actor and audience to my own play, not fully me unless I was with her, and then I was someone else. How far she could be trusted, I was unsure, but soon I would have to prepare her for what I had planned, for she was now part of it.

Esperanza came to the snake tent one afternoon with cigarettes. She handed me one, then sat on my cot. Her cheeks collapsed against her gums as she drew on the cigarette. She held the smoke in her lungs for a seemingly endless time, looking at me. I knew what was on her mind.

She exhaled. "So, you are busy."

"Me? No."

"Then you do not like my tortillas any longer, my roasted peppers?"

"Yes, I like them."

"Oh, I see." She took another drag off the cigarette and waited.

"He may cut off your manhood."

I shook my head. "I don't know what you're talking about."

"Your," she said, pointing at my crotch, "*como se dice*—your plaything."

I went to one of the cages and removed a snake, which I carried to the pit. "I take care of snakes. That's all."

"When he is finished, you can have her. He is not yet finished."

"You're being an old woman."

She counted out five cigarettes, which she laid on the cot. "An old woman can be a young friend. I am making enchiladas. Come see me if your stomach growls for them and not her."

Bristol kept a small pharmacy in a chest in the trailer. Eva dumped a phenobarbital in his dinner, and when he passed out, she slipped out of the trailer. Taking precautions not to be seen, she circled the camp and came to my tent. I lay awake, sweating in the stifling heat and suffering the stink of the snakes. She scratched the canvas and whispered for me to come out. She told me what she had done and that we would have the night to fulfill ourselves.

We walked silently into the desert. On warm sand beneath a cutbank, as Bristol squeezed his pillow and honked at the ceiling of his trailer, she and I clutched one another and muffled the sounds of our passion. She braided my hair in the moonlight that filtered through the paloverdes. I wrote her a poem in the sand, which we erased with our bodies. We danced on a flat sandstone in the whiteness of the moon to the rhythm of crickets and the music of insects. We held hands and kissed each other's eyelids, crawled after a lizard's trail, and laughed at a family of quail that happened upon us. We loved, but never said love, just talked around it.

"At twelve," she said, "I learned about menstruation and boys away from my mother and aunts. They told me I would be going to away school, that some of us had to go. I left an Apache and returned an outcast."

I thought of how I left home and returned from Vietnam a half-man. She stroked my cheek and said, "People like us must make our own place. Let's leave." She gripped my forearm in both of her hands.

"Not now," I said, thinking of the money that could be ours after Pyramid.

Afterward, as the dawn threatened the night, we lay beside each other bathed in sweat, grit in every pore. She rested her head on the bow of my thigh.

"We have to go," I said. "It's almost daybreak."

She tightened her hold on me. "We have to leave. I mean, this, all of this. Now."

"Why?"

"He wants to marry me."

"Marry? Marry?" I laughed until I saw the gravity in her expression. I saw my plan dissolve in her face. I wrenched away from her. "I'll kill him," I said, a threat hot as fire but all smoke.

She sat up. "No. Let's just leave."

I considered how Bristol had turned Clyde in, weighed his hold over people. He knew their weaknesses, knew mine. "He won't let me go, and I have no money. He'll send Gabe and Henry after us."

She was by then standing. She came to me, leaned into my chest, and wrapped her arms around my waist. Her hair clung to my chest. Then she pulled away and looked up at me. "We can leave soon. Tonight, tomorrow night."

"How? How far would we get without money?"

I held her by the shoulders. "Find out where he hides the money."

"Money?"

"Yes."

She looked away. "Money."

"Some of it is mine."

"He saved you."

I laughed and shook my head. "Saved me for you. If we have money, we can get far enough away. Without it we'll get to the highway, no farther."

"No. I can't."

"You can."

"No."

I laughed and when she laughed, I forced her to the ground and pinned her shoulders with my knees. I held her like that until she quit struggling. "He knows about me," I said. "He'll turn me in to the cops the way he did Clyde." She tried again to escape my grasp, but I held her and whispered several times that without money we couldn't go anywhere.

"Money."

"Yes, goddamn it. He stole from me."

"For us?"

I helped her to her feet. "For us."

She asked if Bristol really turned Clyde over to the cops. I nodded, said, "Yes. He can't be trusted." I kissed her, then lifted her up. She wrapped her legs around my waist and, standing, we made love. Afterward she promised to find the hiding place.

Bristol swaggered into the tent as I was about to wash up for lunch. He stood behind me and leaned on his stick. "How's it going, Pate?" he asked, his eyes trained on the snakes, his voice indifferent in tone.

"Okay, I guess."

"You look a little tired. Aren't you sleeping well?"

I tried not to read anything into his question. "Could you if you had to smell snakes all night?"

"Is that a complaint?"

"Would it do any good if it was?"

He smiled and placed a hand on my shoulder. "You need your sleep. We can't put on the show without you."

"Show? I thought you were saving souls."

He took his hand off my shoulder and walked to one of the cages. "Are you getting used to us? Are you ready to be dunked for the Lord?"

"Used to who? The snakes? Remember me, the devil's work?"

He turned around, his eyes set on me the way a rattler fixed on a rat. "That's more like you. I was starting to think you were changing."

"Me?"

"You ever think about shooting up?"

I plunged my hands in the bucket of water and began to lather a bar of soap. "You ever think about those rings you took from me?"

He walked up behind me and laid his staff softly atop my head. "You have a hard head, Pate. Or is it a little soft in spots?"

I turned around and pushed the tip of the staff slowly from my head.

"That's better." He smiled. "I want you to think seriously about baptism. I want you to think about God's commandments. About the many sins you carry."

And one more to come, I thought. I kept my back turned to him. "I will."

"And start sleeping." I heard the staff touch the ground and the thump of his shoe from the game leg, and I took several deep breaths.

Henry came in the early evening to say the Reverend Bristol wanted to see me. Bristol called me in as I mounted the steps. He sat at his desk counting ones and fives and stacking them in tidy piles. He motioned for me to sit. He set a stack aside, then started counting out one-dollar bills and setting them on the desk in front of me. He stopped at the count of fifteen.

"For you, Pate. You'll get this once a week and town privileges. How's that?"

"I don't need to go to town."

He nudged the stack closer to the edge of the desk. "Like the others, you have to spend the money on your needs. Clothes, sundries. We're not donating to you any longer."

"Oh." I picked up the money and stuffed it in my jeans pocket.

"We're doing serious work, Pate. I want to know I can depend on you."

I looked at the floor to my right and noticed the rug, a replica of the Sistine Chapel. Was Adam forgiven and destined to heaven? Or did Michelangelo intend something more subtle? I stood and patted the pocket that held the money. "I assume you took taxes out."

He laughed and when he stopped, said, "Don't be insolent."

I began weekly excursions into towns—Wikieup, where I ate homemade apple pie at the Cowboy Café and Bagdad, where copper miners lived in prefab homes all the same color, and Parker, where fifteen dollars netted a few T-shirts with giant cacti silk-screened across the chest and sneakers at a discount price. Wherever I went, Henry or Gabe waited nearby. In Salome I ate five hamburgers under Gabe's watchful gaze, in Ehrenberg five orders of pancakes. Bristol made sure I had nothing more than coins in my pockets when we drove on our return trip. I was not allowed to save money.

My mouth stuffed with white bread and greasy meat or dripping syrup, I would wink at Gabe or Henry, whichever was my watchdog for the moment. They would stare back, contempt in their eyes, but would say nothing. I was, after all, the snake boy. In the truck on the way back I would ask questions of them: "Getting laid, Henry?" "Gabe, How 'bout you and I slip into Phoenix and chase skirts or score some smoke?" The veins on Henry's neck would bulge and his cheeks would redden, but he seldom spoke.

Once he said, "You don't fool me. You're scum."

I was sandwiched between him and Gabe in the cab of a pickup. I thanked him for his comment, which I noted was the kind of charitable and Christian sentiment he seemed worthy of. Then I said, "Henry, have you ever thought that you might wake up one day with a snake or two in your bed?"

He slammed on the brakes. I flew forward and only at the last instant avoided banging my head on the dash. Henry doubled up a fist and prepared to backhand me.

"Don't even think about it," I said. "You get to punch on me only if Bristol says to."

He muttered, "Someday," and pressed the accelerator.

I turned to Gabe. "So, tell me, Gabe, how do you feel about snakes?"

The long southwestern summer set in. I began to wonder if Eva was keeping the secret of Bristol's stockpile because she did not trust me. I told her we needed to be especially cautious from now on, that it was a matter of time now and the question was whether I would get the money or Bristol would catch us first. She and I were too bold, and too many eyes watched us. I began to read things in the way he looked at me, and my neck bristled at his every question, at his every remark.

The journey to Pyramid was long weeks away, which gave me plenty of time to devise a plan. The way Bristol spoke of the event—the volume of attendees, the number of evangelists, music, and lines of converts to be baptized in the shallows—there would be too many distractions for us to be closely watched. I told her we had to make our move then. My plan was uncomplicated—steal the first night's take, then blend into the crowd and escape. The lake was a short distance from Reno, which was a five-hour bus ride to San Francisco. We would find connections in the Bay Area to the underground highways, flee to Canada perhaps. I assured Eva that I had no intention of being greedy. One night's take and scram. That would be more than enough. In the meantime, we needed to be cautious, do nothing to raise suspicion.

As soon as I fixed the plan in my mind, it became real and fear took control of me. It was stimulating, a plot based on tension and gamesmanship. I began to wonder if I was a fear junkie, if I needed risk, and in its absence, drugs. Had I survived Vietnam to no purpose other than to seek risk for the sake of risk?

Then six weeks before we were to start for Pyramid, I blundered. The caravan drove south and west, bypassing Yuma. We camped in the flats between Gadsden and San Luis. It was hot, pushing a hundred and fifteen every day, and humidity from the nearby Colorado River made the nights unbearable. Eva and I had not been together for a week, and each time I saw her—and it did not matter, close or far away—my desire turned to desperation. Not being with her dominated the landscape of my mind. I thought of her in his bed and hated him with the same depth of passion that made me want her.

Bristol kept her busy as a shill in his baptism game. She would stand and walk to the stage as if in a trance, the goat leading the sheep. I loitered at the back of the tent and cringed when he extended his arms to her and led her to the tub of water. When she emerged, her hair flattened, eyes closed, her dark nipples pressing through the white cotton blouse, something inside of me would go cold, and as I stood at the back and watched the ushers pass the plates, I could smell the money even above the sweat. It was too hot to sleep, and late after the revivals I would lie awake on my cot planning our escape.

Outside Yuma, Bristol did not get the crowds he had anticipated. Nonetheless, several hundred took the plunge and filled the coffers. His stash, wherever he kept it, was getting fatter. We moved camp east to the Mexican border in the foothills northeast of Nogales outside the small town of Patagonia. It was cooler there, the thermometer topping at about a hundred at mid-afternoon. The Buick and two trucks left for town, with Bristol and several followers packed in them.

Eva and I had been without each other for more than ten days. We'd had one brief conversation, and that about the money, which she said he deposited in banks on those occasions when he disappeared. That was all she had managed to discover.

I was sunning the snakes when she strolled by and casually looked down in the pit. "I know where he hides it," she said and pointed to the supply tent that we had used for a rendezvous on one occasion.

I watched her hips as she walked to the tent. For a few seconds I let the information settle. Soon, I thought, soon. I imagined the expression on Bristol's face as he looked in his hiding place and discovered he had been robbed. I returned the snakes to their cages and waited until I felt certain no one was watching me. Then, thinking that no one had noticed, I headed to where she waited. I intended only to ask her where the money was, but when I entered, she offered up her lips, and without a word passing between us, we fell into each other's arms and clawed at our clothing.

When Bristol tossed open the tent flap, she and I were atop the flour sacks. He set Henry and Gabe and a third roustabout on us. As Bristol screamed about injustice and insult and vile sin, one of the men pulled me off of Eva, and another sent me to the ground with a blow to the side of my face. Henry laughed and booted me in the small of the back. Bristol told them that was enough for the moment and left. I looked at Eva and she at me. Her eyes said that she had been right. We should have left. My greed and desire for revenge had brought us to this.

Naked and bound, Eva and I were carried to the big tent and tossed at Bristol's feet. Ham Hardy pressed his fingers on the keys of the organ as the camp in full assembly seated themselves facing the altar. Bristol stood over us, lavishly stroking a leather belt, which from time to time he dipped into a pail of water and flailed against the altar. The leather striking the wood sounded like a pistol shot.

"Fornicators! Sinners! The mark of shame is upon them!" Gone was his vainglorious dignity and his beneficent tone. He shouted, "They have entered Satan's fiery palace and shirked the commandments of the righteous!" He asked the gathering to stand and pass by us, invited them to smell us while the sweat and stink of lust still clung to us. "Breathe in the foul odor of treachery. They toil on behalf of Satan to destroy the chaste and the good."

He raised the belt to strike her.

"It was my doing," I said. "Not hers." Just get to it, I thought. I tried to get her attention. I wanted to be courageous for us, but she would not even look in my direction.

"She must face the hand and be saved from eternal damnation."

Bristol whipped himself into a mania as he continued the tirade against sin. A chorus of amens punctuated his every word. I lay on the ground helpless to do anything. He flogged Eva, whipped her until deep red welts crisscrossed her back and then left her twitching in pain to turn his anger on me. I tried to roll away to avoid the belt, but Henry and Gabe shoved my face into the dirt and pinned my arms.

Bristol told them to leave me be. He stepped closer, the belt raised. "Writhe on your belly like a snake," he said. I took the blow on my lips. My mouth went numb. The next struck my neck and shoulders. I heard the Gathering chant off the numbers as he lashed me. He worked me over with the belt until the blood was too much even for the Following to endure and the tent went silent except for the pop of leather.

I called out, "No more, no more. Please." Then I blacked out.

When I came to, I lay on my side, my right eye swollen shut. I blinked until vision returned to my good eye. I saw Esperanza, her hands covering her face. The rest of the tent was a blur. He tossed the belt aside and told Henry and Gabe to lay me next to Eva, facing her. He kneeled down between us and prayed aloud and when finished, ordered someone to carry Eva to Anna M.'s tent for nursing.

"Bring him," Bristol said, meaning me.

We followed him across the camp, Henry and Gabe and two others dragging me belly down. They dumped me on the ground beside the snake pit. I tried to crawl away, but Gabe sat down on my back and said it was time for a little heart to heart. He asked how I felt about snakes. My lips were too swollen for me to attempt a reply. Henry returned with a twelve-foot tent pole used to support walls of the pavilion. The four of them tied me to the pole and suspended me facedown over the snake pit. The unshaded noon sun beat down on us.

Several minutes passed before Bristol came up to the pit. He kneeled down to get a look at my face. "Brought you some company," he said and heaved a snake into the pit.

Judas landed roughly and tumbled to a stop beneath my chest. He reeled himself into a coil and buzzed. His first thrust came near enough that I could see the white roof of his mouth. He hissed and struck again and missed me again. Then he slid away.

Bristol pointed his revolver at my head and cocked the barrel. "I saved you from yourself. What was my reward? I should pull the trigger, Pate. You'd be just another snake boy who got careless."

He left, only to return a moment later, calmer but still waving the gun. "That's the Lord's money you were going to steal."

I managed to mumble, "Thought I could use it better than He could."

Bristol smiled and said, "Pain is a messenger."

He struck me on the head with the barrel of the gun and opened a gash. He touched my cheek with the backs of his fingers. I felt his hot breath nearing me and tried to pulled away. Judas coiled and buzzed. Bristol kissed the cut he'd inflicted and backed away.

"Leave him," he said to the others, "till he atrophies. No, on second thought, poke the snake from time to time. Let him understand that the devil lurks near always."

Henry took delight in agitating the snake. Bare ass suspended above an ill-tempered Mojave rattler, I spent nearly a day drifting in and out of consciousness until Esperanza helped Henry untie me and carry me to the cot, where I was laid on my side. She washed me with a damp cloth. When we were alone, she whispered, "I have money. When you are better, leave. I'll help."

I closed my eyes with something else in mind. I intended to kill Bristol.

VII

Esperanza healed me with menudo and roasted peppers and a salve made from jojoba plants. Bristol visited often to chart my progress. He did not speak, just hovered over the cot. Two weeks later I returned to my duties. I hung my head and looked away when others approached, cowered and shuffled to the side when Bristol approached. I spoke in a whisper. I shaved my hair to the scalp and my eyebrows as well. I nibbled when I ate and soon lost weight. I became, in most every sense, an ascetic dedicating my life to the art of snake keeping. I conversed with them, laid my ear next to their cages and listened, nodding and smiling as if we communicated.

As my behavior increased in its eccentricity, the Following took note. I was shunned like a New Testament villain, a Pontius Pilate or a Herod accepting the platter with John's head. Hunkered alone at the far end of a table, fork in hand, I stared at the red checkered tablecloth, held food in my mouth sometimes up to a minute, as if I'd forgotten I'd taken a bite, then chewed it slowly. Soon others started treating me as if I were deaf or invisible. They gossiped openly in front of me.

"Anna M.'s in a family way," Ham Hardy bragged.

Pregnant, say pregnant, I would think, but I did not speak up. I mocked them in thought only now. Sheep, I would think. Only sheep.

"We're headed to Yuma again, Sister. Better pray for rain."

Pray for thirty days and thirty nights of it, I thought, as I picked at my food and mumbled to myself. I scraped leftovers into a pail and shuffled off, hunched over, a broken thing. Esperanza's skeptical eyes followed me, looking for a sign, but I was a mask.

During the weeks while I regained my strength, I also gained the patience of the saved. My thoughts lingered on Barger, the wingless angel who had played chess and smelled VC in the dark. He was the first true friend I had ever made and the first I had lost. Had I been straight the day he took the RPG, I might have at least moved to save him. Instead I had lain in a blind above the riverbank, glassy-eyed, my M-16 aimed at nothing, while he, shiny with sweat, motioned to me and whispered, "Stay down, Pate." I wondered about his mother, what I would tell her. That he had watched over me? I even pondered that he might still be watching over me. But that was a fool's idea, and I was no one's fool, except Bristol's.

Eva returned to his bed. Her jeweled eyes as dull as any among the

Following, she trailed him wherever he went. She spoke his praises. When we encountered each other, I did not have to look at her to see the contempt in her eyes. Esperanza and she were the only ones besides Bristol who paid me the slightest attention. I wished for all the world she would not. She had become openly cruel.

At an evening meal, she said for everyone to hear that it was time that Bristol get a new snake boy, one who could be trusted. "This one's brainsick."

I stared at the tablecloth for a few seconds and then slowly pushed my chair away from the table, my insides sapless.

One afternoon Eva spread open the flap. "You, Snake Boy. Bristol wants you."

I kept my back to her. "Pate."

Raising her voice, she said, "You, he wants you. Now." As she turned to leave, she said in a hushed tone, "He keeps the money behind a panel beside his bed."

As the flap closed, I tried to see her as she had been when with me. But all I saw was the closed slit in the canvas, a corner of which flapped in the breeze. I thought about what she'd said and concluded that she wanted me to steal the money and be gone from her life for good.

Eva campaigned hard for Bristol to rid the camp of me, but he dismissed her misgivings and insisted that what I was doing was God's work at its best. He mentioned her qualms about me and suggested I perform an act of contrition, an act of loyalty to satisfy anyone's doubts. So on the hottest night yet of the summer, I agreed to take a plunge with him. Not to get closer to salvation, but because we were three weeks from heading to Pyramid and I had to see matters through to the end.

"Relax, Pate," he said. "Let your sins be washed away." I collapsed into his arms. He held me submerged a long while, because my sins were many. I didn't struggle, just held my breath. As my head surfaced, he welcomed me as Brother Pate and asked me how I felt.

"Saved," I said. I asked that he say a special prayer for me because I wasn't sure that I was over sin yet. I told him I owed my life to him, that I realized that now. He seemed touched. What I felt was that I was cool for the first time in days, and what I was thinking was how I could manage to steal his money and kill him without drawing suspicion on myself. I was thinking, Snakes. Judas.

After crossing the River Jordan, I was welcomed into the fold as a respected servant of the Lord, another lost soul who'd been saved. I was humble. I held my tongue. The groveling devotion I exhibited warmed the preacher and endeared me to his flock of Jesus Gypsies. After all, my sin had brought me to Truth. On the other hand, Eva carried hers arrogantly, disappointing the Following, who expected her to display humility and remorse.

Only one other person besides Eva seemed to doubt my motives.

Esperanza cornered me outside the shower and asked what I was up to.

"Up to?"

She said that she was not stupid, just old. "Que pasa, Pa-tito?"

"Nothing."

"Look what happened last time, pobre. You know I will give you money to go."

"I thought you were tired of being an old aunt."

She shook her head and walked away.

Bristol's reputation spread, ensuring a sizable audience wherever we went, even at one-night events in backwater towns along the Mojave. His objective remained Pyramid and the great tent revival. He was healing people now as well as taming Satan. People praised the Lord and threw away crutches, a miracle that Gabe or a new follower named Cecil performed on alternate nights. Bristol shouted how he felt cancer dissolve inside the afflicted; he extinguished arthritic pain. Henry lost his sight one afternoon, and by eight o'clock the same evening Bristol restored it. Eva was cured of a limp. I was tempted to ask Bristol to replace Esperanza's missing teeth—in fact, tempted to suggest it over the dinner meal, but the first thing members of the Following lost when they became born again was their sense of humor, so I kept the suggestion to myself and was content to smile, for smiles went unnoticed, being that they were overt symptoms of the saved.

Some among the Following drove pins through their arms. Others talked in tongues. He brought a whole new chorus line of converts on board, men and women willing to grovel on the ground as the Ghost invaded them. He purged their sins, rid them of the evils of alcohol and drugs and the deadly sins of adultery and fornication. Healing and curing were good for business. But Satan remained the staple of the show, and I the key to good fortune.

"You know, Pate, it's a disappointment to me. The good labor I do for the Lord, and people ask me to pray for . . ." More often now, Bristol talked to me in his Southern drawl. He paused as if to gather himself from the effect of a tremendous struggle and fell into his drawl. "A woman asked just yesta'day to he'p her pray for the delivery of a new Mercedes. Now I ask, is 'at a paltry, mean request? When you think of the things I hope ta do: A sem-n-nary, a grand temple—I'm talkin' cubits, Noah-sized cubits. Why, when you think of the powah of prayer in relation ta all that, this woman should've asked for a Rolls-Royce; don't chu think?"

I wondered if he was testing me, waiting for me to smile, to show that I had retained a sense of humor and shed my meek mask? I bowed my head, and without a tinge of irony, said, "A Rolls is fair."

It was as Esperanza had said it was: Bristol had tired of Eva. It coincided with the arrival of a new child to the flock, a young charmer from Mexico with a gold-capped tooth and a walk that could stir desire in a stone. As his interest in Eva languished, Bristol's trust in me increased. I took on one more responsibility: Three times a week, without fail, I tracked Bristol down and injected him with a diluted dose of venom to ensure his resistance to the snake poison in case he was bitten. It was diluted to degrees he would never suspect.

I watched with Bristol as the snakes fed and guarded the tent from spies whenever he took his new mistress inside to watch. I acted as God-bombed as anyone in camp. I did his bidding as the others did, never questioning anything he said, and I amened with the best of them. Bristol bought Eva a sewing machine. She became the new camp seamstress and moved to her own tent. She watched me from the shadows as I had once watched her. But she watched out of contempt.

Bristol did not let this go unmentioned.

"If you'd waited, Pate, you coulda had her with my blessing. 'Course you might not 'a found the light. You're better off this way. Better off."

"Yes, sir. Better off. I need a canvas bag," I said, "to carry snakes in. It'll be easier."

The next afternoon Eva brought a canvas bag she'd stitched together. She stood at the open flap and tossed it on the ground inside the tent. I was

shaving my head. I looked at her, then the bag, and said it would do just
fine.

"For his money?"

"Money?" I offered her a mindless smile. "For the snakes, Sister Eva."
She wheeled about and left.

One of her new duties was to handle the timing of the show, which
meant telling me what snake to bring and when to appear. Apparently
Bristol had delegated this role to her in hopes of reuniting the two of us,
this time with his approval, a bonus for my loyalty as Snake Boy. It would
restore calm to the camp. How could I not kill him?

VIII

The troupe grew from two dozen to four dozen, and we changed directions for a week and swung east into the Oklahoma panhandle, working a
couple of small towns and farming communities. Since taking the plunge,
I had become Bristol's confidant of sorts. He had learned an important
lesson in Texas and found the powers north of the Red River more recep-
tive to his particular Christian doctrine. Sheriffs and councilmen, eager to
help with the Lord's work to supplement their incomes, gave him permission to perform for marginal considerations. Entertainment tax, he called
it. All was preparation for Pyramid.

When September came, we migrated west and north in trucks and
trailers and Bristol's new ten-wheeled bus. I rode beside the happy
preacher. We stopped to save souls in Tonopah and Hawthorne on the way
to Reno. In Reno we wheeled up Virginia Street on a flatbed truck as Ham
Hardy thumped the organ and a half dozen of the women slapped tam-
bourines against their thighs and sang hallelujahs. Then we headed to
Pyramid Lake, where Bristol had ordered a new tent for the revival, a tent
with bench seats to accommodate two hundred.

We followed the road in, a two-lane highway that passed through a
widesaddle between the basalt mountains. The spare brush bloomed saf-
fron, the only evidence that life endured. The land was primal, Indian land,
the wilderness of the Old Testament prophets. Its bare crust supported
cactus and rabbitbrush and sage, snakes and lizards and coyotes and little
more. At first it seemed the last place on earth one would hold a revival.
Then, as if someone suddenly had raised a curtain, the grand lake
appeared, its deep waters several shades bluer than the sky. It sat in an

otherwise dry bowl formed by foothills that led to ragged peaks. No trees grew on its shoreline, not even tamarisk.

At the lake's edge the encampment appeared like a Hollywood set, a medieval jousting tournament or an image out of Arabian nights. White tents and white pavilions and red and blue pennants rose everywhere over a half-mile stretch of sloping land. Streamers ruffled in the autumn wind. White crosses topped the centers of the tallest canopies. Windows of hundreds of cars and trucks reflected the blinding autumn sun.

Beside me Bristol seemed to shine as he reeled off facts and numbers: twenty significant evangelists and healers of the day, twenty enormous pavilions, and twenty troupes, forty or more sermons scheduled every day for a week. I did the calculations: A lost soul had about two hundred and eighty possible chances to save himself. Thousands would come, and they would leave behind tens of thousands in the collection plates. The scene was about God and God hounders and spiritual capitalism and numbers and more numbers.

He explained that the first night was when preachers established their reputations. A potential born-again needed the theatrical to inspire the turn to salvation. Proselytizers would be the beneficiaries of opening-night praises, or not. Those best at peddling heaven would be rewarded not with flowers or reviews in newspapers but with glassy-eyed throngs padding collection plates.

By three o'clock the sense of urgency had swelled like a blister. Roustabouts pounded the last of the stakes and tightened the lanyards. Others installed benches. Bristol was furious with anticipation, rushing about ordering and organizing and then countermanding his own orders. He cornered me outside of the snake tent. "Judas. Tonight I want Judas."

"Judas?" I had anticipated this.

"Yes. They'll be 'spectin' somethin' spectacular, a show. Look at it, Pate." He pointed at the new white tent, which rose thirty-five feet high, blue and yellow streamers wafting down its sides. His face flushed as he admired it.

"Judas will pay for it." He gripped me by the shoulders and pulled me between two tents, where he embraced me and kissed me on the cheek.

"I'll bring a tamer one," I said. "No sense taking chances."

"Bring two. I feel up to it, Pate. Damn, look at this, all this. Bring three."

He smiled, then rushed off, his limp leg pumping like the arm on an oil well. I had killed before, placed my sight blade on a man, pulled the trigger and watched his head explode. And I had likely killed others. Three, I thought, and no one would be any the wiser. The nature of snakes is to bite. It would appear an accident, nothing more. If I took the money, the finger of suspicion would point at me. I would settle for revenge and, if the authorities identified me, take my punishment for the stealing I had done. Prison might have awaited me, but enacting revenge would console me as I did my time.

I was all but at peace with my decision and content to wait for the evening. I strolled away from camp to take a gander at the land. I followed a trail up to where the ground formed a shelf. Eva sat on a rock. I started to turn away, but she waved me over, seemed to be expecting me. I took a seat beside her, thinking that perhaps we might reconcile and she would leave with me if I was not arrested. She stared at the lake for some seconds before again acknowledging me.

"Here it is. Look."

I looked at her instead. "You were right."

"About what?"

"Two people who don't belong probably belong with each other."

"You smell like snake," she said. "You belong to them."

"I just wanted you to know."

She glanced at me and again shifted her attention to the lake. "Here's where all began when the world was first born. This is where Turtle Woman dug to the center of the world and gave birth to twins, the son and daughter of Coyote. Two giants. The wind came hard through the mountain and turned her on her back. Turtle Woman died in childbirth. And this is where women who lose their loved ones came to cry. The saddest woman of all cried this lake. It is the Lake of Tears."

"A myth?"

"Like your Jesus."

"Bristol's Jesus. If I left tonight, would you go with me?"

She just looked off. "See the rock over there?" She pointed to a huge stone by the water's edge that looked like an old woman. "Sorrowful mother. Frozen here when her tears went dry. She cried this lake."

"I loved you," I said. "I never said as much." I reached for her hand, but she pulled away and brushed a strand of hair out of her eyes.

"The twins struggled for control of the earth. One fell in love with Moon Woman. He became the great waters, and Moon Woman tries to pull him to her and then pushes him back. The other fell in love with the sun and became the mountains, reaching forever to the sky."

"I don't understand."

"This is a place of sorrow and joy," she said. "Of death and life. See how there are no trees here. See how deep the water is. But nothing grows."

I stared at the lake, then looked about at the mountains that formed the walls of the bowl. It resembled the shell of a turtle, one turned on its back. I was struck by the austere terrain, the water and sky in relation to the mountains. I stood to leave, and as I did, I noticed a mother with her two children, an adolescent boy and girl, both wearing sandals. The boy tugged at the mother's hand, trying to urge her closer to the water. He was blond and thin. In many ways he was as I had been. The girl, who was a year or so older, pulled her mother in the opposite direction, and the mother rocked between them.

They stopped and looked back. I glanced down the shore and saw a man waving. The daughter released her mother's hand and ran to the man, who I assumed was the father. The boy broke free of his mother, and before she could catch him, kicked off his sandals and waded into the water. He splashed himself.

Eva looked up at me. "He brought you to this place."

"So what? He brought you here too." I looked again at the mother and son. She seemed to be scolding him.

"If you kill him," Eva said, "you kill yourself."

"What? Who says I'm going to kill him?"

"You will try." She shook her head.

"You don't smile anymore," I said. I looked back at the shoreline. The boy was in his mother's arms, and the father neared them, pulled along by the daughter. The four of them came together and formed a circle, the parents connected by holding their children's hands.

"You don't owe me anything, especially words." Eva had folded her arms in front of her breasts as if to seal herself off.

"No, maybe not."

I took in the lay of the land for a moment, the rugged mountains, the dramatic shadowed arroyos, the rock-blanketed earth, and the intensely blue lake. It was easy to see how the stone mother at the lake's edge could inspire myth, and I thought how badly people need to explain the pain that life brings them. What was it he had said? Pain is a messenger. Then I saw the family strolling and talking as if the only thing they needed was this day. It had been some time since I'd witnessed a scene like this—or was it that I had been merely blinded to them?

"I thought I owed you something," I said, and left her to her myths.

I spent the day with the snakes. I talked to them, commiserated with their caged existence. Twice a few of the Following came to me with messages from Bristol, summoning me, but I ignored them and remained in the snake tent until near dark. Instead of placing the snakes in the pit, I placed them one at a time, all but three, in a canvas duffel bag made for this purpose. I carted them to a nearby ravine and released them. I went to see Esperanza. She did not speak, just stood, walked to where I stood and hugged me.

I said, "I'll take that money now."

She took some bills out of a pocket purse and pressed them into my hand.

Campfires blazed on the shore of the lake. Generators fed power to searchlights that played tag across the black sky. Some evangelists started early. When the commotion began, it ripped the air. Hallelujahs numbed the flocking masses. Organs and pianos dueled, their cacophony almost deafening. Shards of distant sermons floated into my tent. The activity fed Bristol's mood. Twice he came to the tent, and twice he hugged me and asked if I'd seen the crowds. I said I had. The most enthusiastic had gathered long before and a line of lost souls stretched twice around the tent to see the celebrated snake preacher.

As the day descended into evening, I sat alone and thought about the lake, and what I had seen, and the living and the dead. The water ran deep but produced no life in the shallows or on the shore. I thought of the bodies I had seen in Vietnam, the friend I had lost, and drugs I had taken. I thought about something I had never thought of before and pictured myself as an old man. I wondered what I would take with me to my final years. And I thought of what constituted a sin. I thought of how the family had formed a circle.

When the time came for Bristol to mount the stage, I readied myself. She would be coming for me, and I would make one last effort to win her. To accommodate the throng, the pavilion walls had to be raised. I watched through the open flap on the tent. I carefully removed Judas from his cage and the two others and placed them in the canvas bag. Then I waited for Eva to summon me for my role. But she didn't come.

A scream rose above the rest of the commotion. Several of the Following rushed from the pavilion in the direction of Bristol's trailer. I kept my seat. Henry and Gabe hurried past the tent, headed in the opposite direction. A few minutes later Esperanza stood at the entry.

"Come," she said.

I clutched the bag and followed her. She seemed to have shed a decade or two as she marched to the trailer, where a circle of the Following formed a fence near the door. Eva sat on the trailer steps, her face blank, blood smeared on one cheek. As I stepped forward, she looked up. For an instant I thought I saw her smile, but it could have been my imagination. She cast her eyes downward. Esperanza pushed her way through the throng. I followed.

Bristol lay on his back, gasping for air as his rib cage heaved up and down violently. Someone had ripped open his shirt. His face was pale and yellowing, and his eyes, wide with panic, scanned the room wildly. A wound on his arm, perhaps the result of a fall, dripped blood on the linoleum. Anna M. and two others kneeled beside him, praying and crying. Then a man drawn in by the noise pushed past me, kneeled down, closed his mouth over Bristol's, and began resuscitating him.

As he fought for his life, I stared at that man who'd imprisoned me. What I saw was myself as I had been outside of Hue, lying on the ground, squirming, wishing to escape the pain but wanting desperately to live. I wonder if he was at that moment begging for life, and I realized as I looked down at him that I could never have killed him in the first place. I'd killed but never murdered. I wanted him to live, not for my sake but simply because I had once had that same great desire to survive. I tried to speak. Nothing came from my numb lips. I nodded and backpedaled slowly. As I reached the outer perimeter, Henry arrived with two tribal cops, who scurried past me without taking notice. A hundred feet away an ambulance, siren blaring and red lights flashing, lumbered through the crowd that clogged the passage between tents. One of its tires struck a stake and brought down the side of a tent.

Already members of Bristol's Following were packing to leave. Ham Hardy bumped into me and said, "Pate, you best pack it in, boy."

I had few possessions. I gathered together a change of clothes and prepared to flee. I heard the siren die when the ambulance reached the trailer. As I stepped out, one of the two cops passed in front of me. Walking passively beside him was Eva, her wrists manacled behind her back. She stared at me as he hustled her off. Why she was cuffed, I had no idea, but I reasoned that she, like me, had been running from something all along.

It was impossible to distinguish the bedlam coming from Bristol's entourage from the other sounds. Still, I imagined I heard him screaming my name above the furies of the other preachers, imagined him cursing the devil and the snake boy and Eva. Then the noise was all one sound drowned out by the raging siren as the ambulance bounced over the rough earth.

I slipped into the crowds that flowed from tent to tent and made it to the parking lot. I was unsure where to head first. Home? Pay a debt to Stonehands and go to North Carolina to see his mother? Albuquerque to turn myself in? I would get to all of them eventually. I knew it with every step I took. I released Judas and the others in a thicket near the parking lot, told them that their days as symbols were over and they were free now to be snakes. Judas hesitated, balking as I might have at one time.

Watching him slither off, I began to understand what I could not consider a year before, that even if my living were an accident, nothing but whim, my life didn't have to be. I knew what I had to do to be free. A half mile south of the pavilions I stumbled upon a family of four readying to leave in a van and said to the father of the clan that my car wouldn't start. He offered me a ride. In Reno I found the courthouse where the sheriff's office was housed and turned myself in. The sergeant at the complaint desk did not believe me at first. I rolled up my sleeve and showed him my tracks, told him I was a wanted man, a thief.

When the deputy booked me, he asked if I was known by any other name.

"Snake Boy," I said.

"Seriously?"

I smiled and shook my head. In the space for aliases he wrote "none."

IX

Even though it cooled considerably as we climbed the incline toward

Donner Pass, Candace still sweated. She sat with her head tilted back to let the air conditioner shoot air over her throat. She hummed absentmindedly to "Nights in White Satin," which was playing on the radio. I knew what she was thinking as she stared intently at the window. I turned off the radio.

"I was listening to that," she said. She ran her fingers through her hair and looked at me. I pointed to the mountains and said she shouldn't miss them.

Here, I thought, is where a party of pilgrims survived by eating one another, and it is the backbone of Turtle Woman's offspring. The granite faces of the high peaks reminded me also of our original purpose, which was to be together without the distractions of ordinary life.

"Still mad?" I asked.

She shook her head and told me I was due a haircut.

"Not on vacation," I said.

"Why do people insist on taking vacations at the hottest times of the year?"

"Probably to get away from the heat."

"Okay," she said, nodding. She unfastened her seat belt, slid next to me, and leaned her head on my shoulder the way she had when we first started dating, when seat belts seemed less important. "Really," she said, "who was that guy?"

The past has been described as a closet where we store clothes that are out of fashion. I like the idea of the past being out of fashion. Much of mine is. I have told Candace of my addiction and of serving probation for burglary, about losing my friend in Vietnam and nearly dying there. But I never mentioned Bristol or Eva or Snake Boy. How could I, when all of it seemed like an invention even to me? So, he had lived, and so had I. I looked in the rearview mirror to see if my daughter was listening. She seemed intent on the book she held on her lap.

I glanced at Candace and said quietly, "He was a preacher who kidnapped me, whipped me with a belt, and hung me over a snake pit."

"No, really, who was he?"

I looked in the mirror again and caught my daughter looking up. I remembered the first trip we took as a family, when we drove from Bakersfield to Mono Lake, and smiled at her. I experienced again the feeling that had flowed through me that day as Candace sat beside me in the moving car and nursed Angie. I heard again the sound of my daughter's lips sucking the nipple of the wonderfully kind and sometimes difficult woman I'd come to love. The sound filled me in a way I'd never before experienced. It was the first time I felt completely whole in my life.

I glanced at Candace. "You know, we probably better find a restaurant."

"You don't want to tell me?"

I set my eyes to the road. "I do," I said. "I will." I was left to tell her things that I'd never wanted to tell anyone, that I once loved enough and hated enough to kill. She would certainly understand why I'd never told her. I slowed the car and eased into the traffic as we neared the outskirts of Reno. "Do you remember our first trip?" I asked.

"What made you think of that?" Candace said.

"Nothing." I looked in the rearview mirror and caught my daughter's eye. "Angie, would you like to see a lake that was made from tears?"

"Dad, how old do you think I am?"

"But would you?"

"I'd rather ride a rollercoaster. Is there one?"

"Somewhere," I said. "Somewhere."

I lifted my foot off the accelerator. For now we would find a place to eat, take the edge off the trip, have a night's rest. Then when the sun rose, we would visit the lake, see the waters and the desert unsullied by revival tents and throngs of worshipers, see it as it was when it was first born and deer and coyote drank from it. We would walk the lakeshore as one, and I would tell my daughter of the lake's geologic origin, and follow that with the myth of Turtle Woman as I heard it in its fullness after the revival.

The tale is a simple one. As days darkened, the brother, destined to never touch his love, the moon, raged and punished the mountains with flurries of ice and snow that covered her peaks. The sister endured the coat of ice and waited for her love, the sun, to melt away the layers in the spring. For a season she found joy, only to see it give way to her brother's anger. But the summer waters rushing from the high mountains filled rivers that fed lakes so that turtles might live on. It is a sad tale of contending siblings who never find fulfillment. It tells us that all we can do is invent our myths to smooth the harshness and, if we're lucky, build strength from our frailty and abide the seasons.